BEGGARS
AND
CHOOSERS

CYNTHIA KING ❧

BEGGARS

for Carolyn.
  the most talented
percolator of fine
art, tender feelings,
and good ideas I've
ever known —
        love + cheers —
            i sui

Cynthia King
     March 12, 1986

AND
CHOOSERS

࢘ THE VIKING PRESS · NEW YORK

Copyright © Cynthia King, 1978, 1980
All rights reserved
First published in 1980 by The Viking Press
625 Madison Avenue, New York, N.Y. 10022
Published simultaneously in Canada by
Penguin Books Canada Limited

LIBRARY OF CONGRESS CATALOGING IN PUBLICATION DATA
King, Cynthia.
Beggars and choosers.
I. Title.
PZ4.K5214Be   [PS3561.I474]   813'.5'4   79-20184
ISBN 0-670-59758-9

Printed in the United States of America
Set in CRT Electra

"Unfinished Business" originally appeared in *Texas Stories
and Poems* in somewhat different form.

Acknowledgment is made to Alfred A. Knopf, Inc., for permission to quote from *The Fall* by Albert Camus, translated
by Justin O'Brien. Copyright © 1956 by Alfred A. Knopf,
Inc.

For Kit

. . . the heart has its own memory. . . .

Don't bear down too hard on me. I'm like
that old beggar who wouldn't let go of my
hand one day on a café terrace. "Oh, sir,"
he said, "it's not just that I'm no good, but
you lose track of the light." Yes, we have
lost track of the light, the mornings, the
holy innocence of those who forgive
themselves.

ALBERT CAMUS, *The Fall*
Translated from the French by
Justin O'Brien

BEGGARS
AND
CHOOSERS

PROLOGUE ⚜

IT WAS THE YEAR OF THE YO-YO. FIVE MILLION WOOD AND plastic yo-yos, ranging in price from twenty-nine cents to one dollar ninety-five, were manufactured and sold by three thousand toy stores and supermarkets, netting national profits well over five hundred thousand dollars. The New Delphi Toy and Stationery Store sold three hundred of them. The boy stole two dollars from his mother's purse which she kept in the second drawer of her dresser with her silk scarves, and bought four yo-yos in one day. He kept two for himself and gave two to Brian Kaplan, who sat next to him in Miss Barker's third grade.

"Gee, thanks," Brian said. And they practiced with them together all during recess.

When Brian got home from school he gave one to his fifteen-month-old brother Peter who couldn't make it work. Peter dragged it everywhere with him, however, took it into his bath and wouldn't let go of it even when his mother, Linda, put him to bed.

At dinner Brian told his father Peter loved it so much because he could say "yo-yo," which went with "no," the only other syllable he'd uttered.

Linda told Brian he was wrong. "Peter likes it because it's such a nice gift from his big brother."

David raised a dark eyebrow. "He'll sleep with anything you give him. Please pass the potatoes."

"Isn't it all right to be sentimental once in a while?" Linda asked.

"Yes, but not about yo-yos which are only being revived so a toy manufacturer can get rich."

"They're fun," Brian said. "I wish I had money like Rick does to buy things."

David and Linda looked at each other, and at Brian.

"Who's Rick?" they asked at once.

THE LAST DAY ⚜

THE BOY SLOGGED ACROSS THE FIELD, SEEMING NOT TO notice that he was walking through the swamp instead of around it. After two rains the week before the ground was no longer frozen. His shoes, magnets to the mud, were heavy. Hands in his pockets, jacket unzipped though the wind sharpened against his shirt, he headed for the hedge that bordered the field, leaving the woods behind him. He was tall for his nine years and for his slight frame. He moved with no angularity, a natural athlete except that he carried himself like one total shrug.

He knew someone could see him in the field, though he never looked up to notice if anyone had walked through while he was there. He knew someone would find what he had done there, because he had left the shovel standing like a flag and whoever found it would eventually learn whose it was and how it got there. He didn't care. Tomorrow he and Brian would be friends again and he would have someone to walk home from school with. Brian would make his mother say, "All right, I'll let it go this time, but if Rick ever does anything like that again—"

By the roads, the swamp was a half-mile from his house, but much less through back yards and over fences. When he came to his own yard it was nearly seven. It was the end of a long day. He was late for supper, not tired, not cold, not angry any more either. He knew that even being late for supper wouldn't make any difference. He went past the front step, kicking the mat askew, through the bushes around to the back door where the light in the kitchen was bright against the blackness. Every night his mother said, "Rick, go turn the front lights on. Your father will be home any minute." Children went in the back door because of muddy shoes. Children and maids always went in the back door, out the back door, up the back stairs, down the back stairs.

Children and maids used the old television set in the basement, never the new one in the living room where the carpet was gray and the couch soft. Children used ballpoint pens and ate in the kitchen, with paper napkins, and jelly glasses for milk. Rick didn't care what he drank his milk out of. Someday, perhaps, he would get over being a child. He couldn't imagine it—maybe like becoming your own enemy.

He opened the back door and wiped his shoes on the mat.

"Close the door, Rick, it's blowing cold," Addie said.

Rick stepped inside and closed the door. Addie didn't turn around from where she was stirring something on the stove. "You're late for supper," she said.

"I know."

He washed his hands with his jacket still on. He let the cold water stream through his fingers. They were colder than the water and began to itch.

"Hurry up," Addie said. Her voice wasn't mad, just warning him. "Take off your jacket and go in and eat. They're already sitting."

"How come they're in the dining room?" He wiped his hands on his pants and dropped his jacket on a chair.

"Your father's out for dinner, so Mother's eating with you and the girls."

"Oh." He started for the swinging door past the refrigerator.

"Rick?"

"What?"

"Someone's been calling you. Twice. I think it was Brian."

Rick shrugged and went through the door. The fractured light from the chandelier was gloomy like the funeral parlor, but the smell was of baked potatoes. There were sounds in the air that he was used to.

"You're late. Where have you been?"

"Honestly, Mother, his pants are so muddy!"

"Aren't you going to make Rick change?" That was Barbara. "Father wouldn't let him eat like that."

"Father isn't here. As usual." That was his sister Deborah.

"He's supposed to answer you, isn't he? I wish I could get a permanent."

"You're too young." Deborah again. "Anyway, permanents are out. They're dumb."

"I saw Felix hanging around the junior high. I guess he's got a new girl friend." Barbara's singsong voice.

"He's a spaz."

"Deborah!"

"Well he is. Anyway, I've got a date with someone else tonight."

"On a school night? Father'll have a fit!"

"Father's not home!"

"Mother, can Deborah go out on a school night? That's not fair when I have to go to bed so early!"

"Well—" His mother's voice hesitated.

"Aren't you going to make Rick say where he's been? You never make him do anything!"

He slipped into the waiting seat and, as always when he was in the dining room, found himself not hungry. The high-backed chair hit his shoulder blades wrong, and in the dim light his food looked like mud.

He shut his eyes.

"Rick!" Her voice cut the air. "You're not even listening."

"Yes'm."

"Answer me when I ask you a question. Where have you been?"

Pussycat, pussycat, where have you been?

Now he was tired. He closed his eyes and could hear her singing to him. He closed his eyes and tried to think of what to say.

I've been to London to visit the Queen.

The girls' voices were around him again. He didn't have to say anything. If he didn't say anything maybe they wouldn't notice and they would let him go upstairs and the day would be over.

It had started a long time ago.

PART ONE

PART ONE

ONE ❧

RICK LEANED AGAINST THE BRICK WALL OF the school yard looking down at his black loafers. The leather was polished but he fixed that by carefully rubbing the top of one with the sole of the other. His hands were in the pockets of his black cotton ankle-tight pants. He let go of the car in his left pocket and the fifty-cent piece in his right pocket and, with both hands flat on his slim belly, tucked in his white shirt without dislodging the small leather knife case that was hooked to his belt inside his pants. Then he dirtied the top of his other shoe. He paid little attention to the children on the playground, though there were nearly thirty of them, boys and girls.

His teacher came near and spoke. He didn't look at her. In a moment she moved on, hands in the pockets of her loose red coat, pulling it around her against the brisk November wind. She stopped at the other side of the yard and watched the children on the tall swings, shifting her weight from one foot to the other. Rick leaned against the brick wall, a still, slanting stick.

Another child ran close past him. He reached out and caught the sleeve of the boy's red parka and spoke to him. Words were carried off by the wind, drowned in the echoing of high-pitched laughter. The red-jacketed child pulled himself loose with a sharp twist of his shoulders and joined a small group in the middle of the yard. Rick slid his shoulders down the wall until he was sitting, his knees up in front of him. On one knee he balanced the fifty-cent piece. On the other he tried to balance a small green rubber ball. It kept slipping off his knee. He caught it several times before it hit the ground. A few of the children in the middle group looked toward him.

Three girls stood near the group of boys. They had a large red rubber ball. One by one each girl took a turn running past the boys, catching the big ball near enough to graze one of them as she fled laughing and shrieking back to safety.

Rick still sat by the building. He had a ball. They wanted it. Now he tossed it lightly into the air, catching it expertly. He knew if he waited long enough, Brian would ask him if they could play with the ball, and when Brian asked him he would smile and shrug as if he didn't really care and say, "Sure."

Then Brian would say, "Gee, thanks," and "Come on, Rick," and then they'd be friends again. He tossed the ball higher into the air.

He looked at his new loafers and wished Brian had noticed them. He had unpolished them because of the fight. His father had said, "For God's sake, baby, must you dress the kid like a hoodlum? It's bad enough he acts like one." It was weird the way he always called her "baby" even when he was mad. His mother had said, "He asked for them, so I didn't see it made any difference what color loafers he had." Well it sure made a difference to his father. In his day a boy didn't wear loafers, or couldn't afford them, or some junk like that. Rick looked up and saw Brian coming toward him. He tossed the ball a bit higher.

"Can we borrow the ball, Rick?"

"Date this afternoon?"

Brian looked down and away. "We'll give it back, honest."

"Can I play too?"

Brian looked over his shoulder toward the three other

boys. They were waiting for him, watching him. Tommy Marchesi was fat and had a lot of hair that was always in his eyes. Brian knew Tommy didn't like Rick but was afraid to say so. Ralph Jones was a genius at arithmetic and always got picked for the new math demonstration class. Ralph and Tommy were best friends and did everything together, and got good marks too. They were always laughing and saying, "Some joke," whenever Brian came near them.

"What's the joke?" Brian would ask.

"Oh," they'd say, "it's just some joke," as if it weren't anything at all. They would let Brian or some of the other boys play with them now and then but nobody could come close for long. Brian wished he could be friends with them and make it three.

Stevie Murchison was waiting for the ball too. Stevie was always ruffled, always half scared. He'd forget to button his shirt or tie his shoelaces. He was yappy and cute like a toy schnauzer. Everyone liked Stevie. He would do any crazy thing you told him and say it was fun. Brian knew Stevie was afraid of Rick because Rick was taller and older; when Brian was with Rick, Stevie kept a safe distance. Somebody told Brian that Rick had beaten Stevie up on the first day of school, but Brian didn't believe it. He'd known Rick since day camp. Rick got mad and did dumb things sometimes, but he wouldn't beat up a little guy like Stevie.

People were always saying things about Rick that weren't true and this was probably one of them.

Brian stood between Rick and the group. Rick wasn't going to lend them the ball unless they let him play. Brian didn't mind him joining the game but the others did. Rick had always been nice to Brian, giving him things, and he was fun when he wasn't mad about something. Yesterday they'd had one of those I'll-never-play-with-you-again fights, but now Brian couldn't remember what it was about. He watched Rick toss the ball up, catch it once more.

"I'll give you the ball, Brian," Rick said finally.

"Come on." Brian turned and ran back to the group. Rick

slowly got up and, as he walked to join them, he threw the ball to Brian who caught it and tossed it to Tommy who ran around in a circle and threw it to Ralph yelling, "Monkey in the middle!"

"Rick's the monkey," Ralph shouted.

"It's my ball, don't forget."

Someone laughed, and somebody said, "Yeah, but you're the monkey."

The laugh was too loud—Rick turned—was it Brian who laughed?—the ball hit Rick in the eye and then he and Brian were on the ground rolling over and over and there was blood smearing everything. The teacher was there in her red coat trying to stop the stream from Brian's nose with her little lace handkerchief without getting bloody herself.

"Everybody inside," she said. "Brian, go to the nurse's office. Rick, I'll take you to the principal." None of the children said a word until Miss Barker left the room; then everyone started to talk at once.

The nurse told Brian to lie down and she gave him a box of Kleenex. He tried to tell her that he never lay down with a nosebleed (which he had all the time) because then he swallowed all the blood and got sick, but she pushed him back and said, "Don't talk, Brian. Just lie down."

She acted as if something terrible was the matter with him. He tried to tell her that sometimes he only sneezed and his nose did this. But she said, "Be quiet, Brian, and lie down." Brian was quiet and lay down.

He hoped Rick wasn't going to get into trouble because of his stupid nose. Maybe his mother would be able to help. She wouldn't mind explaining about his nosebleeds. Brian had brought Rick home a couple of times and his mother liked him all right. She asked him a bunch of questions the way she always did when he brought somebody new home. Rick never answered them, but that's the way Rick was. He didn't talk to grown-ups much. Some kids jabbered away to his mother telling a lot of stuff, and she would get a funny look on her face. Once Stevie said he was going to borrow

Brian's snake some Saturday morning to wake his mother by putting it on her pillow because she was scared of snakes and she always slept late on Saturday mornings. Brian's mother looked away and said, "Does she now, Stevie?" which Brian knew meant she didn't think Stevie ought to be telling so much about his mother's private habits.

Anyway, he'd have to get his mother to explain about his nose because this idiot nurse, who was new this year, wouldn't listen to him. And Rick was a friend when he wasn't mad about something. He had crazy ideas about things to do, like throwing rocks on cars from the bridge over the parkway and putting flashbulbs in his neighbor's porch light, but Brian didn't know anyone who could be nicer than Rick when Rick wanted to be nice. Like giving him that great pen, the yo-yos, and the cars. And whenever Rick had candy, he shared it. Rick just liked to do dangerous things: to go fast on his bike, to jump from high places and moving trains; he knew all kinds of shortcuts and could climb any fence. Rick said he was going to get a motorcycle in a few years. His sister's boyfriend had a motorcycle and gave Rick rides. It was fun being with Rick. You just had to be careful.

Half an hour later Brian was allowed to return to his class-room, pink-nosed but otherwise undamaged. Miss Barker was at her desk; all students but one were at their places with workbooks open. No heads moved but all eyes watched Brian enter.

"Where's Rick?" Brian asked.

"Sit down quietly and open your arithmetic book to page seventy-three," Miss Barker said.

Brian sat down, opened his book, and wondered.

TWO &8&3 DR. GLENNA MASTERSON, PRINCIPAL OF the New Delphi Elementary School, left the assembly quite pleased. The children had laughed at her little joke about Santa Claus being impatient, and they had been quiet and responsive during the cartoon movie on safety. They sang cheerfully as they marched two by two back to their class-rooms. Though they were loud enough to make her turn down her hearing aid, they were not raucous. As Dr. Masterson passed the library she met Joanne Franklin, the school psychologist, and stopped to chat with her. Joanne should have had results of the achievement tests by now. If they were much later the teachers wouldn't be able to make use of them before the Christmas rush. Joanne seemed overworked this year, Dr. Masterson thought, perhaps because there were five new teachers who didn't know the routine. Dr. Masterson encouraged Joanne to hurry with the scores, then went to the lounge for some coffee.

She noticed the Thirds were already on the playground, and watched Catherine Barker, their teacher, stop to talk with the Lang boy. Glenna Masterson hoped things would ease up for him. He wasn't reading fluently yet, and until he did he'd neither keep up with his class nor settle down. He was already a year behind his age group, and, though it was fall, he'd tangled with his teacher two or three times. Glenna thought she'd ask Joanne to run special tests on him.

The first time Catherine brought Rick to the principal's office, Glenna remembered, she'd offered to call his mother in for a conference, since Rick was new in school. Catherine had declined. "Leave him to me," she'd said. "I'm sure I can handle Rick. He's just finding his way. I've done well with boys in worse shape. Somewhere he's got a smile he'll learn to use." But Glenna had thought he was a typical trou-blemaker, a boy to be watched. He had a look in his eyes that was at once familiar and strange, something between insolence and boredom. While she talked to him he sat so still she thought he'd gone to sleep with his eyes open. He answered every question with "Yes ma'am," as if he hadn't heard her. She couldn't quite define the way he made her feel, as if he had decided to be somewhere far away, where she couldn't follow. At the same time she felt he was manipulating the conversation, anticipating her words, constraining her to say what he expected. Even so she had not called the mother, but abided by Catherine's decision. Good teachers, she knew, had to feel that they had some power. Besides, this was still fall, not the time of year for turmoil on the playground. She was not worried.

Glenna Masterson had been principal of the New Delphi school for six years and had taught for sixteen. By studying every summer since graduating from the state teachers' college she had finally finished her doctorate, "Freedom and Discipline in an Ordered Curriculum." It had been a rough climb but worth it. Little as she liked what was happening in the big city schools, the growing discontent and power of students, and the increasing threats to the control and safety of teachers and administrators, the fear of returning to her father's upstate farm made her glad to give up summer vacations and to study during long winter nights. By the time she came to New Delphi she had taught in city and country schools and felt well qualified to handle whatever problems the growing exurb might produce.

Her method was simple, so simple, in fact, she dared not tell it to anyone, not even her husband Harvey, an actuary whom she had married just three years before.

The weather, the rhythm of the seasons, was the most important single factor in maintaining discipline in a grade school. If discipline was maintained, the children would learn. If children learned, parents were happy and stayed away from the school. Everything depended on the seasons. So Dr. Masterson, as she did like to be called, had reassured the staff at last week's meeting. Fall was the time when children were alert, energetic, easy to keep busy. In spite of the recent flurries at recess, many of which had involved the Lang boy, there was nothing to worry about.

She left the lounge and started down the corridor. Just as she rounded the corner before her office she sensed, rather than heard, the scuffling sound of someone being dragged.

She turned up her aid and heard a child cry, "I didn't start it. He hit me in the eye!"

She saw Catherine Barker coming toward her with Rick by the arm. His legs were straight and stiff so Catherine had to half push and half drag him down the hall. They both had blood on their clothes! Repressing a spasm of fear and remembering she must demonstrate authority, Glenna squared her wide-boned shoulders and raised her angular chin.

Catherine said something she couldn't hear, and Rick became docile, walking silently by her side. Catherine still held his arm. Just as the two reached Glenna, another child came out of the office laden with stacks of mimeographed papers. She nudged Rick with her shoulder and spoke smartly.

"In it again, Rick, tough, tough."

"Shut up!"

Glenna gripped Rick's other arm, saying, "Another fight, Rick, and after all the talks we've had. Aren't you ashamed? Well, we'll have to call—"

Suddenly the child went wild, tore loose from both women, stamped on Glenna's foot so hard pain pierced her brain and the brown leather cracked where her corned little toe had weakened it.

"Shit!" She couldn't believe the word came from his child-lips. Her fear exploded as he ran into the office with Catherine chasing him like a farmhand after a runaway pig.

"Come back, you swine!" Glenna cried out in pain, and limped after them, ramming her thigh against the corner of the big secretarial desk. She steadied herself with a hand on the four-drawer file, knocking a pile of papers to the floor.

She closed her eyes, opening them a second later to a vision that would remain undimmed for a long time.

The boy posed, half bent, back to the window. In his immature hand was a little knife, blade gleaming; his stance and the bitter challenge on his face a mirrored image of rebels he shouldn't know. They formed a taut triangle, caught, stopped as if in a newsreel still: the large woman, the principal; the small woman, the teacher; and the now-cornered boy, motionless as a hypnotized chicken with its poor beak pressed down to the point of a V scratched on the ground. How Glenna had laughed when her brother showed her how to do it! But the chicken had been stupid and helpless. The boy, though his eyes were empty, held in his hand at the point of the triangle the rebel weapon. Glenna was sweating.

She finally forced out words. "Put the knife on the desk, Rick, and go wash the blood off your face."

"Make me." He made a sudden forward gesture.

She ignored him and turned to the teacher. "Miss Barker, go back to your class. On the way, see if Mrs. Franklin is free." Then she turned back to Rick, who blinked at her. "Put the knife down," she said sharply, "now."

Dumb, he did as she said, and her own sigh of relief was audible when she heard the metal click. She told Grace, her secretary, to take Rick and wash him up, then to get Mrs. Lang on the phone. She went into her private office and shut the door.

Once safely behind her desk she again turned the knob at her chest, closed her eyes, and effectively locked out the world. She wept. How could she have undone—unstrung— in one ghastly moment the poise she had taught herself to maintain for twenty years? A principal is not supposed to show emotion. And she had screamed like a hand. She had long ago learned to suppress all her feelings, to appear calm, obdurate, at all times steady. It hadn't been easy, continually parrying overwrought parents, students, teachers. She didn't know which were more taxing, which she favored, but in the end they were all antagonists. Those parents who thought their children were so special, if they could see, as she did, how alike they all were! Even her own staff seemed to be battling her will, testing her reserve.

She wiped her eyes with a Kleenex from her desk, then undid the lace on her brown broad-heeled Oxford, examined the damaged toe, felt her bruised thigh, and realized that these pains were nothing compared to the constriction in her chest. Her heavily beating heart still thumped, telling her again and again of her failure.

What had gone wrong? What had triggered that boy? She had to find out. She remembered the blood, the knife. Had he already used it? She shook her head to clear it. She desperately hoped not. Surely Catherine would have said something more. But Glenna had misread other signs. Her own timing had been off. Otherwise one child, no matter how difficult, could not have altered the careful balance of her system. How he had done that might take a while to analyze, but in the meantime she had to deal with Rick and with his parents. Her own failure did not change or excuse the fact that a third grade student had been allowed to come to school with a knife in his belt. This incident, she was afraid, would have wider impact than a scrap in the hall.

She saw her phone light flash. As she reached for the receiver she turned up her hearing aid and heard a tentative knock on the door.

THREE 𝕰𝕺𝕾 RICK STOOD IN THE CARPETED ROOM.

His face was clean. The front of his blue shirt had water spots on it; some dark red spots also. He felt tired, but no longer angry. The voice with the questions seemed to go past him. A lump clogged his left ear. He opened his jaw to clear the passage, but it clogged tighter. He stuck his little finger in his ear.

"Where did you get the knife?"

He looked at the waxy end of his finger and opened his jaw again.

"Does your mother know you have a knife?"

The back of his neck ached from lifting his chin to hear the questions. There were never any right answers. The tall people never seemed to hear the sounds inside him.

"Look at me!"

He heard the big-boned woman's questions, and he saw her teeth and wondered how they could all fit in her mouth.

"Who gave you permission to have—"

Permission. He heard the steam popping in the radiator, felt sweat on his face. Permission. If one of them gave permission the other one took it away and they'd yes and no all night until they'd forgotten what he'd asked them so long ago. In a world of crashing voices it was silence he wanted. He found it within his own tightly sealed lips, his "yes'm" or "no'm." Only when it was quiet inside him could he make a friend.

Deborah's boyfriend Felix had left the knife in the cellar one day after a terrible argument, and Rick found it. Rick sat on the cellar stairs listening, and when they got through Deborah was crying. "I'll never let you touch me again," she screamed. And Felix said, "Who wants to?" and stamped up the cellar stairs, out and onto his motorcycle. Only the smell of gasoline and the knife on the Ping-Pong table was left of Felix. Rick was sorry, because Felix had said he'd teach him something new with the knife. He never got time. Rick was sorry for Felix because he knew what Deborah said about him at dinner. "Really, he thinks he's so smart, so smart, but he's mental." He took the knife to save for Felix, or to remind him of Felix, or—he thought after a week of no

Felix—just to have because it was the easiest way to get the kind of knife he'd always wanted. He didn't go around asking stupid permission for things.

Rick was sorry about the fight, and that the roar of the motorcycle and the gasoline fumes were gone forever. Everything good went away forever, rivers and friends and the day you were born. But all the threats were never and ever: I'll never play with you again; and if you ever do that again; and never come near here again; and if I ever catch you!

Felix had been nice, talking quietly to Rick, telling him about places he'd been, motorcycles he'd driven. No questions. Once Felix said, "You want a spin, kid?" and had put Rick on the back of the big furry seat. The motor vibrated. Rick held tight to Felix's chest, and the wind rushed against his ears. It was quiet inside him. Of course Felix only took him around the block, but they went past the Kaplan house and Rick dared to let go and wave at Mrs. Kaplan. She was on her hands and knees weeding out the rock garden on the steep bank, and she waved back. When Felix came to the fast stop that nearly knocked Rick's breath out, all the little kids on the block—even the ones who didn't play with him any more—stood at the curb with their arms hanging at their sides, and said, "Gosh, Rick, weren't you scared!"

Rick smiled and tossed the forelock off his eyes. "Me? Scared? Na-a-a." He grinned at the wide-eyed memory.

"Richard, this is no laughing matter!"

He heard the dialing of a telephone, and the hard voice from the place where all the teeth were. "Is Mrs. Lang there, please?"

His heart pounded high in his throat. "Yes'm," he said softly. "Yes'm, I'm scared." But the voice went on.

"When do you expect her? Oh, well, I see. Yes, I'll have to send him home. I'll write a letter. Can you tell me how to reach them? No? I'll write it in the letter. You will be there. Yes, he'll be home within the hour."

"You *will* have to stay home, Rick. I *am* sorry." The voice hit the little words like drumbeats. "I *can't* let you back in school until *we* have a chance to speak with your *parents.* You *do* understand, after what *happened.* I *want* you to see Mrs. Franklin *before* you go."

He woke the next morning early as usual. There was no half sleep for Rick; sleeping and waking were separate, as if controlled by a switch, off, on. The instant he opened his eyes there was the blue ceiling. Turning his eyes to the right he saw his desk, the chewed green blotter, the Dinky Toy jeep, the red pen, the real leather pen stand and calendar he'd gotten for Christmas last year. He'd never changed the page since January 3. On the bookcase next to the desk was the box of one hundred crayons, the pill bottle with a dead moth inside, the neat row of books on the top shelf. The bottom shelf had games: Lotto, Monopoly, Baseball Land, Candyland. All the pieces inside the boxes were mixed up so if he wanted to play Parcheesi (which he never did) he'd find the men from The Game of Life. Each game had been a present. Sometimes he'd take three or four of the games out and march all the men across his rug in teams. When Addie put them away the next day, she never got them in the right boxes.

Turning his eyes to the left he saw the little cars on the dresser lined up in two separate groups; on one side were the cars he played with, traded with friends, gave away, or carried in his pocket. None was new, none bigger than would fit neatly in the palm of his hand. He never kept a new car more than a day. On the other side of the dresser were the cars that he never touched, presents or trades from past friends. He knew how he'd gotten each one. He kept no more than one car from each friend, and set them like tombstones on the bureau.

Rick got out of bed, not bothering to close the window even though it was cold. Rick never noticed the cold. Sometimes he was too hot, in schoolrooms and in the dining room. But cold did not bother him. He'd go out, forgetting his coat, and Addie or his sister Barbara would throw it after him. He lost a lot of coats, in the playground or in a tree or in someone's back yard.

He opened his dresser drawers and took out his clothes, careful not to drop anything or make any noise. He pulled on his pants, put one of the giveaway cars (a yellow Thunderbird) in his pocket, took three ballpoint pens from his desk and put them in his other pocket, closed the drawers quietly, picked up his sneakers and socks, and tiptoed out of his room.

On school days it was important to get dressed first, be downstairs, eat the bowl of cereal Addie put on the table for him, and be out of the house before Barbara and Deborah were dressed. That way he didn't have to talk to them. Barbara was ten and in the fifth grade. She would ask him questions like how many tests he was going to flunk that day. Addie put the Rice Krispies on the table.

"Morning, honey," she said and yawned.

Rick didn't answer. He sat down, leaned over to put on his socks and sneakers.

"What're you going to do today?" Addie asked.

"I've got gym. I need my sneakers."

"You haven't got gym," Addie said. "You don't need your sneakers."

"Huh?" Rick looked up at her.

"Don't you remember?" He frowned.

"Rick, you can't go to school, not till your folks come back. That's what the lady on the phone said, remember?" Addie's voice went right up out of her throat into her nose when she said "remember."

Rick picked up his spoon and started to eat the cold, floating grains. "Have something hot, have some cocoa," Addie coaxed him softly.

He ate his cereal, drank his juice, and didn't want any cocoa. He heard water running upstairs. That meant someone else was up. He went to the closet, got his jacket, and opened the back door.

"Rick."

"What?"

"Don't you go to school now."

"I won't." He stepped on the wooden porch outside of the kitchen door and let the sharp air reach his lungs. That first breath outdoors in the morning was something he looked forward to. He always waited a moment on the porch because of the breath. He took it deep like a smoker. He had almost closed the door when he heard Addie's voice behind him again.

"Whyn't you stay home this morning? You could make a cake."

Rick started down the steps. "Please, Rick, don't go so early today. What're you going to do anyway, with no school?" He turned at the bottom step and looked back up at her. "Please, Rick."

He ducked under the stoop and pulled out his bicycle. He rode on one pedal a short way, and just as he threw his leg across the seat Addie called, "Come home to lunch. Don't forget." But he was already down the driveway with wind against his ears, his unzipped jacket flying behind him. He thought he'd ride around awhile, the way he always did in the mornings. Each morning he rode around long enough to find someone to go to school with. He didn't like to walk through the school doors alone. He wouldn't have said he was afraid, but going from the bright world into the dark corridor, filled with hidden traps and people who expected things of him or challenged or provoked him, set up a series of reactions that he couldn't identify but felt nonetheless.

Going through a door from one part of life to another was terrifying alone, bearable shoulder to shoulder with a friend. Even if he didn't know the friend well, he didn't need to put out his toe to trip someone who walked by him, someone he didn't like or who ignored him. Alone he couldn't stop his thoughts or his toe.

Anticipating his father's loud anger or his mother's quick-tempered slap was clear and easy. Sometimes he found a certain pleasure in setting it all in motion. But going into the school yard alone, rolling the front wheel of his bike into the stand when there were no other bikes, waiting in the asphalt space so everyone who came along could see he was alone, walking out of the light air into the dark tiled hall alone suffocated him. It made him remember the indoor pool at the Y where his mother had left him. Only once was he in that steamy strong-smelling cavernous place. Two men tried to make him put his head under water. He thought he would explode. *A real boy has to learn to swim, so get him some lessons, for God's sake.* He screamed so loud they said wait another year. Though he knew he was a real boy, or thought he was a real boy, he didn't go to the Y again and he didn't bother about learning to swim.

He wouldn't have said he was afraid to learn, or that he was afraid to go through the double doors of the school alone, or that he was afraid to go home at night. But there were places and times it was hard to breathe. It was easier if he had a friend.

This past week he'd waited for Brian. One morning he met Brian by the stop sign at the bottom of the hill from his house. The next day he waited at the end of Brian's driveway by the huge boulder. He sat in the safe shadows of the hemlock close by the rock. He could sit in the shadow, or he could come out from under cover and sit on top of the boulder. From there he could watch the street and also see up the Kaplans' driveway to where it made a turn past the kitchen door of their gray-shingled house.

The last few days he had rung the doorbell just as Brian was getting ready to leave. He would stand inside the warm kitchen and wait while Mrs. Kaplan found Brian's hat and jacket, kissed him, reminded him about looking in the lost and found for his rubbers, handed him his notebook, and said, "Say goodbye to Peter," who sat in a highchair with cereal on his face. Then Mrs. Kaplan would open the door, give Brian another kiss, and pat Rick on the head. It made him shiver because nobody but Gran ever patted him like that, and he hadn't seen Gran in so long that he could hardly remember her voice. Mrs. Kaplan would say, "Ride carefully, boys." Then the door would shut behind them and Rick would be in the fresh cold air for the second time.

This morning Rick didn't know what time it was but he knew it was too early for Brian to be ready to leave for school. He rode away from Brian's house toward the end of the street where there was a turnaround, a few trees, a grassy field, the swamp where the stream cut through. He swerved around on the circle of black road and went back past his own house, number 22, and around the block the other way. He went down Nutgrove Street and stopped by the boulder. The ride took perhaps ten minutes.

He let his bike fall at the foot of the driveway, not bothering to put down the kickstand. It was a lightweight black bike and he'd been proud of it when his father bought it for him because he was the only boy in the third grade who had gears and handbrakes.

"That's because I'm older," he'd bragged the first day he'd ridden it to school. Stevie had come up to him with eyes wide and that half smile that Stevie got when he envied somebody something.

"You're a luck," Stevie had said.

But some brainchild had ruined it all, Rick remembered, by saying, "Ah-h-h, the only reason he's so big is he's dumb and got put back." There'd been some books thrown, and some hard fists. Somehow, Stevie's ankle got twisted. He'd cried and thrown the little red Volks back at Rick. That night Rick put the Volks on the bureau. He hadn't meant to hurt Stevie, who had been his friend and could always be counted on to say something nice. After that, Stevie stayed away from Rick and said his mother didn't want them to play together. Rick just let his bike fall any old way, not minding whether the gears got broken or what.

Rick sat under the hemlock for a while, running the yellow Thunderbird along the edge of a crevice, pretending that it was a mountain highway he'd been on once; he had expected the car would fall off the cliff at every curve. Why didn't Brian come down the driveway? It must be late by now. Maybe Brian was sick and wouldn't come. He had to see Brian. He had to be sure Brian wasn't mad about the fight. Rick had waited the afternoon before at the stop sign, but somehow had missed him.

Rick crawled out from behind the boulder and walked up the stone and dirt driveway kicking loose rocks as he went. He hesitated on the step. When he rang the bell he turned his back to the door. He waited a long time. Finally the door opened. He turned around.

"Why, Rick, you're awfully early this morning. We're not dressed." She was in a blue nightgown and her hair fell over her face from both sides. She held her wrapper around her with one hand and pushed back her hair with the other. He didn't say anything. He knew she didn't want him there but he couldn't move away.

Finally she said, "Well, I suppose you can't stand outside all morning. Come on in."

"Okay." Inside Rick stood by the door, not knowing what to do.

"Brian is dressing and I have to get Peter up and changed. If you really want to wait I suppose you can help me with breakfast. That is, when I come down again. I've got to dress." Mrs. Kaplan talked as if she was telling herself what to do at the same time she was doing it. "Well, take your jacket off." She sounded irritated. He should have stayed outside. She looked at the clock. "Oh, it's later than I thought. I'd better start the coffee. Peter was up during the night and I'm always frantic when I have to get up with him. I don't know what's the matter with him. Not another cold, I hope." She kept having to retie her wrapper, and she kept talking while she put things on the stove, filled the pot with water, got some plates on the table. She handed Rick a bunch of paper napkins and said, "Put these around, please. You don't mind, do you?" Rick didn't mind but he wished she'd stop talking.

She added, "You'll have to wait while Brian eats, of course. Did you have breakfast? Of course you did. I like Brian to take his time in the morning, without being late, of course. It's so important to start the day with a good hot tummyful." She stopped and grinned as if ashamed at what she'd said. "It isn't good to rush. Relax, I always say to him. Relax and eat slowly. Wouldn't you eat something too, Rick? A piece of coffee cake? I'll set a place. Unless you'd rather go ahead. Brian is such a poke he might even make you late. Oh, darn, the pilot light is out on the oven. How'll I heat the cake? Help me light it, will you? Brian usually does—hold the match there."

"I blew it out a couple of times. Boy does that make my mother mad."

Mrs. Kaplan looked at him silently for a minute. "That's an odd thing to do, Rick," she said after what seemed a long time. He wished she'd start talking again.

"Hullo." Brian was in the doorway, his brown hair sticking up all ways and his eyes still puffed and sleepy. "Daddy wants you."

"Oh." Mrs. Kaplan held a spoon in the air. "Okay. Here, Brian, you take your egg off when the bell rings. I've got to get into some clothes. Is Peter awake?"

"Linda!" The man's voice bellowed down the stairwell.

"I dunno, but Daddy wants you."

Mrs. Kaplan pulled her wrapper around her again and started upstairs. "Bring in the milk," she called back. "Maybe Rick could do it for you."

He could hear her still murmuring voice grow more muted as she disappeared into the upstairs, a door opened somewhere, and the sound of Peter's "nonononono" greeting. Then running water, doors opening and closing, footsteps.

Rick and Brian were alone. Brian sat at the table and ate a piece of cake. Rick watched him. He felt uncomfortable being here so early. "How's your nose?" he said at last.

Brian didn't answer so Rick opened the back door and

looked outside. "Where's the box?" he asked. Suddenly Brian was beside him, pushing him out of the way.

"Never mind," he said. "I always do it for her."

Rick went inside again and leaned against the refrigerator.

"Look out." Brian pushed him aside and clanked the bottles into the refrigerator.

"Did he leave any butter?" Mrs. Kaplan was in the doorway, dressed in jeans with Peter on her hip looking big-eyed and messy. He had hair just like Brian's. That's the way the Kaplans were, Rick thought. A messy-haired bunch. His sisters were always combing their hair; so was his mother. *Look out, you'll mess my hair.*

"You boys better get going," Mrs. Kaplan said as she stuffed Peter into his highchair and gave him a spoon, which he grabbed and started banging. "You'll be late. Did you eat, Brian? Hurry now, do. Don't forget to look for your rubbers, and no bloody noses today, okay? Rick, where are your books? It may get warm today. Don't leave your jacket at school." She took Brian's face between her hands and kissed him. "Have a good day, dear. You too, Rick. Be good!"

She patted Rick's head and tucked them out the door. As Rick breathed his back-step breath for the second time that morning he could feel the warm place on the top of his head like a heavy cap. While Brian got his bike out of the old shed at the corner of the yard, he fingered the Thunderbird and thought of the empty morning ahead. When Brian rolled his bike up Rick said, "Date this afternoon, Brian?"

"Why ask now? I'll let you know later."

"I'm not going to school."

Brian stopped. "Cut? You wouldn't dare!"

At the bottom of the driveway Rick leaned down to pick up his bike. Suddenly he said, "How about coming with me? Could we ever have fun! We could ride to the village. They've got some new yo-yos. I've—"

"I haven't any money," Brian said.

"I do. I've got money. Come on. I'll buy you a Coke. We'll go anywhere you say."

"No."

"I tell you what. I'll give you—" He pulled the car from his pocket.

"No," Brian said.

Rick kicked his bike. He didn't look at Brian.

"Rick, please come to school. We can play after three. Maybe my mother will take us somewhere. Listen, after yesterday you'd better be careful. What'd they do to you anyway? I mean, they might really do something bad if you don't go to school."

"What can they do?" Rick's voice became a sneer. He pushed Brian away from him. "Go on. Hurry. You heard what your mother said."

Brian rode off. Rick sat on the edge of the grass in front of the big rock for a long time. He didn't watch Brian or the other children who walked past him, the little ones with red and blue and green legs and short skirts. He didn't look at the cars that blew his hair as they went by.

Rick sat by the boulder with his hands in his pockets. He could have offered Brian a pen. It didn't matter. Brian was the kind who stuck to it when he said no like that. No arguing or explaining would change him. Rick had tried before. He was stubborn. How did Brian get to be so stupid and stubborn when he had the only nice mother Rick had ever met? The only good thing about Brian was he could read and he didn't mind Rick leaning over to look at answers. He didn't make Rick feel dumb or make a big deal about it. He just put the stuff out on his desk where Rick could see it easily. Miss Barker once saw Rick copying from Brian's workbook and asked, "Brian, is Rick bothering you?" Brian said, "No, he just asked me a question so I'm helping him," in such a way that Miss Barker said, "Fine."

"Hey, Rick, you'll be late," called Ralph Jones from across the street. "Aren't you in enough trouble already?"

Rick halfheartedly threw a stone at Ralph who ducked and pedaled faster so he nearly flew down the hill. Rick crawled behind the boulder. He closed his eyes and thought of what he would be doing if he went to school, and then began to smile because the first thing he would be doing would be going to that special reading-out-loud class. Imagine being able to miss that! The worst thing about school was the reading lesson. Arithmetic wasn't so hard because numbers didn't have meanings for him the way words did. Right or wrong, the answers didn't matter. He knew how to count and how much money he had in his pocket. But he wanted to know how to read well and the harder he tried, the worse he did.

When it was his turn to read out loud, Miss Alpert, the special teacher, would sigh and say, "All right, Rick, let's see what you can do." And he'd trip and stumble, like walking pigeon-toed, and when he'd get to a word he didn't know he'd think of other things, and then he'd say it wrong. Somebody always laughed. "Rick," Miss Alpert would say, "I just told you that word. Surely you can remember from one line to the next."

But he wasn't thinking about reading; he was thinking about Brian's mother. She wasn't like other adults, teachers and other mothers, waiting for him to do something wrong so they could get mad at him. Brian's mother didn't get mad, not even the day he and Brian broke the cellar window. She just helped them clean up the glass "so Peter and Sappho wouldn't get hurt," she said. Rick thought of all the hours ahead and what he was going to do until he could go back to school. *Not until we speak to your parents.* It was a phrase he had been avoiding. His left leg got a cramp. He had to go to the bathroom.

FOUR &✧& "BARNEY THINKS I OUGHT TO ARGUE THE

Hammerman case myself," David Kaplan said. "He thinks there's a good chance we'll get certiorari."

"Really?" Linda's car turned itself into the small railroad station, avoiding other fenders by inches, fitting itself into a niche out of the thru traffic lane. Turning off the motor, she remembered the shopping list on the kitchen counter. She tried to remember what was on it, visualizing the yellow scrap of paper with the words she had written.

"He's talking about a class action suit. I don't know."

She left the list, pulling her mind to what David was saying. "What chance do you have?"

"We know the pressure is on Kennedy to use his executive power to ban discrimination in federally funded housing. Sooner or later he's going to move on it. So Barney thinks the climate is right for this case."

"Do you?" she asked, thinking he so often told her Barney's opinion or some other lawyer's or judge's, not his own. Then, "Ouch!"—Peter had crawled forward from the back of the station wagon, having abandoned his oversized kangaroo for Linda's long tail of hair. "Let go, Peter, that hurts."

"Some notion of his that this would be good for my soul. He thinks I hide my talents from the world," David said.

"Nonsense. Barney's trouble is that he loves to talk and feels guilty about always taking public credit for your hard work."

David's slight nod and briefly parted lips acknowledged her compliment. She studied his profile, caught suddenly by the intensity of his need to think out loud in her presence. She heard the rumble of the train and her side vision noticed people beginning to rise and move toward the forward edge of the platform.

David made no motion to get out of the car. She found herself wanting to run her finger over his closely shaved

· 31 ·

cheek, the ruddy coarse-grained skin, knowing without touching how smooth it actually felt. The man was like the face, she thought. His apparently caustic surface hiding tenderness below. He kept so many of his feelings hidden, from himself as well as from her. His wry humor, his extreme rationality, his anti-sentimentality were, she knew, a shield for softer emotions that, once exposed, would leave him vulnerable. Though sometimes his carefully chosen words seemed only to flick at the truth, she read beyond them to the perturbations beneath. During moments like this the steadiness of his eyes and the straightness of his profile said comfortable things to her. Occasionally— today—this wait in the station was like a present. He remained in the car, isolating them from home or world, until the train filled the station, and still longer, until the thickest of the crowd had already boarded, as if he were saying, "I don't want to leave you now or ever."

After a pause she said, "But does Barney really think you might win?"

David's answer was lost in the clatter of the train.

"What?"

He tried again. She struggled to read his lips. "I'll call you." He reached for his briefcase, said "Bye" to Peter, touched her hair briefly, and waited another moment. The crowd on the platform was thinning. Cars were beginning to leave. A few men ran across the street. He would have to hurry.

"You'd better go." She almost pushed him out. He opened the door, started again to say something, waved his hand as if to say it was hopeless, then hurried toward the train. Finally he merged with the remaining mass of gray-suited men with briefcases, newspapers tucked under arms.

Linda watched him, half wishing she were going along and could finish the conversation, half relieved to see him disappear into the dark aisle so she could get on with the business of straightening out this disorganized day. Why were the most crucial words spoken when time was short?

Trains came both too soon and too late. Was there something the matter with her that she was never satisfied? "Chronic ambivalence"; she tried to laugh at the term she'd coined, but was suddenly frightened because the reference seemed clinical. Of course there was something the matter; she knew it. Although it was much better than the year before, no doctor would accept her diagnosis or provide a more appropriate one.

As she watched the last men reach the train, she thought, These commuting businessmen were never ambivalent, confused, or disheveled, but neat and gray, moving across the platform like tin toys. One ambivalent morning she had seen a red-eyed drunk lurch out of the station house, his black tie unstrung down his unbuttoned white shirt, his dinner jacket half off. She had laughed, refreshed. Oh, the men were tidy, but the women who delivered them! None were messier than she, she thought, pushing back the stray hairs tickling her forehead. Well, perhaps some other year she'd learn how to keep her hair in its bands, her hems sewn up. All she could do at the moment was offer peace. For now that would have to be enough. At least for a while David had not had to say, "Why don't you fix yourself up?"

It had been one of those unexplainable things, how she simply couldn't manage to remember to comb her hair or change her shirt. It was easy to blame on Peter. "He climbs all over me." But she knew that it was mixed up with her feelings of helplessness, her depression.

"I'm not going anywhere," she'd snap at David. "I just didn't have time to change."

But she knew there was always time to change, and that the more she flailed at him in anger the further he retreated. And he had nothing to do with the anger. He neither expressed it nor provoked it. Hers alone, a private possession, it came from an unknown source within her and fanned itself like a gas fire on artificial logs. She was the medium, but she didn't have control over the jet nor often over the intensity of the heat. When David turned the petcock experimentally, producing first the explosion and then the flame, he would be surprised, not having realized what the little lever controlled. Yet he had been burned; they both had.

Was this unreasoning anger one of the costs of having married him before she quite knew how she loved him? She had told herself the choice was wise. She knew there was no better man if her yardstick was inner virtue. And nothing in David ever frightened her. She sometimes caught him watching her, his lips in a half smile as if he were laughing at her and hungry for her and surprised by her all at once. She felt—and was engulfed by—the force of his physical passion. They made love freely from the night she agreed to marry him. She was as quickly aroused in love as in anger. As she struggled to control one emotion she struggled equally not to constrain the other. Discovering his vulnerability, she never turned away when his hands felt for her in the night. And, not wanting him to slip away, she taught herself not to say half the angry words that rushed her mind. That was a good thing, of course.

It was becoming easier. She had brought herself to the point where she did remember to comb her hair and have it cut, and she set aside Thursday mornings to wash it. It was, after all, such a simple way to win a smile. She had finished turning up almost all of her hems. It was a question of organization.

She started the motor.

Suddenly, "No, no, no!" Peter began to cry. She turned off the motor, ruffled his hair and squeezed his fat neck. How could she have forgotten! Linda never left the station before the train was out of sight. Silently, ritualistically, Peter watched it each morning. At other times he paid no attention to the passing trains, which, he knew, did not carry his father away from him.

While she waited once again Linda tried to visualize the list on the counter. She couldn't see the words, only the messy kitchen, Rick staring vacantly in the open door at her. She hated anything to break her morning routine—once broken, everything fell apart. What should she accomplish on the way home—cleaners, hardware, food, drugs? She couldn't remember. Again she started the motor and, as the train finally disappeared and Peter's attention returned to her, she drove out of the station to Main Street, past the A&P, the small shops, library, the big white clapboard mansion that housed the post office, out to the highway toward Nutgrove Street.

In the nine years she had lived in this village, she had grown to know it so well that it no longer mattered to her. Whether it had a library or the school a jungle gym, were now issues for others to concern themselves with. She had tried many things, and civic improvement had been the most frustrating for her. She found that people in meetings needed to show their mettle and exercise their egos. When their viewpoints were challenged, they lost the qualities she had loved them for. A friend could become rancorous or, worse, tedious and repetitive. She lived closed within the walls of her own home, as if by isolation she could hold tightly to the peace she had so carefully created. If, another year, she were to put her energy to the world of conflict outside, she thought, it would not be to local problems, which had stirred emotion for no reward, leaving shells of friends like scattered debris on a beach. Now she would not venture out even for broader purposes. She cherished her carefully won cloister of home.

The thing was, she knew she had played her own domestic game of brinksmanship with her life and David's. It had left her—and him too, she realized at odd moments—quite tired. A year before when it seemed as if everything they had ever wanted together was theirs, they had come so close to separation that they had both been shaken. There had been moments when Linda knew that the depression she felt, the words she spoke, the anger she never quite controlled would widen the chasm, but she had helplessly persisted. It was as if, now that their external hurdles were cleared and peace and survival within a hand's reach, she had to create a new turbulence. She had never known why. She only sensed that she had more effect on the temper of their marriage than David. It was the wild swings of her emotions that charged or uncharged the air.

Their most devastating argument had erupted, surprisingly, over her inability to call the plumber to fix a leaky toilet. She had not thought, when she had rather casually said she couldn't talk to Leon and asked why David didn't call him, that he wouldn't simply do so. David's equally casual refusal produced an explosion from her that astounded them both. Suddenly, insanely, they were arguing about men and women, about responsibility and commitment, about life. The leaky toilet meant David had to go downstairs to pee. Dealing with Leon, a coarse-tongued boor, would mean Linda had lost control of her life. Plumbing seemed, crazily, the most elemental and onerous part of her existence. To be required to talk to Leon in a box of a room, smelling his sweat while he dealt with their most intimate physical needs, revolted and incapacitated her. Why couldn't David talk to the plumber? He had to work. Accusations flew back and forth. Arguments went on and on as if each had a store of vexations they had been saving. He lost patience with her; she became irrational. She did not manage the house. He underestimated her effort. She didn't love him enough; he didn't know what she felt for him or anything else. The sounds became more and more dreadful. She had not wanted to be hearing or saying—or even thinking—any of those things. In their anger they weren't even clever.

Clearly he thought she was neither useful nor attractive. "Have you looked at yourself in the mirror this morning?"

She challenged him: "If you think so poorly of me you might as well leave."

The words hung in the air, irretrievable, stunning both of them. He didn't contradict her. Eventually, soundlessly, they went to bed. They did not touch. The next night they discussed divorce.

Days she thought of managing without him. She wept in the shower. She divided up the furniture. She fussed over the meals, but he ate hardly enough to survive, and in silence. To break the silence she made lists of topics that might interest him, but his gray face, though it never masked his suffering, gave her no openings. Despair was palpable. At the station in the mornings he opened the car door almost before she stopped the car, but he walked across the platform like an old man whose briefcase is too heavy. Nights she lay awake with wet cheeks, shivering, knowing she could not say she was sorry—sorry for what?—hoping for the touch of his hand, his foot, any sign of affection.

He found her in his sleep one night and wrapped her in his warmth, fumbling with her breasts, burying his face in her neck, giving life back to her. She turned over, pressing her whole length against him. *Hold me, hold me.* She made no sound. If she spoke he might remember that they were supposed to separate. But he woke and entered her quickly and heavily. She fell asleep with his weight on her still, wishing he would stay there forever.

In the morning she could not meet his eyes and blushed as she had with the first boy who kissed her. Conversation began tentatively, shyly, over Brian's first homework assignment and Peter's crablike crawl. She brushed her hair until it rustled and shone, and hemmed her skirt, and got Leon to replace the leaky toilet.

In the weeks after that she did what she could about her "sickness," which was to try to hide its manifestations. On days when she thought she understood it, she told herself she had too many passions—it was greedy to expect them all to be satisfied. She tried to pull her weight. David returned to his gentle manner, complimented her meals and, finally, one night laughed at something she said. Together they planned to renovate another attic bedroom.

To come back from the edge of marital disaster, to look again across the breakfast table into the eyes of the man she loved and had hurt, whom she had hated, and who had hurt her, to speak pleasantries across the soft brown head of their son, to smile together at the antics of the infant caught between them, had taken the conscious, deliberate, and exhausting efforts of both of them. Now that they were well past it, now that conversation came easily and they did not have to try to be polite to each other, it was almost like exploring a whole new romance. She was determined to let nothing tilt the delicate balance of their existence. No chronic ambivalence allowed.

She made the turn into Nutgrove Street, and smiled at Peter. It was always the same with him. "Nononono," he would say passionately, and she could smile or turn off the motor or say, "I know, Peter, that's just fine," and he would be satisfied. If it were only so easy to satisfy the others! How could she ever be sure what level David was operating on? This morning he had needed her whole mind, and she had been distracted. Yesterday he had phoned and said, "How are you?"

"Fine," she had answered automatically. She had been trying to add up a column of numbers in the checkbook. They didn't add up to enough to pay the oil bill.

"No, I mean how do you feel? I have to go to Washington one night this week. Will you be all right alone?"

What was he worried about? She had never been helpless or frightened. Disorganized, perhaps, but—she tried to reach into his mind and found it difficult. Somehow she had always known what her father meant, even after his stroke when he could only point, tell her things with his eyes.

David had been her strength when her father was dying. He had always wanted her to take over his drygoods store when she grew up. "Rosenbloom and Daughter," he used to joke, "since I don't have a son." Her mother said she should go to college, make something of herself, marry an intellectual. During Linda's first day of classes at NYU she saw no other person, no fellow students. Before her eyes were only the brown setter eyes of her black-haired father. And in her ears no educative phrases, only, "Well, maybe she'll marry someone who'll like the store. Maybe."

She was a year away from her B.A., and had already been admitted to the school for social work with advanced standing for the next year, when her father had the stroke. Momma, who had always been the one to hold a person's hand during a sickness, or to fix the soup when you came in cold, sat at the hospital day and night until they knew he would be all right. Linda took his seat in his office, determined to keep the store alive for him. She sat at her father's desk that first sad day and looked at all the pigeonholes, each so carefully labeled, each so marvelously easy to understand. She did no work. The phone rang constantly. The many people who loved him, salesgirls and buyers and customers and salesmen, all wanted to know what they could do to help. Linda kept the store open and didn't let herself think about the exams she was missing, or Robert waiting for her at the hamburger place longer than the soup would stay hot.

Momma came home from the hospital after two weeks of vigil and said, "Linda, he's going to live, the doctor said, but he can't move and he can't talk."

From her height Linda looked down on her small, dumpy, gray-haired mother, who had quietly shrugged her way through every crisis and every decision. The set lips, the tightly folded hands, plump but ever competent. Her eyes had often been critical but never her voice. Over the years Linda's endless questions had been answered with repeated questions or, "Ask your father. That's for him to say." She looked at her mother now, silent, resigned, but unequipped. She felt no closeness, only barren compassion.

"Well," Linda said finally, "he never did say too much anyway. But he can eat, can't he?"

With swift composure Momma went for her pencil. The shopping list developed like a rhapsody. "Soupbones, celery, rice, chicken . . ."

Her mother took care of her father by day and Linda took

care of the store. At night she read Thoreau's *Winter* to the old man because that was what he pointed to. She remembered him telling her that he, too, had once skated up the length of a river but looking at the fragile creature by her side, not the heavy-shouldered man who had carried her across the high brush in the Vermont woods, she found it hard to believe.

But when Robert said, "You've gone uptown on me. You're throwing yourself away," she remembered what her father had been once.

"I have to take care of things for him," she said angrily, "even if you can't understand."

David Kaplan was the youngest lawyer in the firm that had always handled her father's business. David understood the way her father wanted things done, quietly, with no arguments, no unnecessary litigation. "So many lawyers want to make a big case out of everything," her father used to say. "Not David. He's young, but he might as well be old, he's that wise. He knows right from wrong, that boy."

David spent two days going over the books with Linda, and after that she found herself asking his advice, calling him a dozen times a week. Each night she reported to her father on the day's activities, showing him sales and receipts, telling him who had called, who had placed orders. Always when she explained how David had helped her through one tight spot or another, a beatific smile would somehow come to his lame facial muscles. Robert would have said, "I told you so." But Linda was glad to please the old immobile man.

David took her to dinner frequently, and asked her to marry him each time. "You might as well get used to the idea," he said. "Sooner or later you're going to say yes."

"No," she kept repeating, "no, I'm not ready. There's so much to do in the world. I'm not ready to get married."

"Do it with me," he'd say, but she was afraid she never would. Managing the store absorbed her totally; she had no wish to leave it to others. Her dreams now included the profit margin on hundreds of yards of velvet ribbon and how to keep the pattern stock up to date. In her position she could hire an occasional Jewish refugee, a veteran, blacks and some Puerto Ricans who were beginning to crowd the streets of the West Side, fulfilling some of the promises she had made to herself to work for those less fortunate. She had an occupation as long as her father lived, and he lived thus, telling her with his eyes each night how proud he was of her, for over six years.

After her father died it was just her and Momma, who faded so fast, Linda thought some evenings she could see her crumple like a day lily at dusk. They had never had a lot to say to each other. Eventually they sold the store and Linda tried to study again. But she had little patience with school or with herself. The professional degree glittered in her mind like the gold ring at the carousel. But too often what she heard in the lecture hall had little relation to what was happening on the streets of her city. By day, too many gaunt and dark-eyed children scrambled in filthy gutters and, by night, teenage loungers—who in her youth had played nothing more dangerous than stickball—roamed in armed gangs that threatened each other and made her afraid to walk home alone. Too many mornings the same derelict woman lay asleep beside the curb, her bleeding legs awry. Once Linda had driven herself from Introduction to Social Psychology through Collective and Deviant Behavior, course after course, confident that the degree was the key to her being able to rescue this woman or that abused child, or better, eliminate the despair that drove people to such dissolution. Now she stepped carefully away from the pitiful body, its repulsiveness overwhelming her. Statistics 223 had only vaguely helped her mark down the button stock for the biannual sales; Personality & Culture 304 seemed only remotely useful for knowing whom to hire. In six years she had learned that her instinct was usually trustworthy.

She toyed with the idea of switching from social work to education. Exposure to John Dewey and the manifestation

of his philosophy, progressive education, had led her to believe education could cure society's ills. But what she heard
and read was that progressive education was dying, that it
had failed to provide intellectual and academic training. She
felt a personal loss. That had been one of the roots of her
optimism.

The old apartment was a hollow place after Momma
died. She'd lie awake listening to the life wounds of her new
crowded neighbors, the three A.M. screams for help, the
whining sirens. West Seventy-seventh Street's suffocation
no longer seemed safe. The professorial phrases she heard by
day seemed obsolete platitudes. She had felt more effective
when she ran the store. It became harder and harder to listen in classes, to push herself through the days. She argued
with herself: If you stop again you can always go back. You
did that once. She wanted to live life, not audit it.

Time had a way of slipping by. Many of her friends now
lived in the near and far country; instead of joining her at a
concert or the theater they were raising their children,
weeding their new gardens, joining their clubs and their
PTAs. Though she no longer had business dealings with
David, he was still constant, still taking her to dinner regu-
larly, still saying, "Marry me. Marry me."

One day as she walked through Lord & Taylor she met
the secretary from the bursar's office of the university with
whom she used to chat occasionally. An unwed wasp of a
woman with great hips and sloping shoulders, she was glad
to see Linda and talked hysterically about the sex life of her
parakeets. "I bought them a mating box three months ago,"
the woman said, "and you'd think after all this time, well, at
least I should have an egg or two, but—"

Linda glanced past no-shoulders to the long mirror and
saw escaping from her own beret a wisp of hair that, caught
in the overhead light, could have been gray. Who am I, she
thought, to be saying no so often? That night over the blare

of the trumpet at Nick's, where she had asked David to take her so they could hear some real jazz, she said, "You know, you're really the nicest person I've ever known."

"Don't insult me," he said, "I'm in love with you. Will you marry me?"

"Yes." They laughed together and he bent her fingers over his hairy brown hand and kissed her right in front of the waiter.

Each morning as Linda drove home from the station she kept her eyes centered on the road for the whole half-mile down Nutgrove Street. She looked neither right nor left, avoiding the memory of the woods that were gone. But when she saw the boulder she felt better. It had been the boulder as much as the house behind it that had made them buy. Who ever thought they'd own such a rock! "Imagine me a rock owner," she said to David after they signed the contract.

"Imagine me married to you," David said. "Never mind the rock."

After Brian was born she tried a number of innocuous and undemanding occupations which would not take her mind too far away from baby and home. She joined the Committee for Fair Housing and the League of Women Voters, and when Brian went to kindergarten she addressed envelopes for the PTA. But she found herself exhausted for little product. There was no profit and loss ledger to add at the end of the month. What she wanted was another baby and she didn't seem to be having it. After two miscarriages in as many years she took a job with the Department of Welfare. They called her an "investigator."

"We don't need the money that badly," David had tried to argue her out of it. "I'm afraid you'll get too tired again. You're hardly out of the hospital. Loaf a little. Brian still needs your time. Come to town sometimes. You've been missing the city! Have some fun for a change." But with Brian in school, she had the time, and if she stayed home alone she'd think about the girl baby she hadn't carried past the sixth month. *It really was a blessing, Mrs. Kaplan. Usually the body rejects a fetus for cause.* Being an investigator meant that when she finally got some poor relic of a human being to reveal the hapless chaos of his existence, all she could do was report it to her supervisor, hoping, of course, that she had communicated successfully the kind of need she found so that someone else could help. It wasn't much to do. She wrote the school for social work and learned that she had let too much time lapse. If she wanted a degree she'd have to apply all over.

One morning she followed up a call and found two little girls under a downy bed in a house "that must have cost fifty thousand dollars," she told David. "Their half-crazed mother was screaming drunk because—because—oh, I don't know but I know you just can't do enough!" She burst into tears at the dinner table.

With her napkin, she mopped the water she'd spilled and touched the soggy cloth to her eyes. "I'd have brought them home if I could," she said bitterly, "but when their father came down to the office to get them he had tears in his eyes. He's skinny and weak but he loves them. I suppose he even loves that woman, or once did."

"I wish you'd get a job that doesn't tear you apart," David said finally. "We haven't had a decent dinner in weeks."

"How can you talk of food?" Suddenly nauseated, she escaped to the bathroom.

"I didn't mean to carp," David said later. "Do you suppose you could be pregnant?"

Peter was on the way, and so she quit being investigator. Sometimes she dreamed of those empty-hearted people she had failed so utterly, but she seemed to have more to do than she could manage most of the time. She was elated about being pregnant again. David too. He began tentatively to work on the second attic bedroom they'd started twice before. Linda's doctor was cautiously optimistic. "No reason to suppose there was any connection between the two miscarriages. Circumstances were different." Linda let David speak with the doctor. She was impatient with the medical details. All she wanted was the baby.

Now she had it all, yes, Peter and Brian and no more hospitals. The house would be paid for soon enough; David felt strength in his work; the dreadful depressions of that first year were past. The anger had abated, its fire now more or less under control. She had absolutely everything she wanted. Yet still, on an occasional morning drive home from the store, now and then in a strange gas station or on a supermarket line, she would find tears in her eyes and a reasonless despair, a sense of impotence and self-abnegation so overwhelming that she could wish only to rush home to the noise and privacy of a hot shower. Or sometimes she would use Peter's presence, a buttock to squeeze, a dirty hand to wipe, to save herself from self-destruction.

This disorganized morning it was the sight of her beloved rock around which she had once planted crocus and snowdrops and lilies-of-the-valley that reassured her. As she made the turn into her driveway she swung the car wide to avoid a bike that had been thrown on the ground. Now she remembered having avoided it on the way down to the station also. Who had left it behind? The bike-riding children were all in school.

She drove into the garage at the back of the yard and opened the door for Peter, who crouched playfully on the far side of the station wagon seat, tucking his little body close against the kangaroo.

"Come," she coaxed, "come on, Peter."

"Nononono," he grinned at her. Linda shrugged, then turned toward the house. She left the door open knowing that if she hadn't been weary (at nine in the morning!) she would have taken two or three minutes for the grand game he loved. How long would she have him to play with? To hell with it, she thought, and left him alone to follow her. The dog was barking to be let out of the cellar. Rick had come so early and she had been so late, she had forgotten Sappho, poor thing. There would be a mess to clean up. She looked at the gray sky. The air smelled of snow. Deeply damp. Snow tires—damn! Silly of David to be worried about leaving her alone. Unless he needed her to miss him. Or was he uneasy about what he had to do in Washington? Were his musings in the car this morning an extension of yesterday's seemingly directionless phone call? Even now, with his train not halfway to the city, rushing to put distance between them, she felt him reaching for her, for her mind, felt his caress, his dependence.

David had always taken the corporate part of his and Barney's practice: wills, closings, mortgages, taxes, business mergers. Barney was the labor lawyer, the radical, often taking on cases where there was no possibility of a fee, but a principle to establish, a precedent to set. He and David had been friends forever. Barney, a great fat man with quick small eyes and nervous hands, had brought in many clients, argued loudly, teased unmercifully. But he always concerned himself with moral controversy.

He didn't lose cases often, but when he did, the loss was big. "A dull practice is a dead practice," he'd say to placate David.

"I'm a dull guy," David would answer, "but not dead yet. We do have to eat so I'll stick to business." To Linda, David admitted more complicated feelings. "Someday when I'm sure Barney's on the right side of something I'll surprise you all and join him." Was the Hammerman case the one? she wondered.

Bill Hammerman, a successful screen and TV writer, had helped to start a small woodland contemporary development. The community was an interesting one which Linda and David had talked about joining themselves; but they had been reluctant to live so far from the commuter railroad line, as David's work demanded long and regular hours in the city. A Woodland Place was formed by a select group of architects who kept control of the design of the houses and the rugged land between, allowing almost none of the dense woods to be cleared. The development started at the same time that the bulldozer—which had done such a noble job of clearing for army camps and air fields during World War II—was profitably and busily laying bare the landscape outside of the city.

The day Bill Hammerman discovered that his Negro army friend, John Walker, didn't want to bring up his son in one of the two neighborhoods in New York City open to Negroes, Harlem or Greenwich Village, he had an idea. Although the suburban communities were not opening their arms to Negroes, Bill decided A Woodland Place could become a model not only for small-house design, but for social responsibility. Bill, David once explained to Linda, never had gotten off his conscience the fact that throughout the McCarthy era, when so many of his friends were blacklisted, he continued to make more and more money, first on early paperback novels and then in TV.

When Linda had joined the Committee for Fair Housing she and David and Barney talked long into the nights about ways to break the real-estate lockout of Negroes. The only legislation available to them was the Civil Rights Law of 1866, and although they knew legislation was needed, both Barney and David agreed that litigation was a more appropriate avenue to follow. When Barney heard what Hammerman, a friend from college, was trying to do, he leaped at the chance to handle the case.

The community had blocked the sale of land to Walker at every turn—an ideal situation for testing present interpretation of Fourteenth Amendment rights, Barney asserted. Past interpretations had perpetuated discrimination. Why not argue that opening up private property to public use meant the state was involved, and therefore had to adhere to the Fourteenth Amendment? Would the Supreme Court accept the notion that when a private community became incorporated, its franchise coming from the state, it became an agent of the state? If so, it would follow that the private community was disallowed by law from encouraging or authorizing discrimination.

Linda had listened to the four men talk strategy and constitutional law several times. But why would Barney suddenly want David to argue the case? she wondered. Of course he was involved; his knowledge of real estate was indispensable. But David did not enjoy or shine in court appearances.

She nearly fell on top of the boy sitting on the stone step. This was her home. She never looked where she was going. She could move blind in her own house and yard. At nine in the morning there should not be a classmate of Brian's on the back doorstep.

"Well, Rick," she said when she had recovered her balance. "What are you doing here?"

He didn't answer. He rolled a little yellow car back and forth on his knee.

"Are you hurt?"

He shook his head.

"Well, what, then? Why aren't you in school?" She didn't try to hide her irritation. This was the second time this morning he had invaded her privacy.

He looked at the car on his knee.

She talked into the silence. "This is most peculiar. If you aren't sick—or isn't there any school today? Of course there is. You'll be in trouble again if you don't go. Brian tells me—" She was jabbering again. It was a dreadful habit. She did it whenever she was ill at ease. She had jabbered at him earlier this morning too. A nuisance, his coming early like that. Mornings were clumsy enough. It wasn't the first time either, she realized. He'd arrived too early three or four times the week before. It wasn't good for Brian, made him rush through breakfast. She'd have to explain that to Rick so he wouldn't do it again. But this morning he put her off, just sitting there watching her with those big watery eyes of his that she seemed to look right through. And he hadn't said anything at all. She watched the little car go back and forth on his knee and remembered his eyes.

Suddenly Linda sat down next to the boy, folding her heavy sweater around her legs. "There is something wrong."

He looked at her, and she studied the young face for a time. There was something about it, a reminiscence she couldn't place. His face was a slender, smooth oval, silk falling aslant on his forehead. His mouth was narrow, lips full; lips, nose and cheeks fluid, a sculptor's conception. His wide-spaced gray eyes were almost oriental. He didn't blink. He didn't appear to be seeing her at all. She saw in his face the softness of youth, but the distance in his eyes was vast. What had he seen that had blinded him? She wanted vaguely to trace the contour, forehead to chin, with her forefinger. "There is something," she said again more gently.

"Yes'm." The boy barely moved his lips. She started violently.

"Did something happen to Brian?"

He shook his head no.

"Come in." She got up abruptly. "Hurry, Peter," she called to the little one standing now at the door of the garage, feet apart, staring at Rick. "Come in and tell me about it." She spoke in her best matter-of-fact voice. "I haven't yet had coffee." She had meant to send him away. What she did then, she did without volition.

Linda held open the door while Peter lurched along the driveway, stopping now and then to pick up a leaf, an acorn, study it, throw it, take a turn. He finally made it to the door. "We'll have second breakfast." She put Peter in his chair.

"Why aren't you in school?" The question hung in the air. Rick didn't answer. Linda held Peter's milk cup to his lips. She kept talking, eventually realizing that Rick answered none of her questions. "Did something happen to your bike?" "Are you feeling sick?" She watched him closely. She'd had plans for this morning, but she couldn't remember them. That was one of the strange things about her since Peter was born. Half the time she couldn't remember what she was supposed to do. How had she ever run the store? She tried making lists, but there wasn't much use in starting anything because she wouldn't be able to finish, and it wouldn't be the right thing anyway. If she stood very quietly in her kitchen and listened hard she felt she was the hub of many lives. She could hear them all. She was the pivot, the core, the nerve center. She stood still but everything was in motion around her. If she put out her toe a spoke might snap. I could write a play, she thought, three acts, the history of a civilization, but with one set—the kitchen, an empire, a prison.

She listened to the drip of the bathtub faucet upstairs; the tick-clunk of the grandfather clock in the living room; the muffled thump of the water pump; Sappho still scratching around down cellar; the murmur of the oil burner. Close by, Peter, the loud breather, breathed; a car drove by on Nutgrove Street, its sound dimming slightly as it passed in front of the boulder. The rock was home, a lantern she saw from far down the street, always there in front of the dining room window, protecting her. It was a haven for Brian. She looked again at the boy sitting quietly at the table across from her now, not drinking the milk she had poured. He must have hidden behind the boulder this morning, an invader. The rock was her anchor, her watchdog, her fort, the center of a thousand children's games. She could hear the afternoon laughter coming from behind it. When she died, she thought, she would like her ashes buried beneath it; then flushed to think of the flamboyant tombstone she had chosen.

"Why aren't you in school?" she tried again. "You're so late now. I could drive you there."

He still didn't—or couldn't, she realized suddenly—answer. He stared at her dumbly. Something *had* happened. She frowned. The first time Rick had come into her house he had been a wary, defiant stranger whose eyes averted hers and whose too-proper responses sounded insolent. "Yes ma'am!" "No ma'am!" Something had changed him. Now he seemed defenseless, innocent. She stood up and turned her back and said, "Why are you afraid to go to school?"

Then she turned on the water, barely managing to hear him say, "They won't let me go."

She turned off the water but still didn't look at him. "Oh? Because of Brian's bloody nose? Because of that?" she asked.

"I guess so." She felt a minor triumph. She faced him again. "It wasn't your fault. Just a free-for-all. Brian told me about it." She didn't tell him that Brian said the teachers blamed Rick for anything that happened, even when it wasn't his fault. "Do you like Rick?" Linda had asked. "Uh-huh, he's fun. He likes to do fun things. He didn't mean to hit my nose." Linda had been proud of Brian then, of his compassion, rare, she thought, in anyone so young. So she had said, "It's a lot harder to unmake a bad reputation than make a good one. I'm glad you're a faithful friend."

Now to Rick she said, "Brian wasn't hurt, not even frightened. Perhaps Miss Barker made too much of it. Actually Brian was more upset the day before. He's probably forgotten what you fought about. I suppose you remember." She glanced at him now. Rick's expression didn't change. His eyes showed no flicker of either anger or comprehension.

The interviewing technique came back to her but it had been too long. She was out of practice, so she gave herself time to warm up. As she spoke she reminded herself of the rules:

Don't ask questions. Make statements. If they're wrong the patient will become angry and contradict. Never evaluate what he says out loud. (This child did not say anything. He just looked at her, and on past.) There are some you have to have superhuman patience with, she remembered. If he won't talk, try to say things that will startle him into revealing . . . answer questions with questions. . . .

There were other phrases, rules, empty memories, half

sentences moving against each other, unclosed parentheses. *My life is an unclosed parenthesis.*

"When they told you not to go to school you felt you'd done something pretty bad," she said softly.

"I dunno," he murmured. It wasn't working. She bit her lip, thinking. Children were the hardest, of course, because even when they talked it was ciphers. You had to figure out what they meant by what they left out, or by trying the opposite of what they said. "I hate meat" could as easily mean "I love meat but I'm not allowed to eat it."

"So you're suspended. For a week. A day." She tried by the command in her voice to get him to look at her again. "Until—"

"Until my mother gets home."

"Oh, your mother's away. And your father?"

"Uh-huh."

"Well," she said, "that's not so bad. Someone must know where they are."

"Addie knows."

"Addie." She thought a moment. "Your maid. Of course. Well, let's ask Addie to call them."

"No!" The cry was sharp. His eyes turned on her again, and suddenly he was stripped naked.

There are all kinds of strays, she thought, and all kinds of hunger. She remembered what she had wanted to do—try to design a bookplate for David's Christmas present. Designing took time alone. Pick up the phone, she told herself, he'll never know. Call the school and check the story. If a child came to the door naked and hungry, could she turn him away?

"What would you like to do?" she said at last.

"Couldn't I just stay here?"

She took a deep breath, put the last dishes in the sink, lifted Peter out of his chair and the morning proceeded. Rick followed her everywhere and said no more.

He followed Linda outside when she pulled back the big door to let the dog out of the cellar. Sappho, an ardent young golden retriever bitch with more love and energy than sense, bounded out, mowed Peter flat, and licked his face. Peter picked himself up unharmed and Rick followed Linda down the old stairs where the bare bulb revealed the shambles of torn paper, defecations, spilled tins of nails that had to be cleaned up. Between diapers and this, a great part of her life concerned the refuse of those for whom she was responsible, she thought. As she swept the mess into a newspaper, Rick sat on the stairs and watched.

He followed her out when she dumped the paper, and again when she put Peter into the sandbox. And he followed her in. Finally she handed him a towel, telling him to dry the dishes. If he was going to shadow her she might as well put him to work. What would she do with him all morning?

He followed her upstairs, so together they made the beds. She vacillated between wanting to shed him and remembering his nakedness. As she finished picking up the daily leavings—pencils, puzzle pieces, papers—behind Brian's bed she said, "Now why don't you play awhile. Brian has a new puzzle. Do you build models? He's working on a cruiser, I think."

"I don't feel like playing." He followed her out of the room.

She went into the bathroom and shut the door, but she knew he was outside waiting for her to finish. She ran the water in the sink while she used the toilet. She combed her hair.

When she came out and saw him, hands in his pockets, she felt sorry for him again. She put her arm across his small shoulder. "All right, try and tell me what's on your mind. You're in some kind of trouble. I'm not going to say anything, you know. I wouldn't tell."

He slipped out from under her arm. "The phone's ringing," he said.

She picked it up in her bedroom. "What are you doing?" David asked.

"Nothing. The dog messed in the cellar. I forgot to let

· 53 ·

her out. I think she's in heat."

"So soon? Why must we have a dog?"

"I thought you wanted one."

"I guess I did. I was thinking—" he began.

She interrupted him. "Besides, this year we don't train Peter, so I have a dog to train."

"You do enough."

"Do I?" Suddenly she felt petulant. "I don't know. Why live?" She didn't know where the words came from. He was trying to fill the distance between them but it was too great. He hadn't called to talk about the dog, but to hear her voice, to find a place in her thoughts, to be close to her. She sensed his loneliness, as if he knew she was distracted. His voice touched her but she didn't know what to do with his need; it was like making love to him with her mind somewhere else. She was not alone!

"For posterity." He paused, breathed in her ear. "What's the matter?"

"Nothing. You're supposed to like dogs. Sappho's yours." She was as incapable of telling him what the trouble was as the boy was mute with her. But it was suddenly important that David understand the effort she made. She was on a high wire, trying to balance. She tried to close the space between them. Sometimes they could say more to each other on the phone than during long evenings alone.

"Nonsense," David said. "She doesn't know I'm alive. You're the one she loves."

She felt the caress and shivered. She saw the boy leaning on the doorjamb. "I don't want her to. There isn't enough of me."

"Oh," he said, "I think there is. There's enough of you." His tone became light. Easing up on her, teasing. "But if I ever need a witness—" Linda could hear Barney's voice in the background shouting. Then, "What are we doing Wednesday night?"

"Nothing. What did you decide about arguing the case?"

"I don't know. Nothing yet. Did you get the leaves burned?"

"No. I've been busy." The boy still watched her with unblinking eyes. He tossed the blond forelock back, then looked at his toes. *Have I committed an indiscretion?* She hardly heard what David said.

"It'll be a mess if it rains. I'll try and get home early—if the wind doesn't come up."

She said goodbye, hung up. Turning to Rick, with forced calm she said, "Maybe you could rake some leaves for me if the wind doesn't come up."

"Maybe," he said.

Shortly after noon Brian, pink and puffing, burst in the back door. He went straight to Peter and stuffed him into his highchair like a heavy doll. "Can I feed him, Ma? Can I?" He handed Peter a piece of bread.

"Nononono," Peter said and put the bread in his mouth.

"Take off your coat and wash your hands," Linda said automatically.

"My hands are clean. I washed them at school. You know what—" He stopped and stared at Rick. "What're you doing here? What's Rick doing here, Mom? How come he's here?"

The boy sent Linda a message, a challenge. "I invited him," she said quickly. "I thought you'd like company for lunch."

Brian gave her a look as if to ask, What right do you have to pick my friends? But then he shrugged and sat down. Finally he said, "But he cut school. Did you know that, Mom? Listen, Rick, you're gonna get it!"

"Hush, Brian," Linda mollified him. "He didn't really cut. He had permission."

"Permission!" Brian's mouth fell open. "How come?"

"I'll explain it later. Why don't you eat now."

He gave her another long look and was silent.

"What happened in school?" she asked.

He started to chatter the way he normally did. "You should have been there. It was the funniest thing." Linda didn't sit with them. She listened to Brian's high singsong voice. She felt on and off stage, as if she were looking at a tableau, not quite part of it, not knowing how little or how much she was part of it. She did what she always did, what she had to do. They came. She nourished them. Momma, she thought, a food machine.

Brian was still talking. She heard words, smiled. "Stevie," he was saying, "you know how he talks in a bunch, well he got the teacher mixed up and everyone laughed at her. She said bring your homework tomorrow, and Stevie said, 'Tomorrow never comes,' and then he told her that yesterday today was tomorrow and everybody talked at once, and did you ever think of that, Mom, that today is tomorrow's yesterday and—"

Linda laughed and Brian started all over again, chewing and talking and wiping his mouth with the back of his hand.

"I don't get it," Rick said in a flat voice.

Brian stopped talking.

After they ate, Linda took Brian upstairs and closed the door of his room. "Rick seems to have been suspended. He spent the morning here. Do you know anything about it?"

"No," said Brian. "What did he do? Did he touch anything in my room?"

"I don't think so." Linda tried to reassure him. "He didn't do much. I gave him a book to read but it was too hard. Did Miss Barker say why he was being punished? He doesn't seem to know."

"No. I told you. Nobody said anything. I figured he'd cut. Should I get his work? How long is he suspended? Last year they suspended a guy for spitting in the library. I suppose it was my bloody nose. My stupid nose. The fight wasn't so bad. I mean, kids are always fighting. Should I get his work?"

"That would be good. He'll be here when you get home. Do you mind?"

He paused. "No."

"I thought you were friends."

"We are. It's okay. Only don't let him touch my model."

There was a small crash from the kitchen, the sound of Peter's milk glass on the floor. The grandfather clock struck one. Peter began to bang his tray. Sappho barked. When Linda started down the narrow stairs Rick was already coming up. As Brian pushed past him Rick said, "Date this afternoon?"

"Sure," Brian said cheerfully.

She lay on the big soft bed and thought about the silence. She lay face down, her body stiff, immobile. Tufts of chenille pressed into her cheeks. She stretched, tensing all her muscles, then tried to relax. Drowning, she clung to this hour of each day, let no one but herself decide how it would be spent, whether to do something or nothing, to think or not to think. Lonely, exquisitely loved, sometimes she loved an empty hour as much as she had ever loved any person. Today would be no different. She turned on her back and reached for the newspaper. *Rick is alone in Brian's room.*

"Kennedy sees progress on Cuba. Insists aerial watch continue." *You gave him a book. He's all right.* "Educator criticizes U.S. schools for being lax." "Dutch elm disease claims 100-year-old trees in Riverview." "Realty man ousted in race 'panic sale.' Broker's license revoked after attempted 'blockbusting.' " "Mississippi judge says Kennedy administration moving toward a totalitarian dictatorship." *He wouldn't go in to Peter. He wouldn't! You'd hear him if he moved around.* "Texas town split by Birch dispute." "Nixon ordered by court to say if he supports Bircher." *Maybe you should have left the door open. Listen! No one's moving.*

Her ears, even in deepest sleep at night, were tuned to

every sound in the house. Even when she didn't want to hear or think or listen, she couldn't help it. Once in a while David would take the children out for a Saturday afternoon saying, "Have a nap; read a book; goof off." But when they were out, she never did. She wandered aimlessly, hearing noises of the ones who weren't there. By the time she settled down to a good book the clatter of all of them would be around her again. Chronic ambivalence. How long was it since she'd read a book? *A long time ago I read* Winterset *and walked under the Brooklyn Bridge at night.*

She came back to the newspaper, but she had to force herself to follow what she read. A little war in a faraway country called Vietnam—she didn't read that. A touch of scandal in the city government—that didn't touch her. A rehash of the missile crisis—that was over. The election in California—not her concern. No sit-ins today. No blacks and whites marching side by side without her to raise her guilt. No school revolutions today, no knifings, no breakthroughs. Progressive education was dead and "education in depth" was going to replace it.

While she lay on her chenille bedspread, freedom riders had moved through the South; blacks and whites sat side by side in bus stations and restaurants; James Meredith studied at Ole Miss; a Harvard professor said you could teach anything to any child of any age or stage if you could find the key; an educator said the secret was to love the sinner, not the sin.

I'll be what I want to be somehow, someday.

The phone rang and she almost didn't answer it; she spoke as briefly as possible to a PTA phoner urging her to go to a lecture on left-handedness the following morning. She made a promise, but wondered why she hadn't said no. What would she do with this guilt over all that she said yes to, over all that she avoided, over the lucky fact that her beautiful children were born white instead of black, were smart not dull, were clothed not naked; her luck, her pride, her guilt. She studied the paper again, forced herself to read the continuation of the blockbusting article. "The action taken by the Secretary of State was the first under Rule 17 of the Real Property Law. The law, put into effect last year, bars real-estate brokers or salesmen from engaging in 'blockbusting' activities, that is, inspiring panic sales of homes because of the entry into the neighborhood of persons of another race or religion. The ousted broker had urged whites to sell because Negroes . . ." To start with she would stay informed.

Her knotted leg muscles began to flex. Then she realized someone was outside the door of her bedroom.

"Yes," she said. "What is it?" She heard a murmur. "I can't hear you. Wait a minute." With a longing look at the mostly unread paper and the bed, she went to the door.

Rick stood there, the book dangling in his hand.

"Didn't you like that one? We'll pick out another."

"Peter's crying," he said. So together they went into the little room where Peter stood in his crib, tearstained face smiling at both of them.

"Why don't you read him a story?" Linda made one last effort.

Rick's eyes implored her. Then she saw that he held the book with his finger still at the first page.

"I'll read to you both." She sat on the extra cot with Peter on one side, Rick on the other. They sat quite still while her voice filled the time. Gradually she became conscious of his shoulder touching her arm, of his fair head leaning tentatively on her; soft and safe like any child.

Brian arrived soon after three and she let Rick serve the brownies.

"Did he bake them?" Brian was frowning.

"He helped," she said cautiously. Later the boys were occupied in Brian's room. She walked by the door, feeling free of her shadow for the first time that day. She stopped and watched a moment. Rick lay on the floor rolling the yellow car back and forth. Even in so small a gesture the boy had a fluid grace, a maturity that belied his few years. She couldn't help feeling distaste for his too-slim pants, tight shiny twill where denim would have clothed the young buttocks more appropriately. But whenever she looked at his opalescent-eyed face, she couldn't turn away.

What was the dichotomy between face and body? Between the words he said and the poise with which he moved?

Brian was talking. She stood in the doorway and listened. "Don't you want to play cards?"

"No."

"Let's play army. I'll get the men."

"No."

Brian, exasperated, "Well, what do you want to do then?"

"Let's go down to the river and float boats."

Brian looked at Rick for what seemed a long time. Finally he drawled, "You dummy. There isn't any river here."

The day had gone on forever; an ache began at the back of her neck and didn't end until someplace past her calves. She thought, If there's a cry in the night I won't answer. I'm all used up. The house was quiet except for the last of the dishwater running down the drain. Linda dried her hands and hung up the towel. David's footsteps moving into the living room seemed loud, demanding.

He put a record on the phonograph. "I told Barney I'd argue the case for him," he said and walked to the piano.

Linda came the long distance into the living room. "I'm glad," she said. She didn't feel glad. Strains of Benny's clarinet floated across the room. David sat at the piano and tapped out a beat. Then he began to improvise with the record.

Suddenly he banged a discord and turned around. "I hate talking in public, damn it. Barney knows that."

"Why did you say you'd do it?" She reached into the basket of wool and knitting needles on the floor.

"He said I'd have a better chance to win than he would. He's been too exposed. They've seen too much of him."

"Don't do it if you don't want to."

"I think it ought to be won. The time for these things is just opening up. We do have a chance, but . . ." He paused. "The whole office is mixed up in this case. Barney's just gone ahead. It'll change the nature of the practice."

"It's been changing for a long time," Linda said. "You've moved way forward. People change. Daddy's been dead a long time. You wouldn't still want to be nothing but Rosenbloom's bright young man, would you?"

"You sound like Barney. He treats me like a kid brother. Talks about readiness. Kindergarten talk."

"He does have ambitions for you, doesn't he?"

"I'm not sure I have the same ones. Sometimes you can do a better job if you don't let a case get to court." He was playing an old song, and she couldn't think of the name.

"Or sometimes," she said with effort, "you simply don't feel like pushing that hard; not everybody gets a chance to be useful. Don't knock it."

"I'd never be able to do it without you," he said.

Another present. She realized he meant it. "I don't have anything to do with it." He began to play under the clarinet now, quietly, tuneless but rhythmic, nice.

"I wish I could play the piano," she said.

"You do enough." That was the second time that day he had said that to her. She wondered if he believed it.

"What, knit? I don't do anything. Garbage, trash, leaves, leavings, a human vacuum . . ."

"Darling, nobody can make the bathroom gleam so bright. Where did you ever learn?" He got up and sat next to her, picked up her hand and toyed with her fingers. She felt hot; a lump formed in her throat. He never let her pity herself. He picked up a law review from the coffee table.

"I was thinking," she began, then stopped. She glanced at the wall of fine print in his hands, at his face which had become absorbed.

After a while she came around the heel, slipping the waiting stitches back on the main needle with care. With each sock she did a better job, and when she finished this one she would either go on to argyles or try one of those bulky ski sweaters that she couldn't afford to buy.

When all of the stitches were safely ensconced and she was again on the straightaway she said, "I had an extra child here for the day."

"Oh." David didn't look up from the journal. There wasn't any reason why he would be interested.

"Rick Lang," she persisted. "He's kind of a new friend of Brian's."

"The kid with the money." She was surprised he remembered.

"Um. But he was here all day. Morning and afternoon. He just came to stay."

"Why wasn't he in school?"

"He said he was suspended."

David looked up. Linda continued to knit. "I don't really know too much," she said. "He just didn't seem to want to be home. His parents are away, and they don't even know."

"Sounds suspect to me. What terrible thing did he do?"

"Nothing terrible. He followed me around. Like a waif, a kitten. You know, the way that cat did last summer?" She felt herself talking too much, overexplaining.

David laughed. "I meant what terrible thing did he do to get suspended? I know you're so warmhearted all strays find solace in your presence. You don't have to explain that. An original earth mother."

"Well, you have to admit the cat did adopt me. He would have been ours for keeps if I hadn't found the owner. Every time I sat down he'd be in my lap. Drove me crazy."

"Did this boy climb in your lap?"

She shook her head no. "He just followed me everywhere. He didn't even play with Peter. I overheard him ask Brian if he had the kind of mother who always says yes."

"What did Brian say?"

"Sometimes I do and sometimes I don't."

David laughed again. "Well, he's all right."

"They got in a fight later, with a couple of kids down the block. But when he was alone with me he was . . ."

"Why was he suspended?"

"I'm not sure. There was a fight on the playground yesterday. Brian got a bloody nose. But that's not enough. It wasn't so serious."

"Where are his parents?"

"He said out west. He didn't know what his father does for a living. Do you suppose Brian knows what you do? I have this feeling about the Lang boy. He isn't stupid, but he's so detached. And yet when he stands next to the other children he seems much older, tougher."

"He sounds like something of a menace. He can't be good for Brian. They wouldn't suspend him if he hadn't been in trouble before."

"He's been in trouble."

"I'd get rid of him," David said.

"I have this funny feeling. I can't explain it. He reminds me of something, someone. Whenever he looks at me I feel responsible. I can't figure him out and I couldn't turn him away."

"Why ever not? That shouldn't be so hard to do."

She didn't know how to answer him, so she was silent. It seemed to Linda that David looked at her for a long, long time. She began to decrease toward the toe, counting carefully, four stitches fewer on each row as she knitted round and round. She felt his critical eyes on her, probing, waiting, watching for her to drop a stitch, to say more, to reveal more than she knew. She felt uncomfortable under this scrutiny, as if caught in a lie as a child, someone waiting patiently. *I'm waiting, Linda, I'm waiting patiently.* She flushed, raised her eyes from the tiny loops of wool. Her eyes did not meet David's because his were closed, the journal still at the page where he'd opened it, having slipped to an impossible angle when his fingers loosed their grip.

Warmly, apologetically, she said, "Come, David, let's go to bed. You don't want to sleep here." He hugged her roughly and she turned off the lights as he climbed the stairs.

Tuesday morning Linda stopped to shop before she returned from the station. She had a list, carefully made, that did not include Rick. She would say she was busy if he was there.

The sky was gray again when she got out of the car and she didn't stumble over him. He followed her into the house, polite, quiet, distant, yet even when her back was turned she knew his eyes were on her.

"Look," she said, turning suddenly. "Don't you have something to do at home?"

He shook his head no.

"Isn't there someone at your house? I have things to do here."

"Addie's there."

"Well, why don't you—"

"I like it here."

"What about your schoolwork?"

"They didn't tell me what to do."

She opened the refrigerator, took out the makings of a stew. She glanced out the window and saw Sappho like a sentinel guarding Peter in the sand. She remembered Brian telling her Rick was a poor student. "I help him a lot," Brian had said. "He can't read very well."

"Who at home helps you with your work?" she asked.

"I don't like to be helped," he said.

"Oh, but you'll get too far behind." She stopped. She didn't want him here. She took out a cutting board and washed the carrots. Go home, she wanted to say. Go away and leave me alone. Don't look at me any more. Don't ask me for anything. You don't belong to me and I don't have to stop living my life for you. I have things to do, places to go.

She pushed the cutting board in front of him. "Slice these for me, please." She handed him a paring knife and the washed carrots. It didn't matter in the morning. He might as well stay. She'd send him home after lunch. No playing today, she'd say. She heard again the raucous sounds of his voice in her yard on those days in the late summer and early fall when he'd come to play with Brian. She had never particularly warmed to him. "Shut up!" or "Baby!" would signal his arrival. One day she saw his pointed toe trip Brian as he ran after a ball. She heard her neighbor's daughter, Suzy Mendelsohn, whine, "Rick won't let me play." She remembered the sound of the cellar window glass shattering, his defiant smirk when she picked up the rock he'd obviously thrown through it, his startled look when she put the rock down and told the children to help her sweep up. Before yesterday, she thought, she'd rather have any other child come to visit. Why couldn't she send him away? That shouldn't be so hard, David had said.

In the morning she could be gentle. In the afternoon he would have to go home.

"Do you ever help with the cooking at your house?" she asked.

"No."

"What do you like to do?"

"They wouldn't let me have a knife."

The words didn't make sense. "Surely you're old enough," she started. What was he trying to tell her? Was he saying, in effect, you trust me and they don't? She studied him again as she had the day before. Consolations were at the edge of her thoughts. A boy who said "I don't get it" to an ordinary childish vision had his mind locked up somewhere. Only certain things seemed to get through. She peeled an onion, dropping dry skins in the sink. Wherever he was, it was no business of hers.

"Cut the carrots a little smaller," she said. "Like this. Small enough for Peter. Don't cut your finger." She shouldn't let him use a knife if his parents disapproved. You don't feed other people's dogs or give candy to strange babies. Unwritten rules that govern the behavior of mothers who never meet.

She didn't want him here. "You may stay for lunch," she said crisply, "but this afternoon—"

She felt something on her left arm and when she looked she saw his small hand with its ragged overgrown cuticles, its close-bitten nails, a grubby boy hand touching her arm just below the elbow. She remembered his head on her shoulder, and, "Let's go down to the river."

"Was there a river where you used to live, Rick?" Words slipped past her lips.

His startled eyes caught hers and then looked into a distant landscape.

"There *was* a river where you used to live," she said.

"Down behind Gran's house there was a river where I used to go and sometimes lie on the rock and watch the water go by. Bugs too, and once I brought one to her. 'Look,' I said, 'I've got a present for you.' And when I opened my fist she acted scared, but she laughed. That's the thing that's funny, her laugh. I can't remember anything about her, how she looked or anything, but sometimes when I'm asleep I hear her laugh. Maybe she just pretended to be scared. Once she went down the hill even though she said she was too fat to climb up again and we put the bug back, the little black water bug, and it swam away. She said it was glad to be in the river which was home and I said I wasn't scared to go away from home and—"

"Go on," Linda said helplessly, but there was no need to prod or ask a leading question. She couldn't have stopped the words had she tried. They came like a river running, a rapids of strung-together phrases, sense and senseless, rushing and tumbling and tripping, and for the first time without guile. Through his lips and eyes she learned the bits and beginnings of a lifetime.

When she finally sent Rick home she knew that she knew more than she wanted to know. It was like someone back in the McCarthy days telling you he was a Communist. You didn't want to know those things because just the knowing made you more responsible than you wanted to be.

I don't know what to do, she thought. He frightens me, yet he trusts me so. I want to hear no more. But when she covered her ears and said stop her hands locked out answers to questions that had no answers.

Brian had come home in tears the week after Peter was born. His teacher made him spend the morning in the coatroom because he'd been an hour late for school with no note.

"Did you tell your teacher you have a new baby brother?" Linda had asked him. "I'm sorry I forgot the note."

"I tried to tell her but she wouldn't listen."

If there was anything good in her she would not shut her ears. In *The Fall*, she knew Camus had spoken to her privately. She had read it more than once. Who can shut his eyes to a man with a raw wound bleeding? Who can estimate the depth of a wound without probing? There are some that need surgery, some that a kiss and a promise can cure. Who had given the boy a kiss and a promise?

She uncovered her ears and secrets grew between them.

David wanted her to go to the city for dinner Wednesday night to eat with Barney and the Hammermans, but she couldn't get a sitter. "Weeknights are hard," she told him. "The girls won't go out." David got home late and they were both edgy. They lay in the dark, not touching, not speaking. Tales and recollections fought for release into words but she didn't know where to start. Would he repeat, "Get rid of him"? Or, "Don't tear yourself apart"? Why ask David's advice if she didn't mean to follow it?

Whenever she did anything that took all of her and left her spent by night, David reached out and pulled her back to him. When an infant cried and she left the bed, his arms would try to keep her from going. When she slid back under the covers he would say in his sleep accusingly, "You left me alone!" In his own way he would say, I need you and I need more of you. Of course he did and he should and she cherished that need. Why wasn't there enough of her to go around? Hold me tight and tell me it's all right to listen, she wanted to say this night. You don't kiss your husband and think of other things. Rules for wives.

Why was he deaf to some of the sounds she heard?

I reached for a doorknob that was too high and I got a stool and I opened the door baby they said keep the baby out and when the door opened something hit my head bang baby get out get out she screamed my father was sick but my mother screamed.

Remembering hurt her with a pain as hot as when she had twisted her broken arm; she couldn't stop the sounds in her head any more than she had been able to stop the spasm of pain once it began.

Linda's eyes were wide open to the darkness and she knew that she must tell David all she had heard, and she must ask, "What shall I do?" If she didn't tell him everything, there would be nothing they could ever talk about. There would only be time and space and flesh between them, habit.

"David," she said without moving, "did you ever think of the word 'home' as a blasphemy?"

"I don't know why I don't quite trust Hammerman. I wish you'd been there, Linda," he said from another world. "I don't like to be used."

She inhaled as deeply and as long as she could. She let the spasm run its course and subside. She pushed back quick words, reached for what she could say that would be the bridge. Sometimes he said, Must you pick the middle of the night to start a conversation. Must you, must you. She touched him and he was real and he was hers. He was not young and he was tired. Finally she said, "That's what lawyers are for. To be used. It's all right if you want the end." It sounded a bit pompous to her but it was the best she could do.

How many nights and days, she wondered, did they sit across from each other, thinking separate thoughts, reaching at the wrong time? Perhaps timing was the heart of the matter after all. Sometimes she talked too much.

David walked the mile and a half to the station the next morning because Linda wasn't ready in time to drive him. He caught a nine o'clock train to Washington.

FIVE &&& AT NINE O'CLOCK ON THURSDAY MORNING Linda Kaplan sat in the outer office of the New Delphi Elementary School waiting to see the principal. Peter Kaplan, his snowsuit unzipped, sat straight-legged beside her with a book on his knees and a yo-yo in his hand. Inside her office Glenna Masterson was checking through the morning mail, sorting it into neat piles. She reached for her appointment pad to see what the day had in store. Then she began to compose her list of projects for the day.

1. Get the last of the group achievement tests off Joanne's desk. If she hasn't finished scoring, find someone to help her. *Don't antagonize Joanne. She'd been critical Monday after that business with the Lang boy. "You suspended him?" "Of course. I had to." Joanne should have seen the trouble coming. That was her job—to spot troublemakers before they exploded.*

· 69 ·

2. Talk to Mrs. Callahan about the Thanksgiving assembly. Make sure suitable for all school. Parents?
3. Phone publisher to find out why second grade math workbooks are late. Too heavy a burden on the teachers if they have to develop all their own material. No control over curriculum. *Control was what you learned so carefully and lost so fast.*
4. Prepare outline for staff meeting. Subject: Developing sense of responsibility in children. Call speaker for next week's meeting. Written expression at elementary level. *Maybe you should check with Lang's maid again, see if there's a phone number where parents can be reached. Have you tried everything? If only you'd been able to talk with them, better than that letter. Well, the letter was out. "You suspended him?" Shocked voice. "Of course, I had to."*
5. Find out what Thomas Lang does for a living.
6. Talk with Barbara Lang's teacher. Which class? Dillas. *Well, Dillas wouldn't be much help. Never got to know any of the kids. Strictly subject matter. They learned a lot though. Some of the hard-driving parents asked for her. Good to have one of those around in fifth grade. Ya gotta teach my boy to spell! Dillas.*

The phone rang. Glenna put the receiver to the instrument at her chest and turned up the volume. "Mrs. Kaplan is waiting to see you. She doesn't have an appointment but I thought—"

"All right," Glenna said. "Ask her to wait five minutes."

"But Catherine stopped in. Her class is at gym. Could she come in now?"

"Yes, I'd like to see Catherine." She hadn't spoken to her

since Monday afternoon. She should have, perhaps, but she had wanted time to collect her thoughts. It was Catherine's fault, she decided now. The whole mess was due to Catherine's inept handling of the boy. "Leave him to me," she had said earlier. "I'm sure I can handle him." Well, she hadn't done much of a job. And to drag him down the hall that way, not even explaining that the blood was from a little nosebleed. It was, of course, the blood and the sight of the knife that made Glenna lose control. She rubbed her corned toe, remembering the pain. Even three days later her neck grew hot, tendons tightening at the memory of her own shrill voice screaming at him.

Glenna sensed the door opening. "Yes, Catherine." She did not look up as she spoke. "I want you to make up some kind of summary of Richard Lang's achievement for the first part of the year. Make it as complete as you can. Tomorrow I want to meet with you and Joanne and make some decisions about the boy. We should hear from his parents next Monday. Get the papers to me as soon as you can. Behavior and achievement."

"Dr. Masterson."

"By this afternoon, please, Catherine."

"Yes, but—"

Glenna looked up. "But what?"

"Well, his friend has been asking for his workbooks. I was wondering—he'll be so far behind if he stays out all week. Couldn't you let him come in this afternoon? I could give him some special time. I hate to see—"

"The boy may not come back, Catherine, until I talk to his parents. I told you that. I told him that. I wrote to his parents. We just can't afford a repeat."

"I know. Of course." Catherine looked at her neat black toes. She was young—her third year of teaching—and Glenna knew she was good. When she learned to evaluate, she'd be a fine teacher. She cared. She created. But sometimes teachers weren't effective until they learned to care a little less.

"It wasn't anyone's fault," Glenna said finally. "Send the workbooks home if you want. Perhaps you could even write a note." She went back to her list. Catherine left the room.

7. Start draft of article for paper on New Math program. *Don't forget you've got a whole school to run. Don't let the Lang thing run away with your time and your school.*

The phone rang again. "May Mrs. Kaplan come in now?"

"Oh, yes. I'd forgotten she was there. What's it about?"

"I don't know," Grace said, "but I got Brian's folder out just in case."

"Good." Glenna waited for the door to open. "Come in," she said. She tried to remember what she knew about Mrs. Kaplan; she felt more secure when Grace put Brian's folder on her desk. Her hand stroked the smooth manila folder. Something safe about having some solid facts beneath her palm. This was a part of the job that made her feel most inadequate, this business of dealing with parents. The thing to remember always was to keep absolute composure; no matter what they said, to show no reaction. Be polite, smile warmly so they would talk freely, but always keep a certain distance.

Glenna watched Linda enter the office. A pretty woman with long straight hair tied back like a child's, sharp well-defined cheekbones, a large face with full lips and dark brown eyes that were too big and dark for her light brown hair. She pulled an old raincoat around her even though it was warm in the office. Glenna noticed her sneakers and wondered how she dared to be seen in them. Glenna hadn't worn sneakers since she left the farm thirty years before. Probably came in a hurry, on an impulse. Wary now, Glenna smiled warmly.

"Do sit down." Linda settled catlike into the wooden armchair, crossed her legs, then her ankles. "I haven't seen you in a long time. When was it?"

"Library Committee, two years ago. Before Peter," Linda said.

"That's right. What can I do for you now? How is Brian getting along?"

"I didn't come about Brian," Linda said. "I came about another boy."

"Oh?" Unknown territory. "Bad influence" was the phrase she expected. She glanced at the clock.

Linda's voice tickled her ear. "Sorry," Glenna turned the knob on her hearing aid up a bit, "I didn't hear."

"Rick Lang." The sound cut through this time. "You do know him of course."

"Of course." The tendons tightened in her neck again. The name was beginning to irritate her. "What about him?" Glenna reminded herself to smile. Linda spoke with obvious difficulty. Looks as if she hasn't slept in a week, Glenna thought. That's why her eyes are so dark.

"The child has been at my house every day this week since you suspended him." Linda paused. "You did suspend him?" Glenna didn't answer. "At least he said you suspended him. I mean he said you wouldn't let him back into school until—"

"Until his parents return," Glenna said. "That's quite correct."

"I wanted to make sure. Sometimes children get their stories garbled. What did he do?"

"What else did he tell you?"

"He's—ah—he's not a very happy child," Linda said. "And I have two of my own. Couldn't you let him come back to school? He shouldn't be left alone all the time. I mean even if he deserves to be punished, the child is alone all day long."

"There's nothing I can do, really," Glenna said as coolly as she could. This was difficult. She didn't know how much the boy had told.

"Well, he's not loose on the streets, because I've let him stay at my house. And if he hadn't decided to do that, well,

I'd never be here. I don't want to interfere with the affairs of the school. I've never questioned any decisions of yours regarding Brian. But someone—either his school or his parents—should be caring for him. I—"

Glenna fiddled with the knob as Linda's voice rose and fell. "I'm sure his parents have left him with someone responsible. There are two other children." Glenna started, then stopped. She didn't want to sound defensive. She'd better cut this off.

"Well, as long as you won't let him come to school he'll be with me. He doesn't want to be at his own home. I don't know his maid or his sisters, but I tried a couple of times to—"

"I can see that it isn't easy for you," Glenna said. "He's not an easy child."

"It's not that. But I have two of my own. I have other commitments. It doesn't seem fair to me or to him for you to refuse. What terrible thing did he do on Monday? Boys fight. Noses bleed. If I wasn't concerned about that, why should you take such a drastic measure?"

"Mrs. Kaplan, there's nothing I can do. There was no other way for this situation to be handled."

"No other way?"

"No."

"With both parents out of town there was *nothing* else to do?"

"I wrote them. We couldn't reach them by phone. I wrote them full details." She was almost angry now. She mustn't let it show. She forgot the smile. She held tight to the desk drawer.

"I know he gets into fights. I know he can't read. But that still doesn't explain—"

The little knob between Glenna's fingers seemed to roll of its own accord. What did the boy do? He stepped on my toe. He crushed my toe, my shoe, my shell. Suddenly Glenna straightened her back. He hadn't told! She glanced at the little knife in the top drawer of her desk.

"Mrs. Lang, I mean Mrs. Kaplan, surely you understand that certain things are confidential. Now if it were Brian—"

"Dr. Masterson, the child has been at my house morning to evening for three days. He left only to go home to sleep because I made him. He said he didn't know what he had done. But somebody had better listen to him, be with him, talk to him. You can't expect me to do it all."

"Of course I don't expect you to do anything. You're really not involved." Glenna regained her mastery again; the smile returned. "We've been alert to Rick's difficulties for a long time. We know his behavior is well outside of the normal range. We've spoken to Mrs. Lang, and as soon as she returns we'll all work together to help him. But really, you cannot expect me to discuss further what are confidential matters."

"Then you'll not take him back this week?" Linda stood up. Glenna stood also. Their eyes were level.

Linda looked hard at the greenish eyes, the netted hair, the mouth that strained to close over large teeth. She fingered the car keys in her pocket, felt the softness of the gray carpet beneath her sneakered feet, heard steam popping in the radiator. How did a child survive an interview with this large, rawboned woman? How would she survive this one? Your own child is in this school, she told herself. Leave now.

"No." Dr. Masterson's voice was low, clear, controlled. Linda pulled her coat around her and left the room.

At ten it began to snow. It stuck right away and within a few hours the silent whiteness smoothed the whole small world. Scrappy lawns looked as sleek as tended ones, old roofs as good as new. Children stopped whining that their braces hurt and looked out their windows, dreaming the same dreams. Peter sat quite still in the middle of the driveway with his tongue out catching the huge flakes. Linda, who had never been able to resist a snowfall, happily shoveled the paths.

"My father always says to wait till it stops," Rick said. "Then you don't have to do it so much."

"I like to do it." Linda grinned at him. "Here, have a shovel."

"Okay," he said, and grinned back. He had snow on his lashes. She remembered the bad boy in her class in fourth grade who came smiling up to her one afternoon after his daily session with the school psychologist. "What do you do there?" she'd asked him. "What does she do to you?"

"It's crazy," he said, "she doesn't do anything. I just lie on this lumpy couch and talk." Linda had wondered at the time how that could do anything, but after a year he stopped being the bad boy.

Thursday afternoon they sat in the local service station while the snow tires were being mounted. Rick said, "We never had any snow where we were. That's why my mother didn't want to move here. Because of the snow. But my father said we had to, just never mind, all she'd need were some new boots and some snow tires. I guess she's not going to like it much when she gets home."

"Maybe she never knew how pretty it is," Linda said.

"I guess she's not going to like it much when she gets home and finds out I didn't go to school."

"Would you like me to call her on Sunday?"

He shook his head no.

"Would you like me to talk to Addie before your mother gets home? Maybe Addie could help her understand how it was."

He kicked at the tire that had come off the car. "Maybe."

She touched his shoulder. "I'll do what I can. Get in now and we'll pick up Brian. You kids might as well have some fun in this snow while it lasts."

She took them to Long Hill with two sleds that afternoon. Rick and Brian rode together on one, up and down, over and over. She took Peter on the other.

Long Hill was as wide as it was long and there was an ample flat at the bottom before a sled had to meet the thicket of sapling birches and aspen by the brook. Summers it was golden brushed with pink clover. In the snow it was a Breughel.

Over and over the four met at the top; she felt no older than the two boys, eyes glistening, cheeks bright, snowflakes in her nostrils.

"Can I take Peter down once?" Brian asked her. "Please, Mom, please!"

"No," she said, "he's too little, too young. It's too big a hill."

"He's not afraid," Brian said. "Look at him, Mom, he wants to. Look!"

She looked at her teddy bear infant, already sitting on Brian's sled. He understood everything! She listened to Brian's dancing words. "Just once, Mom. I'll hold him tight." She looked at the wet mouth open in eagerness.

"You can't trust him to hold on," she said. "You have to hold him and steer too."

"I'll steer and hold him," Brian said. "I heard him laugh when you went by." He pulled at her arm. "I just want to take him down once. Just once, Mom!"

"I'll hold him," Rick said suddenly. "I'll go too."

Now she looked at Rick. "No," she said. Rick's eyes narrowed. He half turned away, old suddenly, a shoulder's twitch into another kind of person.

Brian kicked the sled angrily. "Oh, no! You butt into everything! She'd let me if you weren't here."

"If I weren't here you wouldn't have anyone to sled with."

"Oh yeah?"

"I don't care. Go by yourself." He picked up a handful of snow, packed it, took aim.

"Rick?" He looked at her over his shoulder, chin high, lower lip hard as if he said, I should have known. As if he said, You're like the others, daring her to trust him.

She took hold of his shoulder, Brian's too, squeezing them equally hard with her gloved hands. "It's too nice a day to argue," she said playing for time to calm them, to calm herself.

She relented. In the long run if no one was hurt, moments like these made boys whole, made brothers love each other. Living was a collection of moments; she had to let them have theirs. Rick needed to be trusted. Brian needed to give Peter a thrill. She had to say yes and hope they survived.

Infinitely tender she packed the three on the sled. Brian in front, then Peter, and she put his short arms under Brian's armpits.

"Hold tight," she said and kissed the cold red cheek. "Hold tight."

"Nononono," he said, holding tight and pressing his face against Brian's back. Then Rick behind Peter. "If he falls let him roll clear but stay with him," she told Rick. "Just keep him out of the way of sleds. Okay?"

"Okay," Rick said.

"Okay," Brian said impatiently. "Push us off."

She did, with her foot, and they slid away. Too fast, she thought, too fast. She'd forgotten to warn them about the trees. They were going so fast they'd go too far. She'd never get them back. Come back! She had blundered! It was over in a moment, but when she saw them pick themselves up, and she counted three, yes, three tiny figures standing at the edge of the thicket, her chest hurt and there were tears in her eyes.

She had not blundered after all.

She watched them start up the hill. She became exultant. I have done something positive, she thought. Halfway up the hill she saw the gray-jacketed figure, the slim one, put the little one on the sled and now two pulled and one rode. I turned around and I listened, she thought. I put more than a coin in a beggar's hand.

Something creative was happening, something that smacked of a novelist's desire or a potter's dream; something that bordered on the selfish and the maudlin; something in her desire to be Jesus or Florence Nightingale. Why did she deprecate the lofty in herself?

By the time the three reached the top of the hill she had decided to do what she could for Rick. She would see Addie; it might do no good. "Addie's Addie," he'd said. "She never tells." But Linda felt she had to make her presence in Rick's life known at his home, as if it would make an honest woman of her, she thought.

Thursday night she ate early with the children, went to bed soon after they were quiet. At one A.M. Friday the temperature began to rise sharply, as a mass of warm air was pulled over the valley in the wake of the storm. By three-thirty, the thermometer read forty-two and all around was the sound of running water from the melting snow. At three-forty-five Linda awoke. The air in her room was close, and she was perspiring. She was glad to be awake because her dreams had been uncomfortable. But now she had Rick's dreams in the dark with her, and that was no better. She dozed and waked alternately until seven. There was an unknown danger, something she couldn't grasp. She couldn't remember her dreams. Like looking for a key, something you had dropped in the dark of the cellar, your bare hand feeling the rough damp dirty pronged things on the floor. You came out bleeding. Lit dangers were all right. You didn't worry about marked manholes or traffic on the highway. She knew the hazards of interfering with someone else's child. Some traps were posted, locations known. If you looked and knew the way you could be cautious. What was the unknown thing?

She wouldn't have him say, "I tried to tell her but she wouldn't listen." What was living, after all, but listening?

At eight-thirty Linda looked out the window and saw Rick aiming sloppy snowballs at the apple tree. Last week it had been stones. She called him inside. "Did you see Brian on the way to school?"

"Uh-huh."

"When are your parents getting back?"

"I dunno."

"Does Addie know?"

"I guess so."

"What will you tell them?" He looked at her and then out the window. "Rick, the school wrote them a letter. The principal. It tells why you're being suspended. Do you know why?"

"No."

"But you know there's a letter."

"No." He looked at her again, and she realized that he could be telling the truth. There was that terrible distance in his eyes again, that watery emptiness.

"Was Dr. Masterson very angry with you the day you were sent home?"

"No," he said.

What was the unknown thing? Compulsively, helplessly, she had to let herself go down each dark hallway. *I reached for a doorknob that was too high.* There was bound to be a light somewhere. She would find the key.

At three she told the boys to go to the playground for a couple of hours.

"Come on, Rick, let's go." Brian tugged at him.

Rick looked at Brian, then at Linda. She knew what the playground was, that he didn't want to face the children who, by now, knew of his disgrace. Once it had been his home, that semi-enclosed courtyard between the school and the open ballfield. A school playground was a jungle of passion and resentment, relief and constraint, exuberance and violence. There went children who preferred any place to home; there went children who looked for a friend; there went the ones who ran with a pack, whose bodies exploded with energy; there the little ones, with hair in their eyes and noses dripping, stood on the sidelines, waiting a turn or a lesson, always wary, ready to duck if a ball came too fast or a bully sped by too close on a bicycle. But the frightened or the shy ones, the children who didn't know how to say, "Can I play?" and the closely guarded ones, stayed home. The playground had everything, the dullest to the smartest, the fairest to the clumsiest, the gentle and the rough. But some never went; some always went and stayed until dark.

Brian would never go there alone. He'd go with a friend, a group, with a ball or a yo-yo, a purpose.

Rick, before this week, if alone, always went to the playground. There were people there, a bike to put his next to, a little kid to tell a story to, a classmate. "There's always somebody," he told Linda. "I'm always the last to go home. The little kids have to leave before dark. Their mothers get mad if they stay late."

"Don't stay late," Linda said. "I'll be home in an hour or so."

Rick shrugged. "Okay," he said.

Just don't get into any fights, she prayed as she saw them leave. Please don't start any fights.

Linda put Peter in his stroller, got the long leash for Sappho, and the three of them walked to the Thomas Lang house, nearly a mile by the road on the other side of the development. She had not been this way on foot since the houses had come in. When she and David first lived here there were woods, then a field, then another patch of woods on a rising knoll. Now it was ribboned with asphalt, and ranch houses with brick arms and yawning garages sprawled behind new hydrants, lampposts, and tidy curbs. The Kaplans' friends were all in the old part of town.

Linda was not only going to try to talk with Rick's maid about breaking the news to his mother, but she hoped to meet his sisters, to see his house, to find out where truth ended and fantasy began in the medley of story, memory, and dream he had told her about himself, his grandmother, his sisters, and his parents.

The Lang house was the largest on Martin Avenue, and the last to have been sold. It stood nearly at the end of the circle, its brick and glass arms seeming to guard the land beyond. The neatly flagged path curved to a recessed front door with the usual iron grillework of current builder taste. Similar grilles appeared on alternate houses on Martin Avenue, the in-between ones having redwood handrails instead. It was general knowledge that the builder had overestimated his market; the house stood empty for over a year, dropping from the original asking price of $60,000 to a mere $41,500 when Tom Lang bought it.

Linda happened to know of this because at the time the tract was sold she and David had hoped to buy a piece to protect their two acres, and, not being able to afford it, had worked to have the zoning kept at two acres. They had been unsuccessful. They were also unsuccessful in getting the town board of supervisors to accept a provision that certain trees be left standing. The result, she noticed, as she approached with Sappho bounding in front and back of her, was that each artificially bermed front lawn, soggy now with melting snow, had one skinny-armed maple seedling planted dead center. If they were going to put in lawn trees, she thought, they might at least have planted ones that wouldn't kill the grass when they got big enough to matter.

She tied Sappho to the hydrant at the corner of the Langs' driveway, far enough, she thought, from the front door so Sappho wouldn't muddy the place. She left Peter's stroller there too, carrying him on her hip to the door. She rang the bell. The entrance was neat, devoid of boots or other debris. After a bit the door opened. "I'm Brian Kaplan's mother," she said to the young black girl who stood there. "You know Brian? He's a friend of Rick's."

"Yes," the girl said. She didn't open the door very wide. Linda had never seen anyone so dark. She had round crab apple cheeks and round lips, and large round eyes reflected again in her round rimless glasses. Her body was neatly plump, stretching the white uniform, well fed like a college freshman's. "I know Brian," the girl said. "But he's not here now." She made no move to invite Linda in.

"I know. The boys are at the playground. I—I sent them there. Could I come in a moment?" Linda didn't know how to start what she wanted to say, or quite what it was. She knew the girl's name was Addie, but, not knowing the last name, she didn't use the first. She had never been able to deal "properly or realistically," David's mother told her, with a servant. She called everyone she met that was not a friend, Mr., Miss, or Mrs., and that included window washers and people's maids. It was hardest with Negro domestics because sometimes they were embarrassed by her formality. This girl didn't appear embarrassed, nor was she cordial.

"Rick's been at our house every day this week. I thought—"

The round eyes widened. "Oh, I hope he hasn't been a trouble!"

"No, no," Linda said quickly. "May I come in?"

"Sure." Addie moved back. "I knew he'd been somewhere. Some days he just left so early and I never even saw him till dark. I knew he'd been somewhere."

"Didn't he call you?" Linda slipped out of her boots and stood in stocking feet on the heavy rug.

"Oh, sure, but you know Rick, he don't talk much. And it used to be Brian was here a lot in the afternoons, but not this week. I sure hope he didn't cause any trouble."

"He was just fine," Linda said. She registered the heavily furnished hall, the carefully cluttered living room behind. Which department store decorator had "done" this house? she wondered, measuring the obvious accents of color, the matched drapes and upholstery, the too-plush carpeting. The expensive tastelessness gave her a certain satisfaction because it did not surprise her. But she had not come to evaluate the Langs' interior design.

"Rick is frightened about what his parents will say when they find out he wasn't in school," she said at last.

"Why don't you put the baby down?"

Linda did and Addie held out two arms. "Nononono,"

Peter said and hid his face behind Linda's legs.

Addie laughed. "That's all he says," Linda said apologetically.

"I just love babies. I used to take care of my sister's babies all the time." Addie held her hands together as if to keep them from reaching out again, and Linda saw an almost hungry look on her dark face.

"Did you take care of Rick when he was a baby?"

"Gosh no. I've only been here since last year." Addie stooped down and held out a finger for Peter. "I'll get him a cookie."

Before Linda could tell her not to bother, Addie was gone through the doorway behind the stairs. Linda heard a radio somewhere, noticed a pink sweater on the banister. Over the ornate oak table in the hall was a gilt-framed mirror. She brushed a strand of hair off her face. She glanced at the accumulation of mail. Propped by the phone was a long white envelope with a familiar look. Of course; the letterhead of the New Delphi School.

She started when Addie returned with a large cookie and held it out.

"It's awfully big," Linda said. "He'll leave crumbs."

"I don't care." Addie offered Peter the cookie.

"Rick is afraid his mother will be angry when she gets home. What will she do?"

Addie didn't look up. Peter studied the cookie, then finally reached out a small hand. "Eat it," Addie said. "Go on."

"I feel sorry for him," Linda said. "I wish there were something I could do." She waited. "He, well, he didn't ask me to come here but—"

"I've taken good care of him." Addie stood up suddenly. She walked into the living room, turning her back on Linda.

"Do you think it might help if I talked to Mrs. Lang?"

"Mrs. Lang? You can if you want."

"Maybe you could do it better." Linda groped for the right words. "I don't suppose he really did anything so bad at school. He doesn't seem to know what he did. Brian got a bloody nose. His nose bleeds easily. I suppose the teacher was frightened. Maybe if you talked to Mrs. Lang, if we both did."

The girl turned, held her head high, looking through the low part of her lenses. "Mr. Lang knows I do my best. I can't help it if Rick gets in trouble at school. I don't tell them what to do. He don't cut up with me."

"I know. I mean—"

"Mr. Lang knows I take care of his house and his children just fine."

"Of course. I thought perhaps you'd agree that he's been punished enough." Nothing was coming out right. She wanted to say, Have you heard what the boy has heard? Are the sounds in his ears real sounds? But the girl looked at her now with something close to hatred. For the second time in two days Linda knew she had failed. "If there's anything I can do—" She reached for her boots.

"Mr. Lang will be home Sunday. Anything you want to know, you ask him."

The front door opened suddenly, letting in a burst of air, a girl child with her arms full of books, and the sound, "Addie, for crying out loud, there's a beast tied to our hydrant who's brought out the neighborhood hounds. Whose dog?" She kicked the door shut.

"You're not supposed to come in the front," Addie said. "Wipe your shoes."

"I know, but—oh, hello." She saw Linda. She looked so like Rick that Linda was stunned. The same pencil slimness, the soft oval face. Her hair was brown, though, and straight, and she seemed to be very little older than he. Her eyes were opaque, ordinary, unafraid.

"You must be Barbara," Linda said. "I'm Brian Kaplan's mother."

"Hello." The girl spoke shyly, politely, with a proper nod of her head. "I know Brian. He's nice."

"Thank you." Linda studied her. "That's my dog, but she

was alone when I tied her up. I hope she hasn't dug up the lawn."

"No, she just looks funny. I mean—" Barbara frowned. "I didn't mean funny. Addie, is something wrong? Is Rick in trouble again?"

"Nothing's wrong," Linda said. "I just stopped by thinking you children might need something with your parents away. Addie says not."

"No, Addie takes care of us just fine." Barbara walked through to the kitchen. "Anything to eat?"

"I'll fix you something," Addie said. "You'll excuse me."

Linda pulled Peter's zipper up roughly. She shouldn't have come. Addie was insulted. Barbara confused. Linda fumbled with the buttons on her coat, letting go of Peter's hand to hold her boot. He walked toward the door, following Addie. "No, Peter." She strode one-booted after him. Her outstretched arm brushed the phone and the letter fell to the floor. She picked it up, studied the typed address. She thought, I would give my life to know what is inside. The desire to shove the white envelope into her raincoat pocket was so intense she felt her chest constrict; an unseen hand clamped her wrist, forcing it against all her strength to move back toward the table. The struggle made every muscle in her arm and chest ache. Could she hide Rick's sin—whatever it was—in the deep inside pocket of her coat?

She grabbed Peter with the hand that clutched one boot, opened the door with the other, and, holding the door open with her hip, awkwardly tried to step into the boot without losing her balance or letting her toe touch the cold stone. It seemed suddenly impossible; everything did. She couldn't see; her hair was in her eyes.

"I'll hold the door." Barbara Lang had appeared.

"Thank you!" The child stood still while Linda arranged herself. "Thank you," she said again. She started down the walk, exhausted. She looked back. "Don't hesitate to phone if you need anything." The girl was framed, cool and neat, in the doorway. Linda hoisted Peter onto her hip and walked toward the street.

At her hydrant post, Sappho held court with five dogs—an undersized sheep dog with hidden eyes, two spaniels, a red setter, and a basset. All circled, smelled, growled at each other, pranced about her. Sappho sat poised, aloof, glued to the ground, sniffing at one, snapping at another. Peter squirmed from Linda's arms and ran headlong into the group. Frightened, Linda watched him throw his arms around Sappho which she endured as if he, too, were but another suitor.

Linda was cold by the time they reached home and found Brian sitting on the boulder waiting for her. The dogs were all around her. "Hi," she called. "I thought you'd still be at the playground."

"Where'd you get all the dogs?"

"Sappho's attracting them. Lock her in the cellar. I'm afraid she really is in heat." Brian took the leash from Linda.

"Where's Rick?"

"I dunno."

"What do you mean? I thought you were together."

"He went off somewhere."

"How come? Didn't he come home with you?"

"No."

"Brian, was there another fight?"

"No." He sounded irritated with her questions. "He just met someone. Some big kids he knew at the playground. So he went with them."

"Who were they?"

"I think one of them was a friend of his sister. I heard them mention Deborah."

"Deborah's the older one."

"Uh-huh."

"How old were they?"

"They were big. That's all. How'm I supposed to know how old they were? I don't know everything or everybody

Rick knows. You always think I know everything." He turned his back.

The sheepdog was barking at Sappho again, and suddenly Linda was angry. "Scram. Get. Get out of here!" She yelled and ran at them, clapping her hands. "Home. Go home. All of you!"

She took Sappho by the collar and dragged her ahead of Brian. "Bring the stroller up, will you? I'm late. I've got to shower, change, feed you kids, and meet Daddy's train. We're going out to dinner."

"Who's sitting?" Brian asked as he ambled slowly up the driveway.

SIX ❧ THAT NIGHT, FRIDAY, THE TRAIN WAS LATE. Linda kept the motor running for the heater fan so her toes wouldn't grow numb. She arrived at the station early, gaining the choice parking spot in the front of the lot near the narrow exit. She didn't mind waiting. She'd left the children with a new sitter who was young, just fourteen, but eager and clean. Brian was showing off his stamp collection when Linda left. She didn't worry about the children. There was a movie in Stamford she wanted to see, but she couldn't remember the name. She looked forward to sitting in a restaurant and didn't care whether the food was good or bad so long as she hadn't cooked it. It was always fine to eat a meal she hadn't cooked, to sit at a small table across a tawdry candlestick from David, to notice his black brows meet at a point over his nose. It didn't matter whether or not they said anything to each other.

But if the train was late, they'd miss the start of the feature and David would want to eat first. That never worked out too well, because by the time they got through with drinks, dinner, wine, and coffee there'd be the usual Friday-night line at the movie house. The wine always made her sleepy. "You can sleep at home," David would say, tickling her ear with his breath. "Why pay two-fifty for a noisy snooze?"

Think about the line at the movie, Linda. Think about what kind of food you want to eat. Think about the martini you're going to drink. Think about David joggling on that train, sitting impatiently on some stretch of track. Tired. Think about the groceries you bought today, what you're going to cook for dinner tomorrow. Chicken or veal. Save the chicken for Sunday. It's easier and the kids like it better. Nice Sunday dinner, broiled chicken. Rice too. Peter eats rice grain by grain with his prehensile fingers.

Think about what you're going to do next week when the boy goes to school. Think about school, David, movies, presidents, Communists, Catholics, trees, PTAs, second-hand pianos . . . anything.

The boy will go to school next week and his mother and father will go with him and say yes we'll take the responsibility yes we'll see that it doesn't happen again and then they'll take him home with them and his father will go to his room with him and beat the living hell out of him and his mother will cry and his sister will say why do you always make my mother cry.

If you went back to school and got that degree, even if you spent a lot of David's money and went full-time and let some slob take care of Peter all day, even if you learned everything you needed to know, you'd not be through in time to help the boy.

She pressed her forehead against the upper rim of the steering wheel harder and harder until pain came and passed.

Oh, God, why didn't you ever do anything properly, like finish anything you ever started?

How do you know what he told you is true? Maybe he made it all up. Maybe. Go away from it all, Linda, you're not ready for this. You've got other jobs to do. You aren't even half through making your own family right. David's starting something big. You don't even have a degree. Do something right for once; forget the whole week. It's nearly gone. Wait till next year. Go back to school then. There are whole cities full of children who beg and cheat and lie and starve. This one is well fed. Why feel so damn sorry for him?

Those others didn't come and sit on your doorstep. They said to him, "There is no place for you here." But here is his world, and they are trying to take it away. "We could make our world his, David. I know it." But I also know it's none of my business. None of it. I went somewhere I didn't belong. I looked under a rotted log.

"All the boy needs is a little love. It wouldn't be hard. I can reach him. I bet I can teach him. So can you, David." Say it like that. He'll understand. A little time and a little love. That's not so much to ask, to give. He's asked for help. That's the first victory.

The train was twenty minutes late already. There would be no chance of making the early show. The car was too hot so she cut the motor and rested her aching head against the back of the seat. Take an aspirin in the restaurant. If David wants to stop off and wash, take an aspirin at home. How much longer?

Play the game, Linda, the memory game. It was a way to go to sleep when sleep was elusive. It could be a way to pass the time and keep your mind where it belonged. Besides, it was fun. Start at the beginning of something you liked and, as if you're telling the story to someone else, tell yourself every tiny detail you can remember. Don't skip anything.

What about?

How about when Peter was born? There you were on the delivery table with the mirror and you forgot to look.

I can't remember.

How about when you first met David?

Some other time, maybe, not tonight.

Not even the night he proposed?

He proposed every night for months.

How about the first night in your own house?

But that was nearly ten years ago!

But you remember, you always will.

Just the two of them then, and all the flaking blue paint, and the boxes of Momma's dishes she had saved, and the shadeless lamps around the rooms. She had carried her father's Thoreau, four faded blue volumes, up from the city in her lap. Not even a pretty set, but he had loved it so and David had loved him so, and so and so they put the books on the stove next to the coffeepot and said they'd read aloud every morning at breakfast. Then, like two idiots, instead of unpacking they carried a bottle of brandy up the narrow farmhouse stairwell with two different kinds of spotted speckled wallpaper on it, gray and yellow, dirty and scratched "by someone else's child," Linda complained. "Just be patient," David said and took her hand as they picked their way among the disarrayed furniture toward the big fourposter bed they'd bought with the house.

"Isn't it beautiful!" she'd said with a sweep of her hand. She could remember how David's lips felt that night. Other nights go away but that one stays; because he'd never stroked her face, her jawline, her neck, to her breasts with his lips before that night. Sometimes he does it now since he discovered she likes it.

What is in that letter?

It's a funny way of making love, to be touched so lightly, but she always wants him to do that. Sometimes he doesn't and she won't show him that she wants him to because she wants it to be his idea.

What Godforsaken, misguided, demented, meddling, criminal, idiotic impulse made you want to steal that letter?

The next morning when she opened her eyes and saw the bottle on the filing cabinet she thought she'd gone to bed drunk with a stranger in a strange bed. She looked at the bare brown shoulder next to her, and then she recognized the line of black hair all the way down the center of his thick back and started to laugh. She turned on her side and put her arm under his and around his chest and pushed her breasts against his warm flesh. "I forgot where we were," she said against his shoulder blades. "I thought you were someone else."

"Who'd you think I was?" he asked sleepily.

She never answered because there'd been an explosive rat-a-tat-tat right outside their bedroom window. They jumped up naked, hastily pulling a blanket in front of them, and peeked out of the dormer. At first they couldn't identify the noise, but David finally found a couple of men with ropes across the road, starting to saw down a huge elm that must be close to a hundred years old, David said.

"How do you know what kind of a tree it is?" she asked. "It doesn't have any leaves."

"I grew up in the country. You always forget. You'll know the trees too, after you live with them awhile." The sound of the chain saw went on and off all day as they unpacked and put away their things. "I wonder how many they're going to cut down," David said sadly.

They had cut four that year, all sick. And every year after that, she thought, they'd go through the woods and along the parkways and they'd mark all the sick elms with big yellow X's; that meant they were diseased and had to be destroyed. What if they did that to people? *Scat! Scram! Get out! Go home! The dogs were a nuisance. The elms were sick. The boy gave Brian a bloody nose.*

Yesterday morning, when she lay with her eyes open, the fourposter did not seem strange. David's back faced her and she slipped her arms under his, and spread her hands on his chest. She laid her face sleepily against his shoulder blades. She was glad to see the curly maze of black hairs next to her eyelashes because when she closed her eyes she saw the boy's eyes and heard the boy's words. Her head was so full of the tangled images of the young mind that she thought it would explode until she opened her eyes and saw the familiar black curls on David's back. She squeezed him tightly to be safe. Yesterday she hadn't tried to steal the letter. *What was in it? What had he done?*

There was a river where you used to live. The words had opened Pandora's box, she thought, forcing herself to hold her tired, smarting eyes open. The train would have to come soon. She couldn't sit in the dark car all night. But she had to keep her eyes open now, because it was the only way to hold down the lid on the box. The contents were creatures of a brutal nightmare. Truth or fiction? Fairy tales, she thought. But fairy tales were fantasies of a richly endowed mind with pinpricks of reality. Rick's mind too was full of fantasy and pinpricks of reality. There was no telling where one began and the other ended. *Behavior well outside of the normal range.* The two—fantasy and reality—would collide, of course, in some terrifying moment. But in another, softer time they might, like lovers, meet and coyly explore each other, meet and mingle and perhaps merge at an unknown paradise.

Her arm had ached to steal that letter. Her bicep was still knotted from the struggle.

As she waited for the train a group of boys caught her attention. She counted six of them coming along the side of the tracks from the wooded area just south of the station. In the gray light of dusk they appeared as silhouettes, now and then disappearing against the background of dark tree trunks and overgrown shrubbery. They moved as a pack, as wolves, not racing but loping, now one ahead and now another, shifting as if they were one body, not six. As they came into the open area of the station their forms were more distinguishable, their ankle-tight dark pants and open windbreakers almost like uniforms so that again, though they were different sizes, some tall and one almost half as tall as the others, they moved as a single mass. They had the long-legged look of youths; she guessed they were not over high school age.

It was their sinuous, almost sinister motion that held her,

frightening her as the night-roving gangs of boys on the West Side once did. They moved in and about the old stationhouse now, stopping here and there, turning a gum machine lever, pivoting on a pillar, darting into and out of the phone booth.

Three of them suddenly jumped onto the southbound tracks, surefooted, arms out in counter-motion to the long legs. No head turned to listen for an approaching train. The other three followed. Where was that train? she wondered. Why was it late this night?

She held her breath, sensing a leashed evil, a cocked shotgun. Where had these *hoods*—the school-world term jumped into her mind—been? And where were they going? The city's hoodlum gangs should not be loping about her calm countryside!

They easily scaled the iron picket fence that separated north- from southbound trains, then stood for a moment on the top, rocked, one brief glance over their shoulders as the clicking of an approaching train began in the distance beyond the curve. The smallest of the group was the last to leap onto the northbound rail. He balanced on the iron, his pointed toes suggesting to her overwrought mind a dagger balanced on its gleaming point, his arms outstretched like the cross guard. A long lock of pale hair fell like a stripe across his forehead. He tossed his head to throw it off his eyes. Just as he leaped over the ties there came a crash; a glass bottle exploded on the rail by his ankles. Heedless, he ran over the ties a station-length ahead of the incoming train, which had just appeared around the bend. It slowed now to disgorge, among many others, David Kaplan at the end of a long gray day of studying citations and strategy.

Without needing to rush and without effort, the boy put two hands on the concrete platform, swung his thin legs up, and trotted across the plaza after the rest of his gang.

The whole thing took only a minute, but Linda's lip was bleeding. As they snaked among the parked cars toward Linda's station wagon she pushed the lock buttons on the rear doors, as if Peter were there. The six loping figures passed twenty feet from the car. The little one stopped, looked at Linda and smiled the most disarming smile she had ever seen.

"Hi, Mrs. Kaplan!" he called.

"Hi, Rick," she whispered, waved, and watched amazed as he broke into the gangland run and disappeared out of the plaza and into the trees beyond.

She released the steering wheel and blood returned to her knuckles. The train came slowly to a stop. Long past ready to rinse the grit from between their fingers, men with brief-cases began to move toward their cars.

David Kaplan rode in the first car of the 6:08, the last of the express commuter trains that went to New Delphi. His head throbbed to the rhythm of the wheels as the train moved through the darkness past miles of small houses which stretched in all directions from the city. Involuntary muscles of his neck and back flexed with the motion of the car like the leg muscles of a proficient horseman. David held the *Telegram* in front of him but though his eyes registered the words he didn't know what they said. He held the paper to shut out the people and sights around him. His body tensed in perfect time for each stop. The conductor's unin-telligible words were the signal for the body response. The last stop was passed and he settled back, relaxing for the twenty-minute run to New Delphi.

His head ached and he'd have to wait until he got home to take an aspirin. Pain had begun over his left eye two hours ago when he started to leave the office. As he got to the door Barney had said, "Oh, by the way, Dave," and shifted his cigar to the left side of his mouth so he could talk. David couldn't break away. He wished he hadn't taken on this case with Barney. They'd gone over the record and the brief again today, and every time he asked a question Barney would start talking so fast David lost all perspective. Barney was snowing him. The details were becoming confusing, the issues clouded. He knew there were holes in the argument, not enough precedent to be sure of a win. He'd spent the week before in the library and two days in Washington getting papers ready to file with the court. Hammerman, when he was talking with David, seemed not to be telling the whole story. David could stand anything except people who didn't square with him. Why did he sense he was being used? Hammerman would pay amply to salve his social conscience. And if David was being used, wasn't it in a good cause? What's so pure about me? he quizzed himself. Am I above allowing my efforts to serve purposes beyond the obvious? Isn't that what we're here for? To be useful? He knew the answers, but he persisted in the mental dialogue. Control was the critical issue. You had to keep control. If you didn't control the uses of your time and talent you were no better than a whore.

On the surface everything was all right, even ennobling. But a suspicion persisted. He was acting like Linda, he thought. Usually she was the one who looked below surfaces, stirred up trouble. How often he'd said, "Just don't mess around. Don't always look so deep. You make trouble by looking too hard." David accepted the surfaces of the people he dealt with, accepted or rejected them. If Hammerman was something other than an honest man with a social conscience, seeking a chance to change the status quo for the better, why look for more elaborate motives? David was uncomfortably aware of psychological nuances. Something had passed between Ham and his wife at dinner on Wednesday night, some change because of something Barney had said. The memory was unclear, but David suspected there might be some old history between Ham and Barney, and wondered if it had something to do with Ham's wife. She had been sick on and off for years, David knew. The politics in the case was the surface David trusted and it pleased him. If old debts were being paid that were not his concern, why worry? Why did he suddenly remember a history professor whom he had distrusted and disliked saying,

"Nothing is an accident; neither birth nor death nor forgetfulness nor recollection," an axiom David had rejected vehemently at the time?

"That's what lawyers are for. To be used. It's all right if you want the end," Linda had said. He wished for mental quiet. It was Friday night, and even though he was late they might still get to the movie. If she had a sitter. It was always such a thing, just getting out to a movie. Barney had wanted Linda to come to dinner with them in town, but David couldn't stand any more of Barney. He needed his home, his wife. He wanted solace and reassurance. He wanted time to think. He needed time to set down on paper once more the logic of this case. The key to their thinking was a reinterpretation of what constituted state action, since state action versus individual rights was the only way to go up to the high court. There were no laws on the books to guide them, and few decisions. If David could only be sure that Barney was right, that the timing was the essence of their case, that now was right! If he got the yard chores done Saturday, maybe he could put some time in on Sunday and think it through again. He'd need to before he faced Barney on Monday. Another way the world intruded on his peace. Too often he was forced to bring his work home. The weekends were never long enough. Why couldn't he put it out of his mind now? Come to it fresh, he told himself.

Tomorrow he'd walk around the garden. He'd go to the woods for a while. Perhaps Brian would condescend to go with him. David smiled at the thought of Brian in the woods, climbing the sapling birches, pruning the infant pines as David had so carefully taught him. Serious, active, responsible, they were close and like each other, he and Brian. It pleased David to think what a *nice* child he was; what a nice, softly inquiring mind he had. When they were together the burly world didn't exist for David. He loved the glimpses of the natural world through Brian's eyes. He loved the now wondrous, now ponderous, now mystified opening and shutting of the boy's growing mind. "Why is a cloud?"

Brian had said when he was three. When anyone asked David what his son was like, David quoted that.

When David was Brian's age he had dreamed of having his own children. While other boys talked of football or scientific discovery, David imagined showing his own son the world as he knew it, teaching him the skills he had learned from his father; on and on, father to son, the endless, marvelous repetition. The problem for David was that he had to create something besides a home.

He had thought during those months he and Linda had worked so hard to fix up the house, she pregnant and he a new commuter, that the family they built would be enough for her. It hadn't been, he realized almost too late. Or maybe it would have been if she had carried the two babies she'd lost. At times, he thought she didn't have enough to do. Other times she seemed driven. Occasionally he found her looking at him with something close to dissatisfaction in her eyes, as if he was not fulfilling her ambitions, as if he'd set his sights too low. She would champion any underdog, he knew, and in discussions always took the side of the downtrodden. Did she think he could move mountains? His need to be worshiped was fulfilled now by Brian; he had never expected blind idolatry from his wife.

His fascination with Linda had never dulled. That and his devotion were based partly on the fact that she was so different from him. "If the world could be saved by reason," she had cried out to him once, "you'd have been proclaimed the Messiah long ago." He didn't know what she meant. "Isn't reason the only hope, the root of all optimism?" he had replied. She eluded him always, yet he knew she depended on him greatly, and knew, too, that sometimes the canes he offered were clumsily fashioned or wrongly placed. She was the laughter and the excitement and the dangerous unknown in his life.

She was all good things, he thought, soft in looks, sensual in her lanky awkwardness. Her motives were pure, her standards high, her beliefs, though based on passion, were just and, if not always wise, at least warm. He knew there was a hollow somewhere in her life. When existence was serene he didn't think on it. Only when she seemed too restless and irritable, too beset, did he explore that mystery. Sometimes—once—he thought their marriage would not survive unless he got to the source. Sometimes—more often—he thought the underlayers of her discontent were better left undisturbed. He couldn't predict when she would turn her disquiet against him, what word or act would trigger her temper.

He was sure she loved him but he wasn't sure she loved him enough. He knew he wasn't the first man in her life but she never talked about it. Her father had once unhappily confessed that he was afraid Linda was "meeting a goy" and "it would kill her mother if she found out." But no more was said. When David first met her she was, he thought, seeing no one else, just running the store. On the night before they were married he asked her if he was the first man she had loved. She looked so frightened by the question he was sorry he'd asked.

She replied, "No, not the first, but I hope the last."

He didn't know what to do about her moments of despair. He had been angered by the way she had let herself go that difficult year after Peter was born. He didn't know why all that they had wasn't enough for her, or dissatisfied her, or, at times, seemed even to disturb her, as if being comfortable was in some way immoral. Why shouldn't they own a car, a house, buy new clothes for themselves and their handsome children?

Sometimes he saw reasonless tears in her eyes; once he heard her weeping in her sleep. He didn't know then what to do or whom to ask, and felt oafish and dense. The best he had been able to manage was, finally, to withhold critical comments. He had not known it would take so much mental energy to fathom this woman to whom he would always be bound and would continue to love.

He knew his experience was inadequate to understand

her. He forced his logic on her, hoping that she would in time become satisfied and accept his view that the world was so full of marvelous things that we can choose to live among them and leave the others. He wanted to lead her by the hand as he easily led Brian and show her the virtues in his garden. "When you have this," he asked her once when they discovered a wood lily that had chosen to thrive in a corner of their land, "why look under a rotted log?"

As David looked out of the train window, he noticed a commercial laundry flash by which indicated he hadn't far to go. Why indeed? Linda was pleased about the possibility of his arguing before the Supreme Court. If he didn't flub it, he knew she'd be proud of him. She'd been elated all week, as full of vigor and control as he'd ever seen her. Perhaps he would ask her to spend a couple of days in Washington with him. It would be good for her to get away. As the train moved him closer to home his mind moved anxiously toward his family. If the kids were asleep, maybe instead of eating out they should open a bottle of wine. No movie, he thought. An omelet and a bottle of wine at home. And he thought beyond Brian's "Hi, Pop," and Peter's open-mouthed face-wetting kiss to the quiet of the night and Linda's long lean nakedness and her brown silk hair falling over him.

The train whistle blew and there was a giant screeching of metal on metal that split the rhythm as car bumped car back and forth and the segmented carrier shook and buckled and teetered before it shuddered to an unnatural halt. David gripped the back of his neck to stem the sudden pain. Two conductors ran along the embankment toward the front of the train. Flashlight beams swept the brush. The train was still nearly a mile from the New Delphi station. A conductor put his head in the door. "Everyone all right?" he asked.

"What happened?" A number of jagged voices attacked him.

"There was someone on the track," he said. "A boy, the engineer thinks. They're looking for him."

The tired men breathed in as if they were one body. "Did we stop in time?" someone finally thought to ask.

"We're looking for him," the conductor said.

Conversation in low murmurs ensued, and men peered anxiously into the darkness through the dusty glass. David rubbed his neck and rotated his shoulders to ease the knot of pain. Minutes passed and finally he, too, cupped his hand to the window. In the background beyond the railroad strip he could see the framework for a new house silhouetted against the rising moon. Suddenly his fatigue turned to anger. He hated the raw-looking houses that covered what once was his own private wilderness. He hated the crowds that joined him daily, riding to and from the city. Someday, somehow, he'd stop spending half his life on trains. All he ever wanted was to be home and the way of the new world, even this accident, seemed to be a conspiracy to keep him away.

Half an hour later the train pulled slowly into the New Delphi station. David, like the others, peered around to find his car. He saw Linda and threaded his way to her.

"Late again," she said sympathetically.

"Um." He was too tired to do more than grunt.

"What happened this time?"

"Some kid fell on the tracks or something. They never did find him."

"Oh, but he wasn't hurt!"

"I don't know," he said irritably. "They never found him. Probably one of these damn hoods. Kids ought to be home this time of night."

She was silent. After a time, she inched the car out of the station along with the traffic.

SEVEN ᏸᎧᏸ   ADDIE SIMONS WRUNG THE RAG

nearly dry and began to wipe fingerprints at the refrigerator end of the kitchen. She might as well use the time, she thought, while she waited for Rick to come home. It was late, even for a Friday, for him still to be out. She noted whose prints were whose. Rick's on the doorways—he used each white molding as a pivot for his weight as he passed through. Sometimes, too, there would be gray smudges on the low arch over the back stairs. Ten-year-old Barbara's were neatly printed on the edge of the refrigerator door which she held in her right hand while she thought about what was inside. She often stood with it open like that, trying to decide whether she wanted milk or juice, saying to Addie, "Why don't you ever put any Coke up here?"

No matter what Addie served or offered to Barbara she asked for something else. Don't you have any salt butter? Why must we always have egg salad? We have mashed potatoes every night. Barbara ate whatever she got but she always complained. Sometimes Addie wished Rick would complain about the food. Addie never knew whether he liked what she cooked or not, because he just ate it without noticing. Rick wasn't like the children she had helped to bring up back home, Marybelle's boys. Addie didn't know if it was because he was white, or because he was rich, or because he was different. She'd never seen a boy who didn't care what he ate before.

Addie liked to watch kids eat, especially when they grinned at her and asked for more. When she was little her mother always said, "If you eat right you won't be sick and if you aren't sick you'll eat right." At home no matter how bad the fights were, or how sad any of them were, when they all sat down to eat they just got laughing, almost as if the hot food going down their throats made that great high laughter squeeze itself right up. In the Lang house they never laughed when they ate. They just ate.

Like her mother, Addie always fed freely anyone's child or dog who came within her realm. That had been the only thing she and her mother had in common, it seemed, and it had made trouble between Addie and Marybelle, her big sister.

"Addie, you'll give away the last cracker in the house if one of those brats smiles at you," Marybelle said. "We've got to feed them all, don't forget."

Like her mother, Marybelle worried all the time about money and work. When they were little Marybelle would yank Addie off her father's lap where he'd been reading to her and make her help with chores. Perhaps that's why Addie felt sorry for Rick, she thought, and didn't mind when he forgot something or got in trouble at school. He was the youngest, and she knew what that was like.

Growing up in the shanty mud street end of their town on the peninsula, living down the alley between the worst shacks with paper windows and no toilets, and the big brick houses of the white people at the paved end of their street, Addie felt she'd been walking tiptoes on a long fence all her life, just about to lose her balance. It wasn't only her brothers who chased and teased her during that two-mile walk to school, and it wasn't often that she arrived with her hair ribbons and her apron strings tied. In the two-room school she had the teacher to mess with. So far as Addie knew, the teacher stood at the front of the room with her hands together and her lips tight, staring through her rimless glasses at Addie, waiting for her to make a mistake. Breathless, Addie always did. Worse, she asked questions.

"This morning we will find out how many of you know how to tell time. Look at this clock." (She held up a Big Ben.) "How many of you can tell me what it says?" A number of hands went up, including Addie's.

"Addie. You were late again this morning. Tell me what the clock says."

Addie: "Eight-forty-five. Would there be any time if there weren't any clocks?"

Laughter. And then the clipped, nasal words. "Miss Addie Simons, what makes you think you're smarter than me?"

Each time she felt a question coming she tried to push it back, to press her lips together; but it never worked. It was always the same. The words pushed out, and the teacher wrote the note which said "tardy," "insolent," "disobedient."

Her mother would shake her head and say, "When will you ever learn to keep quiet?" Her father would look up from his book and smile at her. "Someday we'll send Addie away to school where she can learn something more than how to sit still and count her blessings."

"Huh," her mother would say. "That'll be the day you git out and work." Her father hadn't had a steady job in longer than Addie could remember. "You and your reading and your mixed-up dreams," her mother would be off again. "If Addie can't get on in school she'll just have to go to work like the rest of the women in this family."

"Addie's not quitting school!" her father would roar, and though the thunder of his voice made both Addie and the wooden house tremble, she loved him softly for standing up for her. "Addie's not quitting school so long as her old man owns the land he lives on." That would quiet her mother for a while, because there weren't many men—black men, that is—who owned land. He owned their house and he owned odd pieces here and there. Sometimes he'd take Addie walking with him and they'd stand together on the corner of a field or in the empty lot behind the cigar store.

They wouldn't have to say a word. Sometimes when there was no food Addie's mother would beg her father to sell off a piece to the white man who came around every month. But her father wouldn't do it. "Someday these old stones and those fences will be our salvation," he'd say. He tried to explain it to Addie, but she never quite understood. The land was going up in price, all around them. White people were building houses, supermarkets, factories. They just couldn't get enough land. If a Negro got behind on his grocery bill white people wouldn't lend him the money, but they'd buy his land cheap, and make a big profit on it. Nobody'd pay a black what the land was worth, so her father wouldn't sell it.

Marybelle was five years older than Addie and never got in trouble. She didn't ask questions and the teacher liked her a lot. The boys didn't bother Marybelle on the way to school because from the time she was twelve until the time she got married at fifteen she and Billy Williams had been in love. After they were married they built a one-room house on one of Father's little parcels of land a half-mile away, and Billy Williams worked in a garage. They had three kids, one two three, and Addie spent a lot of time helping Marybelle with the babies. All of them were boys and Marybelle didn't seem to mind. "Boys work harder than girls," she'd say, looking straight at Addie.

Addie liked it at Marybelle's because of the babies, and because Billy was always full of fun. He had built two more rooms on their house and he was always after Marybelle to have a girl. He'd tickle her when she walked by, and look hungry and say, "Who's going to love me when I'm fat and fifty if I don't have a daughter?"

Marybelle'd smile over her shoulder and say, "That's no reason to go having a mess of kids you can't feed. Three's enough for me. Pick up the baby, will you, Addie?"

Addie was glad she was growing up. She liked the sour milk smell of Marybelle's babies, and she looked forward to holding one of her own. The only pleasant thing about being a child had been sitting curled in her father's lap while he read aloud to her. She was too big for that now. One day when she was in the sixth grade the teacher sent her home because she'd forgotten her apron. Actually two older boys had ripped it off her. She didn't explain about having to run all the way through the woods to get away from them, and she didn't bother to go back to school. She got a job in a radio factory and read everything she could get her hands on.

After she quit her father kind of faded away. One morning he just didn't wake up. Her mother sold all his pieces of land to the white man except the one that her house was on and the one where Billy and Marybelle lived. Addie knew her father had been betrayed but she didn't move out until after Father's Day.

They'd always had a big feast on Father's Day with all his sisters and brothers, and all their kids. Addie and Marybelle and their mother used to kill one of the baby hogs and cook for three nights before. A month after her father died her mother had the feast just the same, only his chair was empty. The next day Addie moved in with Marybelle. She didn't make much at her job but she gave a little to her mother, and a little to Marybelle, and what she kept for herself she spent on books and magazines and newspapers. And she had time to read them.

There was a boy who drove her home sometimes who liked to read as much as Addie did, and who reminded her of her father. He wanted to save enough money to go to college and live up north. Addie didn't talk about him to anyone.

She didn't really know whether she loved the boy or not. They used to take walks on Sunday afternoons across the wide rolling fields and through the thicketed woods. They talked about the books they read, and sometimes about their dreams. Addie told him about one dream she had. She was lost in a library that was like a maze. She couldn't find her way out. While she was hunting for the path through the stacks that would lead to freedom and light, she had to read all the books. "I can't read fast enough," she cried in the dream, and tears streamed down her face. "I've got to go to work." But she opened book after book, faster and faster, and the more she read, the less she was sure she wanted to find the path to freedom and light. It was only a dream.

She was crying when she told him about it and he held her in his arms.

The boy whose name no one knew but Addie went to a northern university and became a lawyer in New York City. He left Addie one afternoon in September at the Union Station in Washington. He didn't say he'd send for her, or that he'd be back. They just said goodbye and he told her he'd write and let her know where he lived. He left her at the railroad station with his one-dollar silver lucky piece, which she knew she would never never spend, in her hand, and Elizabeth planted firmly in her womb. They never talked of marrying.

After Elizabeth was born Addie and Marybelle got on a little better. Billy loved Elizabeth as he might have loved his own daughter. The seven of them made a happy family. Addie and Marybelle worked different shifts at the factory and with the money the three of them made, they lived a lot better than many Negro families around.

Elizabeth was four years old the day Marybelle took the whole bunch of them to the movie *Peter Pan*. The next day Elizabeth fell off the woodshed roof—flew, the children told Addie, like Peter Pan. "Look at me," she called to them, "look at me, I'm flying!" Though not dead, Elizabeth was paralyzed. She could see but since she couldn't speak or move it was hard to tell how much she could understand. Everyone, even the doctor, told Addie she was lucky the child hadn't died. But as the weeks went on, and Elizabeth didn't get better, they stopped saying it. Eventually Addie, who still read everything she had time for, saw the agency ad for domestic workers: "Fine home, own rm, tv, lge pay." Perhaps in the North, she thought, she could make more money and buy some northern doctoring for Elizabeth. The terrible part would be leaving Elizabeth, the best of herself. She couldn't bring herself to answer the ad right away.

The economic situation and the temper of the family changed markedly after Elizabeth's accident. Addie kept working for a while, but in those hours at home she would read to Elizabeth, feed her as an infant, or sit by her bed talking to her in low tones, waiting for some indication that her daughter knew she was there. The beautiful clear brown eyes stared at her mother always. Marybelle would come home and find the boys running wild outside in the darkness, unfed, unwashed, unruly. Half-peeled potatoes turned brown in the kitchen sink, and the water in the kettle boiled away. Addie once had helped Marybelle's oldest boy, Bilbo, learn to read. Now he'd fallen behind again and his next brother teased him. He'd come crying to Addie and she didn't hear him.

One day Marybelle got home at six and found the ironing board set up with the iron burning a hole right through one of Billy's shirts and all the padding underneath. It might have been the whole house next. Addie was in the next room reading *Mother Goose* to Elizabeth, who didn't know Georgie Porgie from the Lord's Prayer.

"It has to stop," Marybelle said to her. "You just can't go on this way."

Addie crumpled up the newspaper ad in her fist and said without looking up, "But Elizabeth can. Elizabeth just goes on and on."

"Take the river," Rick had said to Addie at breakfast that morning, unusually talkative, "you drop a stone in it and it sinks. But a feather or a piece of wood just goes on and on." Startled, Addie felt Marybelle's latest letter in her pocket.

"You take it," Barbara said, "it's too fishy for me."

Rick gave her a dirty look and was quiet. Addie wished Barbara hadn't acted so smart. Rick didn't often make conversation. He finished his cereal and got up to leave. Suddenly Addie said to him, "Wait a bit, Rick. I want to talk to you." He shrugged and went out of the kitchen.

She read Marybelle's letter again, trying as always to learn more than was there. Marybelle wrote long letters but never said enough about Elizabeth to satisfy Addie. They didn't vary much. Thanks for the money. Elizabeth was the same.

(The same. The same.) Now cousin Tammy came in to care for her. Bilbo was reading a whole lot better. Everyone missed Addie. She realized Rick was standing watching her read. She didn't know how long he'd been there. She folded the letter and told him she was glad he'd come back.

"You always leave so early in the morning," she said. "Where do you go?"

"I dunno," he said. "Around." Well, she should have known not to ask. This whole week when he couldn't go to school he'd left so early, come home so late. She hadn't known where he went, but knew there was no use asking. He'd tell her what he wanted to. Rick talked to her now and then so long as she didn't ask questions. Then he shut himself up tight. She supposed if he got into any more trouble she'd hear about it soon enough. She knew he'd been avoiding his sisters, and after the way they went after him on that first Monday night at supper, she didn't blame him.

Barbara had said just as soon as she sat down, "I saw you in the office again. Another fight?"

"Oh, for heaven's sake," Deborah joined in, "can't you ever stop? Everywhere I go people tell me you've been fighting. I'm getting sick of it."

Barbara whined, "How do you think I feel when my own brother's in trouble? The kids are always talking."

"It just can't go on, Ricky," Deborah said, imitating Mrs. Lang.

"Leave him alone," Addie said. "He feels bad enough."

"Why should he feel bad?" Deborah asked. "He couldn't care less."

"He's suspended, that's why," Addie said. And then she wished she'd kept her mouth shut. Rick gobbled his food without looking up and the girls hammered him with questions until Addie got them out of the kitchen and off to their homework. The rest of the week he came home late and she fed the girls early and kept his supper hot for him.

"I'm sorry I told them like that," she said to Rick, "but I guess they'd've found out somehow."

"It's okay," he said. But Addie knew that apologies didn't make any difference to him.

It was Friday night and the girls had eaten. She was wiping cabinets just to keep busy while she waited for Rick. Now she knew where he'd been all week, hanging around the Kaplan house, but she hadn't known this morning. She thought about the morning. Rick had been different, not only talkative but seeming to ask something. She couldn't explain it. What he said about the river had made her tell him about Elizabeth. She hadn't meant to, but he didn't seem to mind listening to her for a while. Sometimes when he looked straight at her without seeing her, she thought of Elizabeth. Addie sighed and dipped the rag in the pail of gray water, wrung it, and began a new section. If she could get all the cabinets done tonight, she thought, she'd have tomorrow to clean the house and cook for Sunday, when the Langs were due.

There was a paperback in her room that Deborah had given her, but she didn't feel like reading now. Deborah gave her all her books after she was through with them. Sometimes Addie didn't think they were very good, but she still read everything that came her way, good and bad.

She washed the face of the blue electric clock over the door and noticed the time: 7:30. She glanced at the chrome clock built into the stove: 7:30. He was late tonight. She'd never seen a house with so many clocks, an electric clock in every room, wall-hung and built-in, and clocks in radios and one in the cellar and, on the mantel in the living room, a mahogany and glass clock with a gold pendulum that Deborah told her belonged to her grandmother. When daylight saving ended, Mr. Lang spent three-quarters of an hour setting back the clocks. "Nothing gets done around here," he said to Addie, "unless I do it."

"I'd've changed them if you'd asked me," she said. Both the kitchen clocks now read 7:40. Where was Rick?

Back home, if the kids weren't home at suppertime Marybelle would work up a worry, and if Billy went out looking for them they'd all get spankings. Addie remembered turning on the water in the sink so she couldn't hear the smack of his big hand landing, or the little ones crying. But she knew that Billy spanked them because he loved them and knew what could happen to little black kids caught out after dark. She knew if Billy'd seen Elizabeth going up on the shed roof he might have made her cry out loud, but she wouldn't be lying so still now. When Mr. Lang took off his belt the night the superintendent of schools called to tell him Rick had been caught smoking on school grounds, Addie turned on the water just the same, but she didn't need to, because Rick never made a sound. She wondered if Mr. Lang would have been so mad if it hadn't been the superintendent; or if the call hadn't interrupted his dinner; or if Rick had cried out loud the way Marybelle's boys did.

Mr. and Mrs. Lang were coming home Sunday. Addie panicked. What if Rick didn't get home? They still didn't know he'd been suspended. The letter from the school was waiting for them on the table in the hall. What had he done?

Addie thought of the boy and his father. Then she thought of the boy and his mother. She tried to imagine them all in the front hall together, as she told the Langs that Rick had been suspended. But in her mind she retreated from the scene, letting the swinging door to the kitchen close behind her. She could hear water running. She turned on the water now, filling her ears with the sound. One of the things Mr. Lang had said to her when she first came was, "You're so nice and quiet, Addie. Nothing ever ruffles you. I know we can trust you because you're so calm all the time."

Nothing the Lang children did ruffled her, she thought as she turned off the water and wrung the rag again, because nothing that happened here was as bad as what happened to her when she was little. Having to make decisions didn't worry her; it was like walking through a forest. If you just took one step at a time there was nothing to be scared about. But if you thought about the forest in all of its dark bigness, then the things you knew lived in the leaves and under the moss would scare you so you couldn't move. Addie made the little pieces of decisions, as she had to, not looking at the bigness. It wasn't always right, she told Rick. Sometimes it's better to look ahead. Each minute was a decision and it determined the next one.

She told Rick about Elizabeth. "I said yes to Elizabeth when she wanted to go to the movies with her cousins. I could have said no."

"It wasn't your fault, was it?" Rick asked. "Nobody told her to fly."

"No," Addie said. "No, I don't suppose it was my fault." She didn't feel she was to blame, but she didn't feel she was not to blame either. That little "yes" to Elizabeth meant she'd been able to get all of Marybelle's ironing done during the afternoon instead of having to do it at night. There'd been a borrowed book on her bed she hadn't read.

When the children came home, Addie remembered, she fed them a huge potful of chicken legs. It was a party. She remembered how many drumsticks they'd each eaten, because they'd raced each other. Elizabeth ate two, Jeremy four, Bilbo and Allie ate five each and tied for first. Billy came in while the kids were eating and asked how those poor chickens were going to walk without any legs. Everyone laughed except Elizabeth, Addie told Rick. Elizabeth never did understand Billy's jokes. There was nothing about that day that Addie didn't remember, no sound, no word. Each moment was so much part of her that thinking and telling about it squeezed the breath out of her.

"Did she hurt a lot?" Rick asked.

"I don't know. She never made a sound after that."

Then she stopped telling him and she thought about what life might have been like if she'd said no to Elizabeth that day. Then she thought about Elizabeth, with her round brown eyes and her nice thick cookie-round nose which Addie used to run her finger up and off when she kissed her goodnight. She thought about how, even though Elizabeth was four years old, she still didn't know there was anything in the world except sweetness and truth. Addie wondered sometimes if her "yes" had really made any difference. Elizabeth might have flown off another roof another day because Elizabeth always believed everything that anybody told her with her whole wonderful loving believing heart.

The blue-faced clock said 7:45. Addie wiped the last cabinet. She didn't know whether she was frightened or angry. She did know that if Rick didn't come in that back door soon she'd have to ask one of the girls to go look for him. She didn't want to do that. When the house was quiet in the evening with only the sound of Barbara's radio or Deborah's voice on the phone, Addie didn't like to stir things up. She washed the tops of the burners on the stove. She dried her hands. Maybe she should call someone.

She went to the back door and opened it. The wall of icy air hit her face. She called into the darkness, "Rick?" Her own high voice sounded like a strange bird in her ears. "Where're you, Rick?"

She shut the door and rubbed her arms. She opened the oven, where the covered plate with one last portion of dinner sat. The warmth caressed her face. With a shiver she closed the oven and sat at the table in the middle of the big room with the cold surfaces: Formica, glass, and steel.

He had to come home sometime. He was only nine, and he couldn't stay out all night. Maybe Mrs. Kaplan, the woman who'd come to see her that afternoon, would know where he was. Brian's mother. Her number was in the book.

That would be admitting she didn't know how to take care of the boy. Mrs. Kaplan had asked too many questions, poking around in Rick's life as if Addie weren't responsible. She could take care of Rick all right. Mr. Lang had faith in her or he wouldn't have left her in charge.

Why wasn't Rick home?

Addie dumped the pail of dirty water, rinsed and dried her hands for the last time. She went to the living room window. The streetlamp in front of the next house cast its empty circle of light on the pavement. She couldn't see beyond the circle. Through the back window all she could see were dead leaves.

Addie went upstairs and knocked on the closed door of Deborah's room.

"Yes?"

Addie opened the door. Deborah was sitting in her pink club chair, feet up in the air, a textbook on her knees. She took a lock of her long brown hair, which she washed three times a week leaving long strands in the sink for Addie to clean up, and held it across her upper lip like a mustache.

"Vat do you vant?" she asked, making her voice hoarse. "Anoder book zo zoon?"

Addie didn't laugh, as she often did at Deborah's dramatics.

"Rick isn't home yet," she said.

"Zo?"

"I'm worried. Go to the playground, would you, and see if he's there?"

"Ha!" Deborah dropped her hair and swung her legs down. "Now that's just about the last thing I'd want to do. You go."

Addie was silent a moment. "I'll go with you," she said at last.

"But I don't care if he never gets home."

"That's not true. He's your brother."

"You're right," Deborah said. "I do care. He's still my baby brother even if he has grown tall and repulsive, as Felix would say. Why I can even remember before he was born." Her voice grew mockingly dreamy. "There was a day, long ago, when someone in this house laughed at him. You'd never believe it, Addie, he was a cute kid once."

"I'm worried about him," Addie interrupted her. "Please help me look for him. Where do you think he is?"

Deborah inspected a fingernail. "Maybe he's out selling junk. How do I know?"

"Oh, you."

"Honestly, Addie, you worry too much. So does everyone. If you all just left the kid alone he'd be fine. As a matter of fact I saw him downtown this afternoon with Felix. He'll be home sometime. I know he will."

Addie went down the front stairs and sat on the bottom step. To her right was the telephone table where she'd put the letter from the school with the rest of the mail. In front of her was the door through which Rick never came; but she could go out that door and look for him. She sat with her chin on her hands and wished for courage. She looked from the phone to the door and back again. Something was wrong.

She went to the table and leafed through the stack of mail, magazines, and ads. Where was the letter? She looked on the floor and under the doormat, behind the table and under the phone. She looked on the tables in the living room and on the buffet in the dining room. The letter had disappeared.

Addie got her coat from the back closet. She found a flashlight on the cellar stairs and went into the cold November night to look for Rick.

Hands in her pockets, shoulders hunched against her neck, Addie walked down the asphalt driveway and turned left. She was cold. Her fine white teeth chattered and frost bit into her nostrils. She couldn't stop the spasms that ran through her body, or stop her mind from racing into places it didn't always go, into and out of dark crevices that she didn't often look in. She shook all over like this on the day she ran away from school and stayed the whole afternoon in the woods alone, crouching, hugging her legs tight to her chest, not daring to go home, finally not daring to stay past darkness. She knew she'd have to stand up sometime and tell her father she'd never go back to school. She could let her mother's "why didn't you" and "when will you" roll off her, and the everlasting laughter of her brothers who teased and tripped and merrily tortured her go past without hurting. She could even laugh out loud when the teasing hands pinched or pulled her hair. She could give as good as she got. But her father's anger or disappointment in her made her ache so she stood limp as a broken clothesline waiting for him to say something, even to hit her. What he did that day was worse. He squinted at her and she saw tears. He turned palms up and licked his lips. She waited for his anger but it never came. She waited shivering; she wanted to scream, "Hit me!" but she couldn't. She opened her mouth but her voice didn't work. She couldn't even whisper she was sorry. He turned away and pulled the old bridge lamp closer to his chair; he picked up his *Saturday Evening Post* and pushed his glasses up on his nose; he started to read. It was a picture in her mind.

Addie walked across a golden hayfield with Harold two years later. The sun went behind a cloud and she shivered. The tremors began when he talked of going away to college and got stronger and stronger. She was cold. He put his hands on her and she was suddenly hot and laughing. He said, "You're always so cold on your outside, Addie. Who'd've guessed at the fire inside you?" Addie was always cold except when she was with her father and for those loving months with Harold. "Who'll you spend it on when I'm gone?" he'd asked her. "Who'll warm you then?"

"Nobody, no sir," she'd said.

They had started home later than usual; it was fall and the light faded early. To reach Marybelle and Billy's house they had to walk through a white village. There wasn't a decent way around it, with a swamp on the east side and thick brambly woods on the west. Rarityville was just three blocks long with a grocery store at one end and a gas station at the other. On each side of the narrow main street stiff porched houses with white lace woodwork and sharply peaked roofs stood like paper cutouts. It wasn't dark yet but the sun was down and only its lingering reflections on the high clouds lit the roofs.

"We're late," Harold muttered to Addie. "Can't you

· 116 ·

walk faster?" He held tight to her hand and pulled her along. While she felt his shoulder near and his hand on hers Addie didn't need to scream. But she was cold again, frightened and starting to tremble.

Rarityville, these three short blocks, was legendary. A young Negro had been shot one evening in the middle of the street, just as the lights went on. He'd been walking through town when darkness fell and the shot killed him. Some said the whites were afraid of burglars. Some said rape. It'd been so long ago, nobody knew for sure except that nobody ever said who did it. At sundown each day, the man of every house in Rarityville would sit out on his front porch with his shotgun on his knee. There wasn't much time between sundown and darkness. If a Negro was seen in Rarityville after dark he'd be shot. Far down at the end of the block Addie and Harold saw a figure come out of a door, walk partway down the front steps off the lace-paper porch, the silhouette of his rifle sharp in the fading light. They walked the gauntlet, hands tight, not so fast that they looked scared. It seemed to Addie that the light raced away from them. It was hard not to hurry. The night breeze slipped up her bare arms and inside her dress. Past the stiff houses, the gas station, twenty steps beyond, forty . . . Run, Addie! Run, Harold! She was so frightened when they reached the turn in the road she clung to him crying, "I'm cold! I'm cold!" over and over again.

"You'll be warm all right," he breathed in her ear and her trembling mounted and subsided as he came against her in the brush.

The cold darkness assaulted her from all sides as she looked for Rick Lang. She pushed her hands deep in her coat pockets and tried to feel invisible. She walked to the end of the block and started down the next street, forgetting how far the playground was. Easy for Rick on his bike to go back and forth. A bike made a boy free. Addie wasn't ever free; she was cold. She moved from spotlight to spotlight and the fear she felt as she moved into the streetlamps' circles was replaced by fear of the darkness when she moved out.

The ranch houses were set far back, full of eyes in the darkness, spies' eyes. Addie's skin, suddenly chilled and crisp, grew sensitive to the rough texture of her coat. Addie had warmth to give and no one to spend it on. It always came to this.

Did she suppose that behind the false stone facades and the insulated layers of wood and plaster, inside the soft warm interiors with thick carpets, muted phones, in all that hot air between slick sheets and thick blankets, and inside heavy tweeds and under furs and soft flannels the bodies of white people were ever cold?

A door opened from a house down the block ahead of her letting a shaft of light fall across the lawn. She stopped, a still target. I hate you, Rick, she thought, for making me go out in the dark. She held her breath as she watched a man walk across the velvet in the path of light, turn toward her, moving closer, into and then out of the circle of light. She held her breath till she thought she would burst. If she lived through this night she would never forgive any of them—her mother, the white people, the school teacher, the Langs—all who had brought her to this moment and left her in it alone.

The man turned into the next driveway and disappeared. Addie breathed again, but heat and cold and sensitized skin made her feel as if she had a high fever. She tried to make her sneaker-clad feet move toward the highway once more. Please, Rick, she prayed, please come home. Please. I won't be mad. I promise!

Far down the street there was a flicker in one of the lights, as if a hand had passed quickly over the beam, a flicker in the next lamp, and then the next and the next. She discerned the flying jacketed figure on the skinny bike. Laughter rose in her throat, choking her; she wanted to scream. Rick!

But the scream never did come because her voice wouldn't work. The boy came near. When he saw her step into the spotlight he stopped and jumped off the bike. She threw her arms around him and almost knocked him down. "You," she said shrilly, "you scared me, you lousy bastard. You scared me!"

He stood passive and still with her arms around him, and suddenly she was embarrassed and let him go. She wiped tears off her cheeks with her coat sleeve and she pulled his jacket around him.

"You'll freeze yourself to death," she scolded as if she'd been somebody's mother. "Now git on home to supper. Quick."

"Sorry, Addie," he said when she let him go. They turned and walked together, she with her hands in her pockets once again, he with his hands on the bars of his bicycle. She couldn't stay mad at him. She'd heard in those two words a tone she'd never heard him use to anyone else. "Sorry, Addie." As if he meant it. Softly, as if he hadn't thought about her being alone in the cold dark or frightened or angry. It was different from the way he said "I'm sorry, ma'am" or "Yes, sir" to his mother and father, as if he'd just practiced the right words and knew that saying them was the only way to get free. With her, Addie thought, he never said much. Tonight he'd said, "Sorry, Addie," as if he'd meant it.

She was sorry she'd yelled at him like that, but glad she'd hugged him. She'd never done that before. He wasn't the kind of boy you thought of hugging. It struck her suddenly that she didn't remember seeing Mrs. Lang hug him either. Most of the time Rick was home Mrs. Lang was out, or in her room with the door shut.

"Where you been so late?" she asked when they were safe in the bright white kitchen. She took his plate out of the slow oven and put it on the table. "Deborah saw you with Felix."

Rick picked up his fork. He didn't look up.

"I think she was jealous." Addie laughed. "I never did trust that Felix. He's a sharp one. I'd look out for him."

"Felix is great," Rick said. "We had a great time."

"He's a lot older than you," Addie warned. But there was a shine in Rick's eyes she'd never seen before. "What'd you and Felix do?"

"We had a great time," he said between mouthfuls of mashed potatoes. "Lemme tell you. It was great. There was this kid—I mean a bunch of them—you know, Felix's friends. I dunno, they were great."

Addie put her chin on her hands and her elbows on the table and grinned at him. She couldn't think when he'd said so much at one time in all the months she'd been working. "Sounds great," she giggled. "But what did you do?"

"Oh, we messed around some. Felix found this old wheel, see. He says I'm okay. I mean he likes me. 'You're okay, kid,' he said, 'cause I rolled the wheel on the tracks."

"Where were you?" Addie asked cautiously, not wanting him to stop talking. She'd seen boys playing along the tracks. But not Rick—please! Not when she alone was responsible for him!

"It wasn't just the wheel; there was a whole pile of junk. Felix says I can go with them tomorrow. There was this kid, see, and he said how about if I play dead, see, and . . ." Rick sounded so like the little boys back home now that Addie relaxed again. A bunch of boys going through a dump; she'd seen plenty of that. She'd heard the tales before, boys so full of words that tripped and tumbled over each other that she lost the meaning in the music of the words, and felt like dancing.

"So you found a dump," she said. "Then what?"

"Well, it was a joke, see, but the train stopped and the people looked so funny running around that Felix and I got to laughing—"

On the tracks with the train coming! Addie's heart raced. She thought of the tracks on the levee near her home, and the pieces of an old wagon caught at a grade crossing flying every which way, and the pieces of the old man who'd been driving it. At home if Billy caught the kids playing anywhere near the tracks you could hear the crying in the next town.

"Well," Deborah said from the doorway, one hip out, "I see the wandering boy finally got home. Whatever made you decide to come back? Boy, are you lucky Dad's away."

"Shut up," Rick said.

"Addie was frantic."

Rick shrugged and chewed in silence.

"She was so scared you'd gotten killed or something she even tried to get me to go look for you. I knew you'd find your way back. I tried to tell her, but she had to go running out after you." Deborah fingered the ends of her hair at her neck. "You should have heard her yelling for you. The whole neighborhood must've known you were out. I tried to tell her you always come home eventually, like a sick dog, but she wouldn't listen. You didn't know, did you, Addie, that he always disappeared, even when he was a little kid. He'd run away and everyone'd go wild for a while looking for him. Mom'd tear around crying like the end of the world or something and Dad'd rant and rage and say couldn't we even keep an eye on the kid for ten minutes. But Rick would always turn up, sooner or later."

She sat down at the table across from Rick, picked up the salt cellar and turned it around in her hand, smoothing it with her pointed fingers. "You know, it's funny. I guess Dad felt special about Rick. I always knew it. Maybe because he was a boy. Or because he was the baby. But Dad got madder at Rick over things, even little things. But when Rick was lost or away with Gran he'd talk about him differently. You know, worry about him a lot and say 'my son' like some crummy movie hero father. But then when Rick'd get home again Dad would blow up because he'd forgotten to zip his pants, or left a truck in the driveway or something."

They were all silent. Addie got up and put Rick's plate in the sink and a dish of canned peaches in front of him.

Finally Deborah said, "You saw Felix."

"Uh-huh."

"Did he say anything about me?"

"Unh-unh," Rick said.

It was ten that night when Addie finally crawled between the sheets in her room behind the kitchen. She reached for the book on the table by her bed, read the title page. *A Night To Remember*, by Walter Lord. Then she remembered that she had forgotten to ask Rick what he had done with the letter from the school. Her throat constricted for a moment. Of course he'd stolen it; she knew that, although he'd seemed not to notice it. How would she ask him? And then it occurred to her that perhaps the Sunday ahead would be easier if she didn't ask him. She could just turn on the water in the kitchen sink.

Addie turned the page. *High in the crow's-nest of the New White Star Liner* Titanic, *Lookout Frederick Fleet peered into a dazzling night.*

EIGHT 🙢🙠 DAVID KAPLAN LEFT THE SATURDAY breakfast table, called Sappho from the cellar, and walked into the garden along the perennial circle. The back of the low frame farmhouse with its two additions—the shed off the kitchen door, and the small bedroom they put the TV in off the living room—formed a wide U, creating an outdoor enclosure. Each time he walked this semicircle it was like reliving the last ten years. He had placed every stone, set in each shrub, tended each plant. Past the garden the lawn sloped up to a stone wall, beyond which were the woods. Every tree in that lawn had either been permitted to remain or been planted by him. As he walked, consciously or unconsciously he knew what lay under each damp leaf. Surprised, he saw a patch of white under an azalea. He touched it with his booted toe.

"It snowed on Thursday," Brian said, "but it didn't last long."

"Hi." David hadn't realized the boy was beside him. "I didn't know." A piece of their lives he hadn't lived, he thought jealously. A family is so close and yet they live separate lives. Lonely, he squeezed Brian's shoulder.

"Ouch." Brian happily wrenched away.

"Was there enough to have any fun?"

"We went sleigh-riding. It was great. But yesterday it all melted."

"All except this."

"And some ice on the playground. Rick and Mommy shoveled the driveway but they didn't have to. It would have melted if they'd waited."

"Your mother's always loved the snow."

"I know. She even went down Long Hill. You should have seen her. One of the kids said, 'Lookit the old lady on a sled!' I told him it was my mother. You should have seen her."

"I wish I had," David said. And then, "She isn't old, you know." Brian shrugged. They climbed over the stone wall and wet leaves slid beneath their feet.

"You said Mommy and Rick shoveled. Why didn't you help?"

"I was in school."

"Oh, yes." David picked up a stick and threw it ahead. Sappho bounded after it.

"Rick didn't have to go to school all week, the luck. They suspended him or something. He didn't even have to do his homework."

"And he came here every day?"

"Uh-huh."

"What did he do all that time?"

"Gosh, I don't know. How'm I supposed to know everything? I had to be in school."

"Don't you like school?"

"It's okay, I guess. Some of it's fun."

"Only some of it? And it's not supposed to be just fun, you know. You're supposed to learn something."

"I know." Brian sounded impatient, David thought. He was changing. He used to be impatient on Sunday nights for Monday to come. David didn't want him to change, to grow cynical. Probing now, he asked, "Doesn't Rick like school either?"

"I don't know. Hey look. That little pine got its neck broke. Who'd do that, who'd break it just like that? Just broke off."

"Broken off."

"Broken then. Can you fix it?"

David opened his knife and began to pare the splintered stem. "It could have been the wet snow," he said. "Was it wet and heavy?"

"Let me." Brian pushed in front of him. "You watch. I'll do it. Where'll I cut? Tell me what to cut."

David showed him how to shave the wood smooth, so no moisture could lodge under the bark. "One of this year's branches will turn up when the spring growth starts. It may be crooked, but a new leader will develop. We'll come back in the spring and see if it needs a stake to start it straight."

"Let's put a 'No trespassing' sign on the road too. There's lots of people who just go through here."

"Let them," David said. "There'll be another tree." He picked up a cone. "See, this one still has its seeds. There'll be other trees in other years."

There were occasional patches of snow on the matted leaves. Within a short time, David knew, the whole woods would be a design in gray and white. This year, he thought, he would try to paint it. This was his happiness. He thought of Barney, his driving energy and sharp perceptions. And then he thought of some of his friends from law school, men who now had far surpassed him. Even in school he had known they would. It hadn't been only his slow methodical mind that kept him at a low middle of his class; even then his ambition to become a good lawyer was primarily a means by which he could be a provider. This woods was his plenty, this scrap of wilderness where he read the seasons his gift to Brian—and Peter too, he realized as an afterthought. But the younger boy still had little reality for him. It was Brian who could walk quietly beside him in the prewinter brush, as Linda used to. Someday, he hoped, she would join him again.

Brian found a tree full of carpenter ants and they watched them work, dropping their sawdust loads over the great bark precipices. They found dead stalks of Indian cucumber and brown fern fronds. Brian disappeared while David occupied himself with a dead birch that had fallen across a young dogwood.

"Look where I am!" He heard Brian call. Looking up he found the red jacket high in a huge beech tree. A sharp pain at the back of David's neck reminded him of the whiplash when the train stopped short the night before.

"I can't look," he called. "I hurt. Come on down." When Brian had joined him again, he said, "Give me a hand in the yard. I'd like to get the rest of the leaves cleaned up and the winter mulch on the roses."

"Do I have to?"

"Yup."

"Oh, all right, but—"

Just once, David thought rubbing his neck, it would be nice if my son would say, Sure, Dad, I'll help. Linda was too easy on Brian. Children had to be taught responsibility from the beginning. It didn't just grow. As they climbed back over the wall David said, "Bring the wheelbarrow and the burlap from the garage. I'll get the rakes."

"Aren't we going to burn them?"

"They're too wet. We'll dump them back in the woods."

They worked side by side for a while, David's rake making great clean sweeps across the damp green, Brian's leaving nearly as much as he collected. Each pull of the rake felt like hot cords drawn taut across David's neck and left shoulder. "I wish you'd gotten this stuff cleaned up before the snow," David said. "It's a mess now."

"Mommy was busy."

"You could have done it." The child's inefficiency exasperated him. "Let the raking go. Just collect and dump the leaves for me."

Brian kicked the edge of the burlap. "Okay," he said. "But you don't have to look so mad."

"My neck hurts." He kept on with the rake; the drive to finish was stronger than the pain. But the thought crossed his mind that more than minor damage might have been done that night. He should see his doctor.

Linda joined them, Peter trailing behind, and the work went faster. David relaxed as they worked side by side. Brian took Peter round and round the house on a pile of leaves in the wheelbarrow. They could hear his squeals of laughter come and go. It was sounds like that, times like this, that made all the train rides, the waiting and fumbling in his brain for words and ideas that wouldn't come, the struggles and dull clients, the old forgotten arguments, and the races lost or won at too high a cost, worthwhile. A moment with a woman and some wet leaves, and your children laughing together. He straightened his stiff back and watched her. As always her hair, brown silk, was in her face, and still she was beautiful. She looked happy today. Her old brown sweater hung straight like her hair and her dungarees clung to her thighs. She raked with the same passion she did everything, as if by furious motion she could beat some kind of devil. She stopped, suddenly self-conscious.

"You're laughing at me."

"Just admiring your energy, and trembling for the leaves you haven't yet thrashed." He wanted to kiss her. By the time they had gotten home last night he had been tired, and she had seemed preoccupied.

"Your neck still hurts," she frowned. He was rubbing it

again. "Maybe we ought to call Dr. Daniels." She put her hand on the tendons that reached down to his shoulders, pressing them. "How bad is it?"

"Not too." He put his arm across her shoulder. She was almost as tall as he and their eyes were nearly level. "It snowed while you were away," she said.

"I know." It didn't matter now what words passed between them. "I wish I'd seen you on the hill."

"Next time maybe you could go." Vaguely he realized Peter wasn't laughing any more, that the sound of his crying was coming toward them but he didn't stop looking at her or take his arm away. How long could you hope for a day as quiet as the night?

"Don't work too late," she whispered.

Suddenly, "Peter, what's happened?"

The little boy was between them, sobbing, holding up a smudged hand. Linda picked him up, still looking at David past the small head which pressed hard into her shoulder.

The sobbing stopped and Linda said, "See what's the matter with his hand."

David felt foolish with the tiny fingers in his, a limp small appendage that seemed detached from the mass of mother and child. He turned it around in his own big hand and moved each finger carefully. Peter was quiet. "It looks all right to me," he said. "He'd yell if it hurt."

"He probably fell out of the wheelbarrow," Linda said. "I wish he'd learn to talk."

"He will when he has something to say," David said. "Where's Brian?" He looked around. The wheelbarrow was at the far corner of the house, tipped up, a pile of leaves strewn on the already raked section of lawn near it. "Brian!" he bellowed. "Brian!"

He knew he was unreasonably angry. "Dammit, where is that boy? There's nothing makes him disappear so fast as the smell of a little work. I wish—" He heard a scuffling noise and, looking up, saw Brian's red jacket appear on the roof of the house near the chimney. Just behind Brian was another child. David's fists became knots; his head felt double-sized. Why couldn't Linda train and control these children so they stayed where they belonged? Who was with Brian? He turned away from her, knowing that if he saw unconcern on her face, his anger would explode at her.

The roof of his house was not a playground! Though the slope of the farmhouse roof was not acute, those boys were thirty feet above the ground. If they fell—if another man's child broke a leg falling from his roof—David's mind raced, envisioning hospital scenes, courtroom testimony. Would this juvenile caretaking he did on weekends have no bounds? Did other people's children have to play their catch-me-if-you-can games on his property? This was Rick, he supposed, who had lured Brian away from leaf-raking. And probably got him up on the roof too.

"What the hell are they doing up there?" he demanded. Why couldn't he, on a Saturday morning, clean his yard and kiss his wife without having to deal with the irresponsible children of strangers?

"They like to go up on the shed sometimes," Linda said. She seemed incredibly casual. "They've never gone higher before. The shed isn't high and I never thought to stop them, but the roof scares me."

"If they don't kill themselves or break a leg they'll break the shingles."

"I never thought of that," she said. "But they never went onto the house before. I'll get them to come down."

"Never mind." He strode away from her, feeling as if his head would explode. It was too much, suddenly, the effort required to keep functioning, to endure Barney's needling pressure, to maintain his domicile, and now to control his anger so he would not alienate Linda or cause the children to fall.

Leaving Linda with her arms full of Peter, he found the ladder on the shed side of the house and called to Brian, "Come down now."

"Why?" Brian asked, looking cheerfully down at him. "It's neat up here. We can see for miles."

"I said get down! Both of you, now." Brian let himself onto the shed and the other boy followed. David struggled to control his anger until they stood on solid ground in front of him. Seeing how upset his father was, Brian began to look penitent, but the other one stared at David open-eyed and insolent.

"Never go on the roof, any roof, ever." He hated the sound of his own voice, the heavy father, pacing words like bass drumbeats.

"You," he said to the long, lean child. "You heard?"

The boy lifted his chin, stared past David, then turned his head with a nod, as if to tell Brian, Let's go. "Yessir," he mumbled.

"All right." David was suddenly tired. "Go on and play." He looked at Brian, saw tears in his eyes, and watched the two as they ambled away.

He heard Brian say, "I told you we weren't allowed up there."

And then, "Your father's a crank. I bet he wouldn't give you a dollar if you asked him."

Brian kicked at the turf.

"Ask him. Go on."

"No."

"Ah-h-h, you're scared." Brian turned suddenly and they were on the ground rolling over and over, fighting. David watched as long as he could stand it, knowing that he shouldn't come to Brian's defense. Finally he separated them by grabbing their collars.

"What's your name?" he said to the boy.

The child looked at him with something close to hatred in his eyes, hatred or boredom, David couldn't tell which. He didn't answer.

Finally Brian said, "That's Rick Lang, Daddy."

"Rick," David said, very quietly now, "go home. I've had enough for today."

To Brian he said, "Go inside and wash your face. Then see if you can help your mother." David put a hand on his shoulder.

Brian twisted away angrily. "I hate you," he said. "You're a crank."

Rick walked slowly down the driveway kicking stones ahead of him. He heard the door slam and realized Brian was inside the house, but he didn't look up to the window. Mr. Kaplan didn't like him. His heavy voice was like the others, suffocating, making him feel the way he did after all the questions. *Go home*, Mr. Kaplan had said, the way they talk to dogs. *Go home.* He didn't know where to go. Addie would still be washing the kitchen and Deborah curling her hair and Barbara saying, I'll be the mother and you be the child. But he wasn't anybody's child, not when he was on the roof.

On the roof he was king of the world and Brian his friend, assistant king. "Geez, look how far we can see," Brian said. And Mr. Kaplan said, "Come down now." She never minded when they were on the shed roof so why not higher? Why did kids turn the other way when he rode by their houses after he gave them things? Why did Mr. Kaplan's voice, which wasn't even loud, sound like his father's?

He crawled under the hemlock where, earlier this morning, he'd waited patiently for Mrs. Kaplan to be up so he could ring the doorbell. He knew when she was up because he heard the milk bottles clink when she took them in.

He reached into his pockets, fingers searching, and found a coin in one and a car in the other. He tried to guess which car it was. He couldn't remember putting it there. He wished he could have stayed on the roof with Brian. It was like touching the sky and hiding all at once. From the roof he could see his father come home. He could be taller than his father. Everything looked small from up there, like being in an airplane. On the roof he was taller than Felix, who let him go along even though he was half-size. "But he's okay,"

Felix said to his gang. "Yeah, let the kid stay. He's okay."
Felix gave him stuff for his pockets and took his money and
was glad to get it. Last night he was the only one who dared
when Felix said, "I dare anybody to lie down on the tracks."
When he felt the train coming, Felix said, "Run, kid." It
wasn't anything to get up and run, so he didn't know why
they fussed over him, saying how brave he was. Addie so
mad when he got home, as if he'd died or something. He'd
never seen her so mad. What would she do if she saw him
on the roof when his father got home?

The wind blew hard up there, and with so few leaves on
the trees they had seen across all the housetops to the
church steeple in the village. Down in the cellar of the
church was the Sunday school and down the dark hall was
the choir practice room. He'd forgotten choir practice yesterday. He remembered it too late when he'd left Felix and
gone home. Sunday they'd expect him to put on the black
coat and the white shirt (if Addie found where he'd thrown
it on the floor of his closet) and sing. Sunday, the day of
questions.

He noticed his bike lying where he'd let it fall. He looked
up and down Nutgrove Street; the air still smelled early. It
wasn't Sunday yet and he didn't have to hear the questions
yet. If he went home now Deborah or Barbara would be
there and he wouldn't be able to breathe. That was the
trouble at home, it was so tight around him he couldn't find
air to breathe. On the roof there was more air than anywhere, but Mr. Kaplan had said, "Come down now." And
then looked as if he hated him, said, "Never! Ever!" *Goddammit the baby.*

He'd known it was different the moment he rang the
doorbell this morning, like being at a different house. Nothing good stayed the same and nothing good stayed. She only
pretended to like him, and Brian was a sissy. Where would
he go? He would find Felix. Maybe he'd tell Deborah how
neat Felix was and she'd stop crying about him or saying
those things. Or maybe Felix would ride his motorcycle

around to their house again. But Felix said, "Shit, no, I won't mess with your sister," and, "Listen, kid, it's not so bad to be suspended. Maybe in the end you won't have to go to school at all. Where did you say the letter was that'll get you fucked?"

He'd known there was something different this morning when he rang the bell and she didn't say, "Bring the milk in," or "Hi, Rick," or anything else but "Oh, it's you, Rick. Yes, of course." Then she'd smiled in that don't-bother-me-now way and pushed the hair out of her eyes and told him Brian was out for a walk with his father and she had to hurry and get dinner for some company. "Is there anything special?" she asked him. "Because Saturdays are kind of busy around here, and unless there is something special, well, I really don't have time to talk."

"No," he said. "There isn't anything special."

He went out back but he didn't see Brian, so he walked around to the front and crawled behind the boulder to wait for him. After a while he heard some noises and Peter laughing. He crawled forward and there was Brian pushing Peter in the wheelbarrow. The sound of the baby's laughter made him remember something, made him do what he did. It was strange this week, during those long mornings with Mrs. Kaplan he told her things he didn't know he remembered. Now Peter's high-pitched happy squeals made another connection so it was himself he heard.

Yes, he was just getting out of bed and he almost fell because the bed was so high, but he went out of his room and into Deborah's room. He hid behind the flouncy white curtain and said, "Where's Ricky?" At first she didn't say anything, and so he said it again louder. "Where's Ricky?" He held his breath. Then he heard the sheets move and her voice, sleepy, say, "In the closet?"

"No."

"In the light?"

"No." He held his breath tight.

Then suddenly he knew she knew because he heard, "I see his toes!"

"No!" He screamed with laughter and her hands were all over him tickling him and he pulled away and ran screaming laughing out of her room and she caught him and he fell.

"Dammit, can't you ever learn to be quiet in the morning!" A hard hand hit the side of his head. Dimly he heard the voice go on, "Deborah, you're old enough to keep the kid quiet so I can get some sleep!"

He tried to sneak back to his room, but just as he got to the door her girl's hand caught his shoulder, squeezing so he felt her sharp nails.

"Now see what you've done. I wish you'd never been born!"

He felt wet between his legs and when the wheelbarrow came rushing by he put out a pointed toe in front of the wheel and over it went. The laughter stopped.

Rick came out from under the tree and watched while Peter picked himself up out of the leaves. He stared at Rick before he started to cry.

Brian said, "Gosh, I hope he isn't hurt. Are you all right, Peter? I don't know what happened." But Peter was already on his way to his mother in the back yard.

"Oh, let him go," Rick said, "he's just a baby. Come on. Let's go up on the roof."

David's sore neck made him irritable all that Saturday, Linda decided, short-tempered with Brian and later critical of her for being too easy on him. "Make him stick to these chores, Linda. He'll never grow up with any sense of responsibility if you are so lax." And so, because he was critical of her, she became critical of the boy, and by late afternoon Brian had turned against her too, saying petulantly, "You're always telling me how you love me but you sure don't act like it!" Words she kept hearing. She was upset about the roof episode. David had been too angry. It was more than the danger. Brian put his life in jeopardy every time he climbed a tree. David knew you constantly had to set new limits with children; you couldn't predict what they would try next. No, David had been ready to explode, not just at the boys but at her—as if she had sent them up there, or given them permission. Still, she tried to understand his overreaction; it was unlike Brian to climb on the roof without David's help, or at least his permission, or even to disappear with a friend on a Saturday morning when David was home. Rick wasn't easy to absorb on weekends. She was glad he'd gone home of his own accord.

She was gentle with David, rubbed his neck, and Brian calmed down after an early supper. They got through the business of food and children and arrangements for entertaining friends. In the evening the living room was full of smoke and voices. Though Linda laughed, answered questions, carried brimful plates, she realized she was detached; the hours of talk neither entertained nor changed her. She was, once more, a spectator; puppets moved about her house; she saw another tableau. They came. She nourished them. Momma, she thought.

Sunday sounds of churchgoers woke her. A car backed out of the driveway across the road; the staccato footsteps of some children in their Sunday best went by. Rick and his family went to church, she knew, for he had told her about being in the choir. In her mind she saw the sweet-faced choirboy in his frock, but under the frock was the juvenile delinquent she had seen lope through the station on Friday night. Which boy would be in church this morning? Early morning reveries were hard to control. What did Brian—or all of them—miss not going to church? She and David had arrived at their unorthodoxy separately and had been content to live consistently with their agnosticism. The issue of church came up briefly when Brian was five, and talked of his friends who were in Sunday school. Did he want to go? Was it a deprivation for him to stay home? Would he grow up in some way hollow? Separated from his community? David made the family decision. "We can't send him alone, and I certainly don't want to attend services I don't believe in. Which temple, or church, did you have in mind?"

Linda didn't know; she didn't want to go to any of them either. They had been comfortable with their decision, so why was she even thinking about it now? If they all got up on Sunday morning and dressed and went to church together would it truly make them closer? Would David's neck hurt less? Ridiculous! She wondered as she turned over against his warmth if being in church was as nice as lying in bed. She heard Peter sing softly to himself through two closed doors, "Nonononono."

They found the smashed bricks after breakfast when, before dishes, they took a turn around the yard. A few years before, David had lined the front walk with bricks set diagonally, one against the other, just two inches into the ground, and behind them Linda had planted myrtle. All of the bricks had been removed, and so many were smashed that the walk was a red gravel dump.

"Somebody had a sledge hammer," Linda said, hearing her own voice as if it were a stranger's. And then neither she nor David could say a word.

"But who, who, who would've done it?" Brian kept asking.

"Are you sure you didn't see anyone around here yesterday?" David asked him.

"You sent me inside, remember, Daddy? You sent me in when you sent Rick home."

"You did what?" Linda asked.

"I told him to go home." David was startled by her tone.

"How could you be so cruel?"

Time stopped. A collection of syllables—staccato airwaves—crossed the space between them, changed the size and shape and texture of that space as a shaft of sunlight slanting through an empty room changes the texture and design of the air, creates a diagonal rift, suddenly illuminating dancing dust as if the rest of the air were particle free; dust only in the yellow stripe. Six words thrust diagonally across the void.

She closed her culprit lips, touching the villains with her fingertips.

"I, cruel?" His eyes became listless. "However do you mean?" Of all the qualities David possessed—those that pleased or irritated—cruelty least described him. Yet she had used the word. Though she wished to withdraw she could neither explain nor change what had happened. Could she say that his judgment had been too swift? He had acted in honest anger. She couldn't quite say the same of herself.

She looked from David to Brian; the boy was scuffing the brick fragments with his toe. She touched his shoulder as if for support and sent him off on a false errand.

"I'm sorry," she said at last, knowing how inadequate that was.

David shook his head and frowned. "I don't know what you're talking about half the time. If you're angry with me, let me know what about."

"I'm not," she said, to end it.

He shrugged and turned away.

"If Rick has done this, I'll deal with him," she said to bring him back. "Why did you send him home?"

"He was rude to me and encouraged Brian to be disobedient; they ended up fighting. Not my idea of a way to spend a Saturday."

"You didn't tell me."

"I saw no need. You were busy with Peter. That boy had already wrecked half the day." He pointed to the red devastation at their feet. "His father must be told about this."

"No," she said, "not his father or his mother."

The long Sunday oozed by, each tense moment bringing its own twinge. The children, sensing the alteration in the atmosphere, were noisy and intrusive. Peter's nos turned to wails and Brian's too-frequent questions rattled against the walls. When in the evening the house was finally quiet, Linda's knitting needles echoed in the low-ceilinged room. David gathered a fistful of chisels and knives and brought them and the hone to the living room. Carefully he began to drop oil on the stone. When there were difficult things to talk about, disturbances, each found a way to keep his hands busy. If David had played the piano that night Linda might have left him, and he knew it without knowing why.

The hands had to move. Explanation could so easily slip to accusation, question to excuse, insight to anger. The anger was easier to delay if their hands were busy.

Finally David the lawyer spoke to the point. "Why did you say I was cruel to send the Lang boy home?"

Softly, "I don't know."

"I don't want Brian to play with him any more. He's obviously a vicious, vengeful little person, an impossible child well on his way toward delinquency. He's a bad influence."

"You'd condemn him without a trial," Linda flared.

"I'm hardly condemning him to anything but his own home."

"Home, to him, is the flame."

"A blasphemy?"

She tried to pull back from her frontal position, realizing that to win she must retreat and find reason and intellect to rely on. "He's had a bad week," she said. "I told you. I guess when you sent him home he decided you were on the side of his enemies. You see, he's been fired upon in every place he's gone except this house. Until now," she added.

"I only told him to go home. I could have said much worse. He was very unpleasant."

Linda picked her way carefully through an underbrush of arguments. She talked of his difficulties at school, of the way he had appealed to her for help. She couldn't reveal the secrets he'd entrusted to her because David would be frightened by them, because she was frightened by them. Too often her words seemed to work against her. She groped.

She explained that whatever Rick had done in the past to antagonize the adult world was someone else's responsibility. But now, because he had appealed to her for help, she had to be an ally. "I could feel his anger," she said, "when I talked with Dr. Masterson. She's an imposing, unrelenting woman. I felt as Rick must have felt, small and guilty. I couldn't help it, though I know that doesn't make sense. Someone has to try to understand the boy!" Then she added, "It was such a crude revenge."

"Why you?" David persisted.

"Why me?" She played for time. "Well," she tried again, "if every door he looks through slams in his face it's not much of a future. For a boy of nine or ten."

"I'm sure you're exaggerating. I'm sure his parents are fond of him. He has sisters—"

She thought of his parents walking in the door. They must be home by now. Hearing from Barbara of his suspension. She thought of the nightmares Barbara whispered to him in the dark, of the letter she had not dared to steal. *Once Linda had dived from the high dive.*

David was saying, "Damn, Linda, can't you leave the boy out of our lives? Can't you? Even if he is as badly off as you say. What about Brian? Rick's a rotten influence on Brian. I heard him telling Brian to get money out of me."

"No one should condemn another human being. You'd give him up for lost." *She had dived deeper than she meant to, her breath was gone. Would she make it back to the surface?*

"I don't want you to be his savior at Brian's expense, not to mention our property. The boy's destructive."

"You hardly know him."

"But you admit you didn't like him at first."

"I was wrong to judge him so quickly."

"Just what do you think you can do? You're not his mother, his teacher, or his doctor."

"We could be his friends."

"You're dreaming. It's just like that insane idea you had before Peter was born. You're no social worker. You're not trained."

The needles clicked together harder than ever, and if a purl slipped among the knits, she didn't notice. "A little time and a little love," she explained as she had rehearsed. "I know I can teach him. I can reach him. I have to try, at least, without giving up before I start. You see—"

"I see you're all wound up in somebody else's child."

"It's like the orange at the bottom of the crate, going bad. Maybe it rots because it was always at the bottom, never allowed to get the light."

"Maybe it started off rotten. Besides, what can you do?"

"We have so much, he so little."

"He's hardly what you'd call poor." His words repeated arguments that had raged within her before. But she'd moved beyond him. They had lived separate lives for a week.

"He can't read properly. He hates himself for that, gets further and further behind. If he could begin to read . . ."

"Why must you take him on? Why not his own parents? The school? They have specialists."

"The school and its specialists are failing. They turned him loose."

"You've more to do here than you can manage. I've got this new case on my head. I could use your help on that, though I suppose what you do with your time is your own affair. Still, I don't see why I have to put up with having unpleasant children around to spoil my weekends. I don't like him."

"All right then," she said, "I'll keep him away weekends. But I can't turn him away altogether. I'll let him come in the afternoons, and perhaps while Brian does his homework I can help with his reading."

"If what you see in him is there," David said cautiously,

putting out feelers for peace, "and all he needs is a little time, a little love—but be careful! You always get so involved."

"I'll be careful. I promise."

She watched the little knife blade go round and round on the oiled stone, remembering, "They wouldn't let me have a knife." Slowly, exploring the idea as she spoke, trying it on herself as well as David, she said, "*The Children of Sanchez*—remember—it was not only the physical deprivation that made their skins hang on rattling bones like sheets on a clothesline. There was no one to talk to. *No one ever listened.* No adult heard what a child said. There was nobody but other empty-headed children to try a thought on. Mexicans may not be the only starved Americans."

"At what age do you suppose a starvation case becomes hopeless?" he asked. "If an organism has been starved, deprived enough from too early in life, it can be too late for a therapeutic diet to revive it."

She was startled. "I don't know," she said. "And I don't know how starved Rick really is. But I would be less than worthy if I didn't try to find out. He did talk to me; he even smiled once."

She stopped now because she was swimming against the current again.

"I suppose the word 'hopeless' isn't in your vocabulary. But there is substantial evidence, you know, that with early and prolonged starvation, there is no possibility of recovery."

But she was not hearing him. She was remembering her involvement. What had Rick done to deserve Dr. Masterson's anger? Had there been any real danger in keeping him at school? She remembered Dr. Masterson's hand turning the knob at her chest, and knew that the woman could have faulty perception as well as faulty hearing. It was impossible now to explain her feelings further without revealing to David how disturbed Rick really was, and how deeply she had been affected by him, so deeply that she had, on three occasions, nearly lost control of her own actions. If he knew how close she had been to stealing! She felt his eyes were on her, waiting for her to continue, but she had already said too much. The parallel to the Mexicans had perhaps been ill-advised. She remained silent, caught, so to speak, at the door of her own conscience. He watched and waited. Did he know that she knew more than she was telling? Was he ever sensitive to how much of herself she withheld from him?

Finally he said, "My mother wants to visit us at Christmastime. Do you think you could manage to put her up for a couple of weeks?"

"Yes. Of course." Always, no matter what he asked of her, she answered yes. Always. "It would be nice for Brian and Peter." She was being careful again.

He said, "It might even be nice for you if you let her take over the children sometimes. You and I could have more time together."

"Yes," she said. "Yes, I would like that." She wasn't angry with him any more, so he came back to where they were.

"If you take on Rick's problems, his reading, if you let him and Brian be together so much, will you do something for me?"

"What?"

"Speak with his teacher, with anyone at school who is involved with his affairs. Let them know what you're doing. Maybe the psychologist."

"They won't tell me anything. You know, confidential stuff."

"Of course."

"But I could try Catherine Barker. We're sort of friends."

"Try."

"All right." She watched the little blade in his hand go round and round. "And I will call his mother," she added. The blade grew sharper and sharper. There was something she still had to say. She wanted to do what she wanted to do, but she wanted his approval too. She picked up her knitting, letting a new flow of words fill the air without watching them or him. "I may not be good for much, but sometimes there's just one thing you have to do. Maybe arguing Barney's case is your thing. You don't want to do it but you said yes. You have to do it and you don't want to but you said yes, I'll do it. Maybe you think it's your chance for greatness and you're afraid it might be the only one. A blown leaf caught in your rake and for some reason that might be its beauty, or might be a vague fear that it is the last beautiful leaf, you save it from the fire. Maybe you have to do it because someone needs you. Maybe once in your life—maybe never—someone reaches out a hand and says please. Maybe it doesn't matter that what you try to do is too little or too late. Maybe you fear that you'll fail. I can live with someone who tries honestly and fails. You have to do some of each in every day. But I don't think I'd have loved you at all if you'd turned your back, or pretended not to see what you did see, or not to care when you did care."

"Be careful," he said. But she wasn't finished.

"Someone said something to me. A leaf is caught in my rake. I must love myself as much as I love you or Brian or Peter, and I couldn't if I pretended that I haven't heard what I have heard."

"What have you heard?" He was frowning, but his words were a whisper on a breeze that went astray. If she had known how completely David expected her to fail, just as he often expected himself to fail, she might not have put away her knitting. Optimistic, she visualized only her success and deflected his fears. She thought of his question in the night, and her answer. It's all right to be used if you want the end. The thing that would hold her to David and him to her was their continuing to believe in the same end.

Time, and an end, and some blown leaves might make a life between them after all the words were done. You had to be free and constrained at the same time. You had to believe in some fairy tales; you did not always have to chart the course between fantasy and reality. She had not stolen; she had avoided lies. At least, she thought, his father will not know about the bricks tonight.

Life, to be bearable, needed a villain or two. Tom Lang could do for now.

NINE ✑ VIVIAN LANG SHIFTED HER WEIGHT FROM her left hip to her right, recrossed her legs, pulled the tight tan flannel down to her knees, and let her head rest on the big worsted shoulder at her side.

"Don't," Tom said, "it's uncomfortable enough in this damn plane without your leaning all over me. I wish we'd gone first-class." His big knees hit the back of the seat in front of them; his long legs twisted to the side.

"Sorry, dear," Vivian murmured and let her head rest against the steel window frame. She watched the cumulus clouds travel past until her eyes burned. Once in a while the plane dipped, her heart and lungs dropping with it, but most of the ride was smooth; the monotonous roar in her ears became noiseless. She thought of the seven days behind her. Each meal had been an adventure (Shall we have abalone or crab?); each decision a delight (Shall we take raincoats or?). Every one of those fleeting minutes that Tom was with her she—consciously or unconsciously—pretended that years had not existed. San Francisco was exactly as it had been when she first met him. There had been no birthdays, no houses, no doctors, no schools, no people asking what she couldn't give, touching where she hated to be touched. She had tried to tell Tom so he would pretend too.

"It's just the same, remember?" But he had been distracted, and too often his words had gone past her into the music at the black-mirrored bar, into the fog, or to some place beyond that her mind couldn't follow. During her few afternoons alone, when Tom was at business meetings, she had shopped, bought delicious clothes for the girls, but had been unable to decide what to buy for Rick. On the last day they had met with the lawyer for the final disposition of Gran's will. Vivian never bothered to read what she signed. Tom told her there was something for each of the children. How had Gran managed to save so much? With the lawyer paid, the fees and taxes and doctors and debts settled, there was still a thousand each for the children.

For the second time as a plane raced her away from the California sun, Vivian thought of the box they had watched being lowered into the ground the year before. Would she forever see the contents of that box, the skin-cloaked collection of bones that had been her mother, when she closed her eyes? When those dark-suited men threw dirt on the box, she buried her childhood, past, connection, conscience. The thud of dirt hitting wood left her naked, as if so long as her mother lived she was clothed, shielded, warmed. What would they, would she, would any of them, do without Gran? Where would Rick run away to now?

Once during Gran's last days she had taken Rick with her to the hospital. Already there were bars around Gran's bed; she had barely been able to speak. Rick, for whom Gran would have done anything, wouldn't even look at her. Vivian had nearly hit him in that hot tiny room, she had been so angry. Thoughts of Rick unbidden (her flesh, her monster) brought tears to the edges of her eyes. How could she feel such anger at the boy over something he did so long ago? And she cruising at thirty-five thousand feet.

She wrenched her thoughts away from the child, back to the city they were leaving, to the memory of sun and salt fog. She opened her eyes to the land below. Already the peaks of the coastal range were behind her. There was something she had forgotten to do. No, not forgotten, postponed.

"It's nice about the money," she said.

"Um." Tom did not look up from the thick book he was

reading. He was always in the middle of a book, it seemed, and always some history or biography—Churchill, Roosevelt, Lincoln. She couldn't remember the many men whose names she had seen on the backs of his books. Sometimes he tried to talk to her of what was in them, but her mind didn't follow. Sometimes, she remembered guiltily, she would doze off, lulled by the sound of his voice as he read out loud. It had been a long time since he had done that.

"It was so nice in California, so warm. I'd forgotten."

"What?"

"I almost forgot why we left. I mean, home comes at me too fast now." She waited for him to say something. Anything. He was silent. She was sorry they'd left the west, but perhaps it would work out. California was warm and familiar. The east cold and strange. Tom had said, The money's in the east but the ideas are dead. She didn't know what he meant. He was doing well, she thought, not knowing what he was doing. He had opened up an eastern office for his investment company. He made business friends quickly. Once in a while he brought people home, but none became her friends. She had been lonely, she supposed. Was it Gran she missed? Or the sun?

"I heard on the news it snowed in New York. I don't have any boots."

"Get some."

"Will you talk to the woman at school? I forget her name. I should have told you before."

His lips tightened. He slipped a finger into his place. "What woman?"

"The psychologist. She called me just before we left. She wants to do some kind of tests on Rick, maybe put him in a special class. You'd think they'd have taught him to read by now, at least."

"Have you tried to help him? Spent some time with him?" He still held the book open.

"Oh, I tried," she said, "but he always gets mad. You know how he is with me. I just can't do a thing."

"The boy's smart. I know he is."

"Yes, dear," she said. She shouldn't have mentioned the boy. He always came between them, even when he wasn't there. Whenever Tom was impatient with her she thought of Rick, and when she thought of Rick whatever she said came out wrong. If she complained about anything he did, Tom accused her as if it were her fault he'd been born bad. For that was the truth. Rick had been in trouble since he was born. All her fault! Tom was the father.

She tried a different tack. "I'm sure if you talk with Rick he'll straighten out. He's behaving better these days anyway. He has a new friend."

Tom closed the book. Truman would wait. It seemed there was nothing any more that his wife could do for herself or for him, even let him read. All right, he'd have a talk with his son. Get to the root of the problem. All the boy needed was a fresh start. If the school was willing to help, he'd talk to anyone. To the psychologist. The teacher. To Rick. He'd start with the boy. He imagined the scene, alone in the car, perhaps, or by the fire in the den. Perhaps he could take Rick out to dinner, a treat in the city. The boy'd had a hard time, first Gran dying, then the move east. He'd give him a present, make him feel better. He'd tell him about the money Gran left. They'd talk about Gran. They hadn't, he realized, in the year she'd been dead. Maybe that was Rick's trouble. "I loved her too," he'd say. "You and I were the ones. She cared most for us. She was in great pain. It's a mercy that's over, but she cared for you. She left you a thousand dollars!" The image of the boy grew in his mind. He pictured Rick, so constrained with him now, frightened no longer.

Something had gone wrong when he'd told Rick about Gran. The boy sat so stiffly on his lap, his bony buttocks pressing into Tom's thighs. What right had his son to be so thin? He was well fed! He'd tried to hug him but the boy had squirmed away. "May I go now?" he'd asked. "Go! Go on, dammit!" He'd pushed him away. Not roughly. He hadn't meant to be rough, but he'd been upset, Vivian and the girls upstairs crying. He should have been more patient. Well, he'd do it right this time. The boy simply needed a little more patience. Big Tom would open his arms and give his son refuge.

"I'll talk to the woman," he said aloud, "and to Rick. You'd never do it right anyway. You never did understand or spend enough time with him. That's why he loved Gran so much. Remember how he used to run away all the time? She was more mother to him than you are."

"Yes, dear," Vivian said again. "I wouldn't know what to say to the psychologist. I'm so glad you'll go. They always scare me, and I never know what to say."

"Just listen for a change," he said. "Don't say anything and they won't get a line on you."

She relaxed. His tone was no longer hostile. "I—I always feel like a scared kid when I go down those marble halls. I get all dressed up, put on my face, and all the time I tell myself they can't hurt me any more. I'm grown up now, but—"

"You never grew up. You never will."

She bit a small piece of flesh from the inside of her lower lip, held it between her front teeth. "I guess you're right." She barely said the words. Once on a fog-strewn night they had stood together on a rocky shore listening to the ocean. He had held her close and carried her safely and so lightly across a treacherous chasm. "Baby, don't ever grow up," he'd whispered against her cheek.

"What did you say?" he asked opening the book again.

"Nothing."

She waited, strained her mind for something to say that might bring him close. She rested a tentative finger on his cuff, touched his coarse-haired hand. "You aren't going to read," she said.

"What else do you expect me to do for six hours?"

She chewed on the bit of flesh until it was nothing between her teeth. Then she opened her purse, took her pocket mirror and straightened a piece of hair. She let her forefinger trail across the slightly pocked part of her left cheek that she covered with extra makeup. She shifted her hips again, looked out the window, pressed her forehead against the cold glass to see down through the double panes. She let her mind drift down to the black hills that rolled by below, still not completely comprehending that she would be home in a few hours.

For Vivian Lang, home was a plush-lined obstacle course. The obstacles were mountainous intellectual problems she couldn't understand, sounds she couldn't still, tasks she couldn't master, peace she couldn't maintain. The plush was the moments she spent with Tom when he wasn't angry with her.

They'd met in a bar in San Francisco where she'd gone with a friend from the shipping office on the way home from the movies. That's how it was during the war, talking to soldiers, to people in bars and railroad stations, and nobody thought it was wrong. Tom was a tech sergeant in the Corps of Engineers. He looked the same then except his skin was a little smoother and there wasn't so much flesh under his chin. He stood over six feet tall and his chest was enormous. His eyes were small slits and suddenly a month after he'd left for the Philippines, she burst into tears at her desk because she couldn't remember the color of his eyes.

When she started to cry she couldn't stop and her makeup ran down her cheeks. Someone finally got her to the couch in the ladies' room and she fell asleep. The next day, her mother took her to the doctor, and he told her she was pregnant.

"I just couldn't be! I mean, I never thought—"

"But you knew you'd missed your period," the doctor said.

"Well, yes, but I thought if I waited it would get better. I thought just some little thing was wrong."

"We'll work out something," Vivian's mother said, taking Vivian firmly by the arm out of the office.

Once home Helen Conner poured them each a glass of whiskey. "I can't decide what to do about the baby," she said. "I might know someone who could do an abortion, but it's risky. It's not that I don't like babies. If your father hadn't died so young we would have had more. But to bring up a child and not even know who the father is! I thought you'd have more sense."

Vivian was looking through the amber liquid in her glass, letting her mother's anger wind around her, and wind down.

Finally, "Which one was it?" Helen asked.

"We're married," Vivian said softly. "There's no problem about that. It's just that I never thought about having a baby. I don't want Tom's baby. I just want Tom."

In the days ahead Vivian let her mother do what she had always done—the thinking and decision-making for both of them. Uninterested in the growing fetus, Vivian worked as before, but lived each day for the mail. Tom wrote at first and she answered letter for letter. By the time Deborah was born Tom had stopped writing. There were no telegrams from the government; the allotment checks continued to come; Vivian never wrote Tom about the baby, and she never talked about him after his letters stopped. If her memory grew dim, her yearning never lessened. All she wanted, then or now, was the man, and she knew him not.

Deborah was nearly a year old when Vivian read an item that told her Tom's outfit was returning. She went alone to the dock to wait. Although she had attended church with her mother as long as she could remember, memorized psalms and prayers as needed, now, pressed against a warehouse wall by an anxious crowd, there was no prayer that helped her. She blocked from her consciousness the messageless time, or the possible reasons for Tom's silence. If he was alive he would return by this ship and be hers to hold one more night. If he were dead, she would have been notified. The idea that he might be alive and not return to her was so painful that she did not allow it.

She watched the American President liner turned troop transport glide against the dock. She stood on tiptoes to see above the heads in front of her; she bit the flesh from the inside of her lower lip and held it between her teeth.

Tom Lang stood at the stern of the troopship which had crossed the Pacific in twenty-eight days, most of which he had spent under a lifeboat planning what he was going to do with his life now that it was his to plan. He wanted money. He wanted professional respectability and cash. He never wanted to be poor or uncomfortable again, or to take any more orders. Tom didn't know where he wanted to work, but he knew what he wanted to avoid.

The son of a Chicago slaughterhouse laborer, Tom Lang had spent most of his childhood trying to escape from it. His Irish immigrant father had deserted his mother when Tom was eight. At ten Tom went to work, but by his own cunning managed also to stay in school. He knew he was lucky to have his brain. His eighth-grade history teacher had kept him after class one day and told him, "You seem to remember everything you read. Not many of us can do that. A quick mind is precious. Place high value on it and use it wisely. You didn't eat lunch. Are you hungry?" For that year and part of the next, until his mother died of pneumonia and the home he was placed in sent him to a different school, Miss Pryzbywsky fed him sandwiches and books and sent him to museums. She taught him the value of education.

As Tom watched the fireball on the edge of the ocean he tried to forget the east, the heat, the disease, the dead, the big-eyed hungry orphans who reminded him of himself. He tried to believe that the old ship had crossed the endless sea, and that he was finally free to shape his next years. He knew there were new industries growing at home: plastics, electronics, construction. He was determined not to let the boom pass him by. Business school would be the way to start, he decided, preferably in California where it was clean, rich, fast; where he'd had more fun in two weeks than he'd had all his life; where he'd met Vivian Conner in a black-mirrored bar.

Vivian Lang. She was the part of his future he couldn't look at. It had been such a lame-brained thing to do, marrying the girl like that. He barely knew her. Just a feeling he'd had at the time, the way she looked up at him, listened to him. Nobody had ever listened to him like that. For a while after he got to the dank jungle of Central Luzon it had seemed fine that he was married, writing to her, "Dear love, dear Vivian," but the months were too long and the memory of skin-soft nights grew faint and foolish. A stranger's letters came to him in a child's neat handwriting. "I'll watch Mom cook dinner tonight so I can learn how to cook for you. She's a real good cook. Which do you like better? Movies about war or love?" Simpleminded sentences that embarrassed him. She wrote of her mother a lot. She was a child, he decided, who had never left home. He didn't need a child bride or a mother-in-law in his life.

He tried to keep writing but after a while he couldn't make the pen mark the paper. He thought if he didn't write she'd find someone else. She was pretty enough. With each mail call he hoped for a letter which would be his freedom. But she stopped writing too. Perhaps she thought he was dead. If he didn't think about it, like not writing and not talking about her either, maybe it would be as if there were no such marriage recorded in the San Francisco City Hall.

Tom walked slowly down the ramp looking at the faces in the crowd below. Over the ringing in his ears he heard shouts and laughter, names called out, horns and music. But the men who moved down the gangplank close by him did not push or hurry. They held back as a mass, a hesitating march of reluctant non-soldiers, blinded by a glittering mosaic of open mouths and expectant eyes, kerchiefs and brightly covered shoulders. It would be so easy if she wasn't there.

He was at the bottom where he had to look at his feet to

step off the ramp. He was acquitted. Then he heard her voice.

"Tom!" like the wail of a child. "Tom Lang. Over here!"

He turned; seeing easily over the crowd, he found her in a doorway. Magnetized, he pushed his way through the damp bodies until he was by her, looking down. He took her hand and pulled her out and away and into a side street. They stood at arm's length. He stared at her, starting with the gray-blond hair in a cotton cloud about her face, wide eyes, soft oval face so smoothly molded the features were hardly raised, almost oriental. Her shoulders were surprisingly square for a girl so slight, breasts high, pushing toward him through a soft sweater. His eyes traced the body he once had wanted all the way to her feet, one patent leather toe rubbing the top of the other. Then he looked back to her face. He shivered. She loved him! She was biting her lip like any punk kid, waiting for him to say something. Scared. A little scared kid waiting for Big Tom to come home! He'd never thought about her loving him. He opened his arms and knew as he closed them around her that he would do some quick rethinking.

"Baby," he said against her ear, "baby, where do we live?"

Together they walked away from the sea and the ships and the fish smells and the abalone shells, straight up the narrow hill and somewhere along the steep he began to think he hadn't been such a lame-brain after all. They walked and didn't notice that the fog had turned to rain. They touched each other.

It wasn't until they woke several hours later that he noticed the crib and the string of bright beads on the night table. He turned and looked again at his wife, suddenly comprehending that it was not he alone who kept secrets. How long would it be before they knew each other?

At five o'clock the doorbell rang. Vivian pressed the buzzer, opened the door, and they waited, Tom hearing footsteps of a relative he'd never met; they were actors, they were dreamers. He felt Vivian's small hand in his, seeking comfort. He held it tight for support, knowing there was nothing to lean on.

Words came to him from a distance. "Mom, this is Tom. Tom, Mom." He nodded, saw a small gray-haired woman half his height in front of him. He searched her eyes suspiciously, but found light and humor; he didn't know why. He looked at her and thought, She feeds other people's dogs and laughs at rules and gives candy to strange children who knock at her door. He put out his hand and she looked at him straight as he looked at her, looking, he knew, to find what manner of man had taken her daughter, then held her hand to meet his.

"Helen Conner," she said. "Vivian didn't tell me you were a giant. I don't know where we'll put you in this tiny place." Then, finally, she stooped and pushed forward the new-standing child.

"This is your daughter, Tom Lang."

The baby managed to walk all the way around him. He could see the top of her head, which reached to his knees. She went around once more, stopped finally in front of him, reached up and with one tiny fat finger tried to touch his brass belt buckle. He was glad he'd shined it that morning.

"Deborah, this is your father." Helen picked her up and held her facing him. The baby stared so hard he wanted to turn his head.

"Not yet," she said quite clearly.

Helen Conner, relieved that her son-in-law turned out to be strong and intelligent, did what she could to make life pleasant for the two young people. She continued to work and take care of the baby as often as possible.

Tom enrolled in the business school at Berkeley, devouring the information, the contacts with people whose cultural lives had been richer than his. He soon learned that sweet as Vivian was, she would never keep up with him. In the early years of their marriage, proud of her selfless devotion and her sexual excitement, he was gentle with her. He liked her dependence and the way she deferred to his judgment. He enjoyed all the times they were alone together, dancing, drinking, swimming, making love. He was proud of the way she looked and dressed. For a long time he felt a certain pity for friends whose wives were aggressive, creative, active. "I'm glad you're not like that," he'd say. "Don't ever get too smart."

But as his interests widened, the sexual hold she had on him began to abate. More and more often he was annoyed with her lack of competence, her inability to cope with an idea, a book, or the complexities of their home. Tom's interests went well beyond business, into history, politics, philosophy. He used everything he learned for some purpose. He outgrew his jobs quickly, so in ten years he held five jobs for five different firms, each a leap in size and responsibility.

When Vivian became pregnant with their second child he was already earning enough to put a down payment on a house. Barbara, a placid infant, was born there and too soon afterwards another child, Rick. When Vivian had three children and a house to care for Tom realized that even with her mother nearby she could not function. Unfolded wash mounded around her like drifting snow. The new baby's colic and constant crying confounded her; the year-old exhausted her. With the help Tom bought her and continual detailed instructions on maintenance, she eventually learned to run the house so he didn't trip over the children's toys or dirty clothing in the front hall. But still he found evidence of her distractibility—a half-eaten apple by the telephone, a hairbrush on the stairs, food half-prepared and discarded testifying to unsuccessful kitchen experiments. If it hadn't been for peanut butter, he once thought, his children would have gone as hungry as he had.

Occasionally he tried to talk to Vivian about whatever idea he was working on that excited him, but she would curl like a kitten next to him, petting him, placing her finger on or between his lips. He didn't resist her. If she responded with words she invariably changed the subject, cataloging her troubles, or rather the trouble the children got into. When Vivian's complaints ran too long Tom would retreat into a book until bedtime, and sometimes long after.

Tom was uncommonly proud of having three children, especially a son. Their pink-tinted eight-by-ten framed portraits were prominent on his desk. He brought home books for them, but tools and trucks and other boys' toys to distract Rick from his sisters' dolls, which he stole and broke when left unwatched. Vivian had not wanted this baby. Had Rick turned out to be another girl Tom might have shared her annoyance, but he was stirred by the thought that even he could have a chance at immortality. Tom's disappointments grew in proportion to his expectations. The boy looked more and more like his mother, slight, thin-shouldered, pale. Tom watched him closely for signs of intelligence.

By the time Rick was walking Tom had formed a niche for himself in the community. They had joined a church and the local civic club. As the three children were tearing Vivian's life apart, so Tom was methodically building his own up, memo by memo, meeting by meeting. He began to think about going to law school. He could study at night. He thought it would be fine to have a judgeship in his old age. He had an impressive and impeccable record, a handsome family; it seemed there was nothing he couldn't achieve. If his work kept him away from his family more and more nights, he knew it was in their long-range interest. He knew where he was going. When trying to decide whether to go home at six or work through the dinner hour, he might not have admitted that arriving home after the tears were dried, the bathwater let out, and the infants asleep, to a freshly showered Vivian with a drink ready for him, was infinitely more pleasant than cries and chaos. He did sometimes admit that the dinner company he found was nearly as satisfying sexually, and certainly more interesting intellectually, than his family.

He knew Helen was critical of the distance he kept from his children, but often the time he spent with them miscarried. Patience was not instinctive with him. What he said and what he meant to say were often disparate.

He still read extensively. When he spoke in public he quoted heavily from his readings, appearing as an expert to whatever audience. If he knew there was a philosophic barrenness to his existence he did not admit it and could not have defined it. He was the leader in his family. All of them except Helen cowered before his rages, believed in his strength, worked for his comforts, tried to second-guess his desires and thus avoid his anger.

But too often the sound of anger eroded his home, and he could not control it. Tom was on his way up and whenever wife or child interfered explosions occurred without design. Tom Lang suffered the tortures of the insecure, the socially mobile man. Rick was the last victim of Tom's mobility.

By the time Rick was six Tom was vice president of an investment company that had interests in educational publishing, land speculations, and construction on both coasts. He had maneuvered his way onto the local school board, and had already begun to seek admittance to law school. The dean of the school he had chosen was a minor investor in their company, he had discovered. That would not be a disadvantage, he thought.

Three things changed Tom's plan. First, instead of Rick's becoming easier he grew more and more difficult. He broke things, got into fights with neighborhood children, and continually ran away. Most often he was found at his grandmother's house, but on several occasions the police brought him home. He was not learning to read; the school reported him a behavior problem; Tom worried that he had inherited Vivian's slow mind as well as her slender frame. A dull-witted woman was one thing, but what would he do with a dull son? The school wanted to hold him back but Tom wouldn't hear of it. He demanded special teachers. As a member of the board he thought they ought to listen to him.

The second thing was that Deborah, at the outrageous age of fourteen, had gone star-struck, boy-crazy, and worse. One night while Tom was out of town she was arrested with her current boyfriend while drag racing in a quiet street on the back of his motorcycle. Some stolen watches and a half-empty pint of Four Roses were found in the pouches of the cycle. Although Deborah was still too young to get her picture or her name in the paper, she was held overnight. The judge who talked to Tom the next day when he went to get her was also on the school board.

Then Tom learned from Vivian that Helen—Gran as they had all come to call her—was dying of cancer. He didn't know what they would do without her.

Gray Abernathy, the president of his company, who had opened doors for Tom, admiring his energy and his quick action, guessed some of the problems Tom attempted to keep hidden. He suggested that Tom open an east-coast office. A financier in a little town called New Delphi, an hour north of New York City, was interested in some of Tom's development ideas. New Delphi, Hokum Falls—it couldn't matter less. It was a new beginning.

When Tom decided to take his family east he finally accepted that there were four people he simply could not shed. They were his, like the stubble on his chin each morning. He had made his successes and failures with them and in spite of them. He couldn't leave them behind. Besides, he had long known the importance of being flanked by an attractive wife and three well-washed children.

The school in California had been all wrong for Rick, he thought. The boy had been treated badly. And Deborah needed to be taken away from Hollywood, hoodlums, motorcycles, and booze. With Gran dead there was nothing to hold them to the west any more.

On the whole he had been satisfied. The work was moving nicely for a first year's start. He was pleased with his house, the community, and Rick wasn't doing any worse than before. If the school was interested enough to call Vivian, that was an improvement. Vivian complained that it was too cold, that she didn't have any friends. But they joined the church and the boy was in the choir which certainly ought to do him some good and, well, Vivian complained a lot.

It had been good to revisit the west coast together. It gave him perspective. He thought about Vivian, so lacking in strength, so unwise with their children. But he had to admit that she had never wavered in her feelings for him. Whatever he asked she gave to the best of her ability. He felt guilty for being short with her. He covered her knee with his hand, stirring her.

"I'll see what I can do for the boy," he said. "I'll talk with his teacher too. Maybe we'll look into private schools, if he isn't making it where he is."

"Oh, I'm sure you can help, Tom."

"I'll spend more time with him," Tom went on, remembering the smallness of his son, vowing not to be impatient. "You know," he laughed, "I used to get mad because he couldn't catch a ball. Remember? I gave him the mitt?"

"He was only four," Vivian murmured.

"Maybe he could catch a ball now, if he tried."

"Maybe," she said.

He went on, "There's a lot to growing up in a big family. I mean, look at the Kennedys. No wonder those kids grew big. A lot of money, but beyond that. Somebody around to play ball with. A boy really does need a leader, someone who cares enough to show him how."

He opened the book again.

"Yes, dear," Vivian said, closing her eyes as the plane rushed them homeward.

TEN ❦ ADDIE'S KNOCK BROKE INTO RICK'S SLEEP

like the sound of chipped brick. His eyes opened to the blue ceiling.

"Rick?" Her voice was soft in the hall. "Rick, wake up." He heard the latch click open.

"Yes."

"Time for church. Up you get." He saw her face in the doorway, shiny as a black marble above her short white dress. "You're late this morning. Tired?"

He pushed back the covers, not noticing the early cold on his legs. He was surprised to see the time. Usually he was up and dressed before her knock, but this morning the sound had startled him, reaching into an unusually deep and dreamless sleep. Time had a certain thickness, and last night piled minute after minute of thick time, blotting and blocking memory, so that now with Addie's knock he didn't recall the events of the day and night before, only felt the kind of exhaustion that comes from complete expenditure of passion. He sat motionless on his bed. His head felt too heavy. His lips felt thick and swollen; the stiffness in his jaws and neck felt as if he were going to get sick but wasn't sick yet.

"Quick now," Addie said.

He stood up. *Hurry up,* Felix said. *If you run you can keep up with us. Quick now.* He walked to the closet and saw his white shirt hanging freshly washed and ironed. He turned to face Addie behind him.

"I found it on the floor," she said. "Why don't you put your dirty clothes in the hamper?"

Rick didn't answer. He went across the hall to use the toilet. "Don't forget to brush your teeth." He heard her voice through the door. He turned on the motor of the electric toothbrush, ran the water in the sink, wet the brush, turned off the motor, turned off the water, put the brush back into its slot. It was usually Barbara who said, "I felt the brush and it was dry."

Addie was downstairs by the time he went back to his room to dress—white shirt, navy blue Sunday suit. As he adjusted the elastic-backed black bow tie he remembered that there would be questions from the choir leader because of missing Friday's practice. He was used to questions. Felix was older. You couldn't say to Felix, "Excuse me. I have to go to choir practice."

Barbara was at breakfast, complaining because Deborah wasn't down. "What makes her think she doesn't have to go to church? She has to go, doesn't she, Addie? I mean, isn't she supposed to take care of us too? What would Daddy say? When are they getting home? What time does the plane get in, Addie?"

Rick put his fork into his fried egg and watched the yellow flow into his plate. "Where were you yesterday?" Barbara was talking to him now. "Fighting at the playground again?" Sundays, even though they left early for church, Addie made eggs and bacon; sometimes there were muffins. He liked muffins hot so he could crumble them between his fingers, letting the butter melt in a pool in the middle. He looked at Addie's face when she put a muffin on his plate, seeing her smile. He broke the muffin. Crumbs fell on his plate like pale brick. He put a lump of butter into each half, watched yellow spread through the whole crumbly world. He knew without tasting it would be gritty between his teeth. It would choke him. He didn't look at Barbara or speak to her. He didn't look up when he heard Deborah come in.

"I know he was with Felix again," Deborah said, her voice cool. "I heard the motorcycle."

Rick tried a bite of egg, catching the dripping yolk with the muffin.

"The only reason he bothers with you is so he can get me back. He won't ever do that. I'll tell you that. You can tell him too, if you want. He's rotten. He's a bore. Thinks he's so great because his father's a famous lawyer. He's just a—"

"He looks like a hood," Barbara said.

"Shut up."

"Okay. Only you said—"

What's the matter, kid, Felix had said. Somebody steal your last nickel? Here, have a dime. Get yourself some candy. What'd you say? Somebody you don't like? Somebody threw you out? We'll fix him! Come on.

The girls went out the door ahead of him. He felt Addie's hand on his arm. She held him back. "What?" he asked.

"Rick, where's the letter?"

He looked at her. She wasn't smiling now. But she wasn't angry. He looked at her brown eyes through rimless glasses, magnified eyes, as he felt her finger on his chin, tilting his face gently up to hers. He remembered the way she said she talked to all those children where she came from. I always give it to them straight, she'd told him, those reckless kids of Marybelle's. I always loved them like they were mine. No fooling around, I say, and they don't fool. Laugh! Oh, do they ever. "Tell the truth, Rick, no fooling. You know about the letter. I know you do." *Let's get the letter, kid. Let's see what the old bag said you did.*

"What letter?" He shrugged, feeling her eyes on him, knowing her smile was waiting; she didn't use it now. He felt her fear, like smoke, envelop him.

"Your folks'll be home today. You'll have to tell them."

"I know." He pulled, but she still held him by the arm.

"What did you do with the letter, Rick?"

He trusted Addie the way you trust a kid, a friend, some but not all the time; the way Felix trusted him. But not the way he trusted Felix. *Get this, kid, what a laugh! "Outside the normal range!" Man, if that bag only knew! Hey, I guess I've lost that knife for good, huh? You'll never get it back from her now. Don't worry. I've got others.* You don't tell everybody the same thing. You don't tell anybody everything. Some friends you don't tell what you don't want the whole world to know. Addie wouldn't try to get him in trouble but he felt her fear.

"What letter?"

She frowned, grabbing him roughly by the shoulder, pushing him out the door, but holding him so he couldn't go. "The lady who called me from school said she'd write your father a letter, and there was a letter from the school that was sitting in the front hall till yesterday. It isn't there any more. Your father'll find out about you anyway, and if he finds out there was a letter and if he knows you took it—"

"I didn't," he lied, but that wasn't anything. What Felix did or told him to do wasn't like doing it himself. Addie was just Addie; it didn't matter what he said. She was all right.

"Oh, go on with you." She pushed him hard this time, almost making him fall. Her voice cracked as if she were crying. Halfway down the walk she called to him, "But you come straight home from church, hear? You come straight home. None of your wandering around today. I want you home!"

"Okay," he said. "I'll come home." He walked a safe distance behind the girls, long smooth hair down the two neatly coated backs, wanting to run but not, keeping that distance all the way to the stone church on the hill.

He liked being in the choir. Not the practices which were held in the low-ceilinged music room in the basement, but being on the side of the vaulted brown-beamed space; feeling the great void, bounded by stone and wood and colored glass, as part of himself; feeling himself, a speck of dust, among the shifting shapes of light that traveled across the distant and mysterious dark ceiling. Safe on the hard bench, cloaked in his nobody gown covering all but his head, he was, then, nobody nowhere. Bach organ sounds filled his chest, trembled through bones and flesh. Reverberations became part of him, so when his voice, separate from himself, rose high and clear, it merged with the air-filling deep-throated chords; soprano tones from his own throat catapulted his self high into the brown-beamed cross-hatched light-split vault above. Nobody, nowhere, unseen, unheard, at peace.

When it was over, he undid his gown, dropping it where it fell. He sifted between the people unnoticed, untouched. He had somewhere to go and someone to find. He walked across country, across yard and fence, avoiding streets and Sunday strollers. Time slipped by him; all the long cold day in his Sunday best, sounds of Bach still filled his ears. Sermon sounds—*Our Father watches you, finds you, follows you.* He heard an airplane fly low over treetops; looking up he saw another far off and a jet's white contrail stripe the blue ceiling. *Your Father follows you.* And he walked a thousand miles and looked at strange houses, but he didn't meet Felix though he searched for him. Time and again he found himself walking past the gray-shingled house on Nutgrove Street, at first seeing no one, and then seeing the dark-haired cranky father sweeping shattered bricks. *Go home.* And so he walked some more. He didn't think about being able to walk up the path again, or not being able to. He finally went back for the last time, unhungry, crawled behind the boulder under the great hemlock and went to sleep.

I tried to sleep with my head on a rock but crackled leaves shouted in my ear, so I lay still. In my home bed rolling, I fall on the hard wood floor. Tonight I'll roll down the scrambled brambled mountain to the river. Please trees, be bars around my ground bed. Star ceiling hold me tight. I won't be afraid of the quiet night . . . I am! Tell me again I am old enough to sleep where the trees sleep.

Tell me again, tell me again. Someone long ago in the short lifetime had read and read that and other lines to him, told him again and again he was old enough. *Why Rick, what are you doing here so late? I came to visit you. Come in, child.* Gran's lap rose and fell under his head when he heard the poems and the endless stories. Her soft legs alternately moved up and down and the droning of the sewing machine sounded through bones in his head. Now treadle sounds and church sounds merged. With his head pressed against the granite, in a delirium, he remembered the stories, heard them over and over. Together they made the story of his life, which he knew because he'd heard it, not because of what he remembered. In the story his father was brave.

"Tell me about the war, Gran. Did my father have a gun?"

"Of course he had a gun, silly. All soldiers have guns."

"Where is it? Did he shoot people with it?"

"When he came home he didn't have the gun any more because they took it away from him before he got off the boat."

"What boat?"

"The big boat he came home on, silly, and when your mother went to meet him and brought him home he'd never even met his own daughter. He didn't even know about Deborah, and she so pretty. Such a pretty baby."

"Get to me. When did I come?"

"After the war and after your father went to school and got all those letters after his name, and—"

"Hurry up. Get to me."

"You have to wait your turn, boy; after we moved and Barbara came first, you know. Your father always wanted a son. All that time, and all those hard-working years. Well, he finally got what he wanted when you were born, Rick. You were the son he dreamed of."

"Father dreamed of me?" Loving the sound of it, loving it but unbelieving. A story that didn't fit with what he knew. And so because it didn't fit he'd ask again. "My father dreamed? Of me? He never—"

"Hush," she'd say, knees going up and down, "Of course he did. Every man dreams of having a son."

And so, walking to the barber (away from the scratchy Saturday sounds of cantchu keep clean for even a half-hour) down a sunny street he put his hand in the big man's hand by his cheek and said, wondering, "Did you dream about me before I was born?"

"Dream about you?"

"Uh-huh. I mean, when you were a soldier and had a gun. Gran said you dreamed."

"Listen." The hand tightened on his, crushing it. "There is no dream, day or night, that I ever dreamed in all the nights and days I was home or away that was strong enough to kill the smell of rotting flesh. And don't forget it. Nobody dreams of anything because if you dream you know you'll wake up. I never did dream then and I don't dream now. It's a waste of time."

It was the longest speech his father had ever made to him. He didn't forget it.

I won't be afraid of the quiet night. I am!

When he opened his eyes it was dark and he was frightened. "Come straight home." Addie had been afraid for him, Addie balancing on a tightrope, walking between himself and the angry people. He was sorry it was dark, sorry because the image of Addie falling, arms out like in a cartwheel, flashed through his mind, falling away from him though he reached to hold her. Or perhaps it was Elizabeth who had fallen. He shook his head, straightened his knees and they hurt. His head had a sore place where it had rested on the rough granite. Still remembering the dream that was not a dream but a memory he crawled out from behind the rock, feeling the damp needles on his palms, and walked down the long hill, around the dark blocks, and on to his own street.

He knew they were home when he came round the corner, because all the lights were on. The house loomed down the dark lamp-lit street like a fallen giant, arms reaching wide, waiting and ready for him to enter, waiting to embrace him. He came to the front walk and saw through the storm door that there were suitcases in the hall. He walked around to the back door, wiped his feet on the mat and let himself quietly into the white kitchen. Addie was there; her glassy eyes were not smiling.

"I thought I told you come straight home!"

He looked at his feet, moved his shoulders. "Where've you been so late again?"

"Nowhere."

"Oh." She turned away from him. "Just this once I thought—oh well, go on in. Even the girls were looking for you. But where?"

"Nowhere. Honest." He held up his hand as if to offer her balance. How could he tell her the truth? "I wasn't anywhere."

She nodded toward the door. "They just got home. Go on."

"Ricky? Is that you?" He heard his mother's voice from the hall, sensing in her tone, in the name nobody but she ever used, she was untired, unangry. "Come in and say hello." Suddenly it seemed he had never heard her before. He went through the kitchen, out past the stairwell into the hall.

"Aren't you going to kiss me?" A velvet-voiced crooner. He blinked in the flickering chandelier light as if he'd come out of the dark. He looked at his mother. He had never seen her before either, never noticed the softness of her eyes or the whiteness of her skin. She stooped awkwardly in her tight skirt, high heels, her stockinged knees bent sideways, pushed back the hair from his forehead, and looked past him at, he supposed, Addie, who had followed him in. Fur-jacketed arms were spread wide, like the arms of the lighted house, and from one wrist hung her large shiny pocketbook.

"Come," she said, "kiss me." He felt his father's heavy hand on his shoulder. "Hello, Rick," rumbled above his head. He leaned forward quickly and kissed her powdered cheek, almost wanting to stay and be fur-wrapped. But the moment passed and she stood straight again. They all went into the living room. Barbara and Deborah were already there, talking, opening boxes. He sat on the couch silently, waiting for the questions he knew would come.

·

Tom Lang rested one elbow on the mantel, keeping his left hand in his pocket fingering his change. He surveyed his family.

"I have news for you," he said. The hubbub in the corner over the dresses Vivian had brought did not stop. Rick sat still on the corner of the couch looking small, staring at a point far past Tom's shoulder. Tom wondered what the boy was thinking. Waiting for his present, no doubt. He'd give that to him later when they were alone. Tom looked toward the girls again. Noting his distress, Vivian shushed them ineffectively.

Tom tried again. "I have some good news for you." Then he stopped. He felt a great distance from all of them suddenly. He was a visitor, tolerated, unknown, observing. "Jes' standin' lookin' "—the phrase from the old song went through his head, as lives like rivers swept past him. He had made them all, yet was not part of their lives. He had sustained them but could not understand or control them. He wanted their attention and respect, but he didn't know what they liked or disliked. He only half knew that he didn't care. He felt used, fleshless, a power transmitter, a skeletal giant on a shorn hillside holding aloft the source of light; an empty steel tower through which many winds blew, untouched and untouchable.

Deborah, so womanly that sometimes he had to look away from her, was beautiful and hard. She didn't like him now, nor had she from the first distrustful day they met when she had inspected him and found him wanting.

Given a certain freedom of choice he would not have surrounded himself with critical women. Deborah had learned, when she was eleven and first began to spend hours brushing her hair and practicing in front of the long mirror, to raise her left eyebrow without raising her right one. He had never realized until the first time she tried it on him that a half-grown child could, without saying a word, stop a dinner conversation. She did, one night, when Gray Abernathy was eating with them. Tom was explaining to Gray the benefits of a mechanistic approach to their enterprise. He looked across the table to see Deborah's left eyebrow poised in a high inverted V, not even pulling the other lovely shapes of her young face out of line. Gray was staring entranced. Tom stopped in the middle of a sentence. Gray stared until Deborah relaxed the fuzzy symbol. Gray picked up his fork and mumbled something about children growing up too fast these days. Perhaps Tom knew that Deborah didn't trust him any more than he trusted her. They were not unalike, and they did not get along. Half the time when he caught her out drinking or motorcycling he suspected she did what she did only to irritate him, to prove he had no control over her.

Barbara, on the other hand, whom he had known since her birth one hot August night, had been cuddly from the first. He felt grateful that she caused no trouble, but he also knew her perceptions were neither as sharp as Deborah's nor as sensitive as Rick's. Another Vivian, he thought, as silly but not as tender. She had learned cruelty from living with other children. But would he have the patience to be as protective of her later, when she would need it, as Helen had been with Vivian? At least Barbara, he thought, did not cause him public embarrassment.

"Wait till you hear about Rick."

"Oh, Mom, it's beautiful, the yummiest color!"

"I thought you'd like the green one. They had it in your size in yellow but . . ."

"Damn it, be quiet!" he roared.

The hush was instantaneous. Then softly he said, "I thought you'd like to know that your grandmother left each of you some money." He was relaxed now, controlling them once more.

Perhaps it was the news that made the evening go so uneventfully. Perhaps it was that they were all on their best behavior because of the week's separation. Eventually Barbara did report the news that Rick had been suspended. "We never did find out what he did, though. He wouldn't tell."

Tom took a deep breath, determined not to lose his temper on his first night home. Vivian bit her lip and said, "Oh, Ricky, not again!"

Deborah said, "Well, leave the kid alone for once. He acted well enough even though they wouldn't let him into school."

"What did you do, Rick?" Tom asked. He saw the boy's eyes panic and then grow dull as they all looked at him.

Rick felt them stare at him. "I dunno," he said. "I wasn't so bad. Some kid tripped me and . . ."

"Another fight!"

"Forget it," Deborah said. "Addie'll tell you he's been good."

"Is that all?" That was Tom's voice. Rick looked up. His father was frowning, questioning, but not angry enough to hit him. "You were suspended? For a fight? There must have been something more."

Addie announced dinner. Tom said he'd talk to Rick later, and told Vivian she should get after those people at school. Vivian chattered as fast as she could as if trying to drown the subject in a sea of words. The girls loved their dresses. Dinner smelled good. The house was clean. Tomorrow she would think about having to take Rick to school to find out what he had done. She hugged Tom's arm to her as they went to the dining room. For a whole week Rick had not come between them. If they could just get through the evening without a full-blast blowup; if Tom would be tired enough from the trip to come to bed without a long evening behind his book, she could bear almost anything that Rick might have done. Tom mad at Rick invariably became cold and angry with her. Please, she thought, not tonight!

His voice sounded too loud. "Vivian?" She took her seat at the end of the table.

"Yes?"

"That school principal must be irresponsible or crazy or both. Send a kid home from school and not even tell him why; no word, no message, no letter to the parents, nothing! You get to the bottom of this, all right?"

"Yes, dear."

Barbara opened her mouth and started to say something but Tom cut her off. "Rick?" His voice was rising.

"Yessir."

Vivian twisted the napkin in her lap and bit her lip.

"Just once it would be nice to come home and hear something good about you. One week shouldn't be so long for you to behave."

Vivian held her breath. No one moved; it was like the stillness before dawn, before the first cannon blast.

Rick's mumbled, "I know. I'm sorry," was barely audible. Still they waited.

Suddenly Tom, as if he were remembering something, put his fingertips on the white-clothed table's edge. "We'll talk about it later. Light the candles, will you, son?" Vivian started chattering again about California. The girls started to eat.

Addie, having spent the better part of the day working on dinner, served it on tiptoe, waiting each time the swinging door closed behind her for the explosion she had heard so often—a hand slamming on the table, a dish shattering, Mr. Lang's thunderous voice. But it did not come. The meal went well. She was glad she'd decided not to tell anyone of the missing letter. If its disappearance became a problem later she would explain whatever she was asked. Nothing more.

Perhaps the most remarkable thing—to each of them—about the quiet in the Lang house that night was that Rick himself did nothing to provoke anyone. Even his silence, which only Barbara tried to break, was not looked upon as insolence. Something had changed.

Monday morning Rick mended his fences with uncanny skill and timing, an actor playing old parts.

At eight-fifteen he waited for Brian at the stop sign, turning the front wheel of his own bike as Brian rode close, so the wheels locked.

"Get out of my way," Brian said.

"Date today?"

"Get out of my way."

"I got something to show you."

"I don't want to see anything of yours. I hate you."

Rick looked down the street. He toed the pedal of Brian's bike. Finally, "It's only a gun. I guess you wouldn't be interested."

"I hate you. You broke my dad's bricks."

"No I didn't."

"Who did, then?"

"Felix. My father brought me a gun."

"A what?"

"A real gun. He gave it to me."

"You're kidding."

"No I'm not. I told Felix not to do that. I'm sorry he broke the bricks."

"I don't care. Get out of my way."

"I'll let you try the gun."

"You're a liar."

"I'm not. Honest. Come to my house. At three. I'll show you. I'll let you hold it. He brought it from California."

"He wouldn't let you load it."

"It's mine. I'll let you aim it."

"My mother wouldn't let me. She said I have to come home."

"Do you have to do everything she says?"

"Well—"

"Like a baby?"

"I'm not!" Brian paused. "Anyway, I don't believe you."

"Well, I don't believe you either."

"About what?"

"About your mother saying you couldn't have a date. I bet she'd let you if you ask her. Ask her."

"No."

"I'll ask her then."

"What kind of a gun?"

"A twenty-two." Rick reached deep into his pocket, brought up an empty shell, and put it in Brian's hand.

Brian's eyes shone. "Thanks!"

"Come on." Rick straightened the wheel of his bicycle. "We'll be late. Hurry." The two bikes, one with the gray-jacketed rider, one with the red, flew swiftly down the divided highway to the old brick mansion that would shelter them for the next three hours.

Glenna Masterson sat behind her desk, not hearing but knowing the early sounds in her school—greetings between teachers, chattering children passing in the hall. She sensed someone outside her office, feeling vibrations through her shoes, her bones, her palms on her desk. Her flesh could sense even the minute trembling of a carpeted floor. If a door opened, the air on her cheek would change. Once a very long time ago she had not been deaf, but the memory of music, direct sound on her eardrums, had long since gone.

Now she hesitated. She was not quite ready. She turned the page on her calendar, studied handwritten memos, checked the in-box—no new material since Friday. The morning mail was not yet sorted. The Richard Lang folder was still on top of the pile by the pen stand. There were sharp pencils in the drawer. She reached for a Kleenex, blew her nose, and then said, "Yes?"

It was Christine Jensen, the nurse. "I have Rick Lang here. May he go to his classroom?"

"Not yet," Glenna said. "I want to see him first."

The boy stepped into the room and stood at attention in front of her desk; his hair was well-combed, his shirt tucked tidily; his gray eyes steadily watched her. The only sign that he might be ill at ease, she noticed, was that the toe of one foot began to rub the instep of the other. Otherwise his manner was so calm, unfrightened, and unwary that Glenna was disconcerted.

"Did your parents get home, Rick?" she asked.

"Yes ma'am."

"Did they have anything to say?"

"No ma'am."

"No?" She looked at him sharply.

"I mean, I said I was sorry, ma'am."

"Did you tell them what happened?"

"Yes ma'am."

"Did they understand why you were suspended? Did they get my letter?"

"I don't know, ma'am. I guess they understood all right."

"Do *you* understand, Rick?"

"Yes ma'am."

"And you won't do anything like that again?"

"No ma'am."

"You understand we have a very strict rule against bringing any kind of knife or even a toy gun to school?"

"Yes ma'am."

"All right, you may go to your classroom." Glenna turned away from him, pushed the buzzer, and picked up the phone. "Get Mrs. Lang for me." She hung up, saw Rick still standing in front of her.

"You may go, Rick."

"Excuse me." He held out a slip of paper. "The nurse said you have to sign this." It was the admittance slip.

"All right." She initialed the corner and handed it back. She watched him walk out straight and slim, his shoulders squared. Was it possible, she wondered, for this to be the same child she had tangled with ten days before? Poised and properly penitent, even though the "ma'am" was lip-service discipline, he seemed to be fully cognizant of what she was asking him. She almost sighed in relief. Perhaps her anger had not missed the mark, as Catherine had seemed to imply. Perhaps it had even produced beneficial results. Everyone had been so critical of her suspending him, but she must have been right. Of course. All it really took, she reminded herself, to deal with wayward children was an ability to be firm, to make quick decisions, and to stick to them. She had always known that. There had been no reason to worry. She felt the buzzer ring; that would be Mrs. Lang. She reached for the phone.

It was nearly ten after twelve when Brian came in, cold and excited, red-cheeked, begging to be allowed to go to Rick's house at three to see, of all things, a gun he said his father had given him. What kind of lunatic was this Tom Lang? Well, maybe the story wasn't true, Linda thought. She told Brian she didn't want him to go, but that Rick could come home with him. "I must talk to Rick about those bricks," she told Brian. She turned off the heat under the soup.

"Oh, that's all right," Brian said.

"What's all right?"

"He said he didn't do it." Brian sat down and bit into his sandwich. Linda stared at him, pot in her hand.

"And you believe him."

"Uh-huh."

"You believe he doesn't know anything about it."

"He didn't say he didn't know anything about it. He said he didn't do it. Felix did. When can I go see his gun? You never let me go anywhere any more."

Linda poured the soup. Brian made no move to eat it. "He's a luck," Brian went on. "First he gets to stay home all week, then his father brings him presents, and now everybody has to help him with his work."

"Who's everybody?"

"Oh, you know Miss Barker likes him, and the special reading teacher takes him in her class. And I have to help him. He sits next to me."

"Doesn't that interfere with your work?"

"Well, sometimes I don't get done because he asks me all

those questions. It's weird, he's older but there are so many words he can't read."

"I know." She paused. "He seems to like being here. I thought I might try to help him in the afternoons. How do you feel about that?"

"I don't mind, I guess, but I wish he didn't have to be here for lunch too. Why can't he eat at his own house?"

"He certainly can," Linda said. "He certainly can eat at his own home."

Rick arrived before Linda had a chance to respond to Brian's other complaints. She must not forget them, she thought. She became fascinated by Rick's manner; he was on his best behavior, true, hanging up his coat as she'd asked him to many times, picking up a cracker Peter had dropped. But she had never seen him appear so natural, guileless, simply childlike. Things are not always as they seem. He was neither angry nor tense, neither frightened nor depressed. No sign now of the tragic figure she had described so painfully and at such length to David the night before.

The boys' chatter filled the room and Peter joined in, mimicking their sounds. She found the noise irritating, as if she were perched in a treetop amid a flock of starlings. No, she suddenly realized, it was not the sound of them that irritated her but the normalcy of the sound, which left her, so to speak, high in the tree she had climbed to rescue the boy, only to find he was quite safe, quite content. He did not need her compassionate arms, her guiding voice—her love—to help him to safe ground. Chiding herself, she recognized her disappointment in his good health.

Evidently nothing terrible had happened when his parents came home. Had they not seen fit to punish him? Or had the hours he had spent with her given him strength to handle it? Had it indeed already been worth putting her own life in mild jeopardy for him? Perhaps. Perhaps she was not ever to know.

"Brian tells me your father brought you a gun," she said

in her best matter-of-fact voice, "and that you want to show it to him."

Rick glanced quickly at Brian, then to her, as if to say, You dummy, why did you tell her? And in the furtive movement she knew again how easily he could slip one way, then another. She must continue to be direct, she decided. There were matters that had to be clear between them.

"Can I go, Ma?" Brian wheedled.

"Not today," Linda said. "I want you both here this afternoon. Rick, I need to talk with you alone." She took him by the hand into the living room. The place had a formalizing effect on him, which was what she wanted.

"What do you know about the broken bricks on our front walk?" she asked.

She watched him closely, waited for his composure to break. It didn't. He looked straight at her. Cool, she thought, unevasive.

He said, "Felix and I came back after it was dark and we broke the bricks with a hatchet he had. It was his idea but it was my fault because I told him where to go."

She didn't know until she heard the words how much she had been hoping he would deny all connection. "Why?" she asked out of the pain in her throat, no clinician now.

"I don't know."

As ever when she was hurt or caught unprepared in unknown territory, she filled the void with her voice. She talked about friendship, his for Brian, hers for him; she talked of destructive urges, of anger unexpressed. She was conscious of the extreme control she used over her voice, keeping the pitch well-modulated, but knew the phrases she used were beyond his grasp. And sometime during the passage of word-filled time she saw his eyes go from cool to cloudy to bored to uncomprehending. To bring him back she said, "But you must have had some reason. Someone, something you were angry about." She didn't believe he wouldn't remember David sending him home, but she knew she must not suggest it or the revelation would be useless.

"I don't know," he repeated. "I just didn't have anything else to do."

The phrase stung her. The final declaration of a hopelessly resourceless child or, she thought, a generation of rootless children, bored and bereft. With all of the new educative phrases and innovations, from cuisenaire rods to team teaching, children could make havoc and say, "I didn't have anything else to do."

She couldn't remember ever having nothing "else" to do. What did these boys of eight or nine need to fill their hours, feed their hungers, expand their consciences, and excite their minds? What did Brian need beyond food and space and clean air and nature and friendships made and lost, a ball to control, a yo-yo, comforts of love, perceptions of the universe, mind food and body food and a house warm in winter? What robbery had transpired in this ideal place organized for children's health, when the idyll produced destructive vacuity?

"Nothing else to do?" she echoed aloud, not hiding the dismay she felt. She had said nearly the same thing to Dr. Masterson not a week before. Was she so out of step with her time that she could not justify anyone's actions, young or old? Were these two in some weird drama together beyond her comprehension?

"Nothing else to do," she said again, replacing dismay with incredulity, "but deliberately destroy the property of a friend?"

He looked at his toes. He shifted from foot to foot. "Will Mr. Kaplan hit me?" he said at last. "Will he call my father?"

"No," she said, startled. "Mr. Kaplan will not hit you. Nor will I." She could have added, he doesn't hit other people's children or his own, but he would eliminate you from his life if I let him. Then she said, "And afterwards, how did you feel? How do you feel now?"

"I'm sorry," he said immediately. "I was sorry afterwards."

She didn't believe him, and as soon as he said it she knew what she had done, what they all did to him—brought him to his knees, to the point at which he became visibly penitent. His relief at saying "sorry" was obvious; relieved of his burden they would let him go and leave him alone. He knew in the end what words would bring him release from adult inquisition. At least she saw her error and knew too she must give him an avenue back or, she thought, banish him. The secret, she remembered, is to love the sinner, not the sin.

"Neither Mr. Kaplan nor I will punish you," she said, "but we will ask that you try to set things right. This afternoon I'd like you to sort the bricks, stack the good ones and put the pieces in the dump. It may be too late to fix the walk before the ground freezes, but in the spring—"

"All right," he said.

From the dining room window Linda watched the boys-on-bicycle shapes grow small as they sped down the hill back to school. She had the odd thought that in some way she did not understand Rick had controlled the conversation, as if he had been forcing her to humble him. She brushed her hair from her face. Ridiculous! She shook her head and took Peter upstairs for his nap.

PART TWO ✤

ELEVEN ❦

THE LAST OF THE LEAVES BLEW OFF the great oaks in the woods and a snow came that did not melt. It bothered David that they had not finished clearing the back lawn; those matted leaves would lay till spring, rotting and suffocating the grass roots beneath.

The children who passed by Linda's yard wore their hoods up, all except Rick, and there always seemed to be an odd mitten or boot lying on the walk. Peter's nose dripped and his chin developed a red rash that Linda knew would persist until April. Days were too short. David often worked late, carrying home with him the burden of his impending argument, so there was little time to spend together talking. Sometimes he phoned in the middle of the day and talked of household or money matters or of Christmas plans that they needed to discuss but never got around to at home. Linda became so preoccupied with overseeing life in her back yard that little else had reality for her.

Her preoccupation shaped each day or hour or sometimes even a fraction of a minute. It was as if she worked at a stroboscopic puzzle, the pieces unpredictably changing form, color, and dimension. From her window she kept a vigil over her back yard that fascinated and exhausted her. She measured and interpreted the play and byplay that caused the constantly moving children to group and regroup—a winter ballet. There were interruptions. The soup boiled over; the washer threw a handful of nuts on the cellar floor and blew its fuse; Sappho's teats developed a faint swelling, making them wonder which of her many suitors had gotten to her. The phone rang.

Once it was Jean to say she'd noticed the boys on the shed roof.

"Yes," Linda told her. "David said that was okay."

"Well, I don't want Suzy up there." Jean sounded testy.

"All right," Linda said. "I'll keep an eye on that."

This time it was Stevie's mother phoning to ask if Stevie was there and would Linda send him home.

"No," Linda said, "only Rick and Brian are here today."

"Listen, I don't care where Steve is so long as he's not with Rick Lang. That boy is trouble! And the kids think he's fun until they get hurt. I was delighted the day Rick tripped him up and then punched him. Steve limped home with a badly sprained ankle and a skinned elbow. He was so mad it saved me the trouble of throwing Rick out. I heard his sister was arrested in California, and she runs around with a hood. Be careful!"

"I know," Linda said, "but you can't believe all the stories. They get exaggerated. However, I am being careful. And I do keep Rick under my watchful eye and under control." Was he really? she wondered.

During those vigilant after-school hours she felt she held invisible reins to each child who came within her vision. Most often she relied on instinct to tell her the strategic moment to remove a child, to discover a rare rock, to suggest a trip to the village, or to bring Rick inside and read to him, thus start him talking again. Sometimes she wondered if the world he told her about existed.

"My mother has a whole drawer full of scarves and when she gets dressed to go out to dinner she tries them on one by one to see which fits. But I've never seen her laugh. Only sometimes after I go to bed I hear somebody laughing and it must be her. Deborah told me that when I was a baby they played games with me. I don't remember. I hate to read. If I could read, it would be an albino cinch."

"What's an albino cinch?"

"It's when something's so easy that even the albino who's the dumbest can get it, gets it, then it's that cinchy. Father says if Deborah doesn't stop running around with Felix he'll send her off to boarding school. He tried once but they wouldn't take her, or she wouldn't take it. 'I've always bailed you out,' he said, 'but no more.' "

After Rick was reinstated at school, Linda was lonely. That first week, with no gray eyes following her, no shadow, no stream of a small boy's consciousness in her ears, she was at loose ends. Just she and Peter and bounding Sappho, wet-nosed and loving, and the house that suddenly needed her. With a passion of energy she scrubbed the old pine floorboards until they were soft, and then waxed them, and waxed the tables and cabinets until her hands were raw. By Thanksgiving Peter was fussing, Sappho whining for a run, and she felt better.

The rhythm of her days was holding her together as nothing had for a long time. Clearing hours and mind for Rick, that job, made her get through those other chores with an efficiency she hadn't known she possessed. She read everything she could find by people who were concerned with moral issues in education, with delinquency, with disturbed children. Some who despaired at the growing foment among the young were finding fresh ways to deal with, and teach, young children. If her theory that Rick's emotional emaciation was caused by the fact that he had not been listened to, those who listened to children should help her with him. Sometimes merely a phrase, a germ of an idea, would give her enough to go on for a week. She applied everything she did and read and heard to Rick.

He was there every weekday, noon and after school. On days he ate at home, he arrived so soon after lunch that he might as well have shared their food. Brian, having forgotten he once wanted to have lunch without him, now seemed to accept Rick's constant presence almost as he would a brother's. And, Linda decided, his bursts of jealousy were as normal as if they had been brothers close in age, competing for her attention. It might even be good for Brian, she told herself, to have to step aside for someone else now and then. She only half realized how her thoughts seesawed.

One night as they lay in bed she tried to tell David how her method worked, spelling it out to herself as much as to him. It continued to be as necessary for her to have his approval as it was to succeed. She told him about some of the things she'd read, adding, "Each time Rick is allowed to show his anger in an undestructive way he becomes freer— to learn, to believe in himself, to do something constructive." She was conscious of overexplaining. David, in a light mood, teased her as she talked, stroking first one nipple then the other.

"I wish you'd listen!" she said, pushing his hand away.

"You mean that if I showed all that understanding when you got mad at me you'd paint the house?" He put his leg across her belly and she moved under the warm weight.

"Oh, be serious!" But her legs opened for his pressuring knee and she held his hand hard on her breast.

"Don't you think we've talked about Rick enough for one night?" He kissed her. Rising toward him, she closed her eyes.

Gray eyes watched her from the doorway.

On the carousel in Central Park she used to ride the pink and silver horse, which rose and fell on its bright steel rod and rocked as well. She always wanted the gold ring, so she'd ride and ride, circling faster and faster to the music that grew louder and louder, its pitch higher and higher; she'd hold the rod with one hand and reach for the ring at the end of its painted gray shute with the other, leaning perilously, fearful of falling, racing round and round to the mechanical honkytonk tune. Sometimes she spent all day and all her money riding and riding, and never got the gold ring.

Now the eyes were sad.

She was round again; she leaned so far she almost fell. She missed and clung to the horse's neck, steadying her heartbeat for another try before the music stopped.

Goddammit, the baby!

David surprised her by returning to the subject of Rick at breakfast. She had not thought he'd been listening.

"Where did you learn all that stuff you were trying to tell me last night?"

"College mostly, and from reading. You know, I probably shouldn't have quit." She surprised herself.

"I never knew you had any regrets."

She shrugged. "I didn't. But that doesn't mean I was right."

He shook his head. "We've been married ten years and I find out something like this! Sometimes I feel I hardly know you! If you want to get a degree, do it. Why waste any more time?"

"I don't know." Chronic ambivalence again, she thought with a shudder. But added, "Going back now won't help Rick. He can't wait that long."

"At least if you're going to work all that hard you ought to be paid for it. And I don't like Rick being with Brian so much."

"Brian's all right. I'm sure of it."

"Good."

That afternoon as she waited for the boys, and Peter sat happily in a corner building taller block towers, she began to read *Summerhill*. She was excited about what she found there, particularly the idea of the country setting. Reveries of a summer idyll went through her mind; two weeks on the Cape with sun and salt water, or a month in Vermont on a grassy meadow. She saw five of them together. It was a painted dream.

The phone rang. A man said, "Mrs. Kaplan, there's someone on the roof of your house." She didn't recognize the voice. He identified himself as an elderly neighbor who lived a few houses down the block and across the street. "I was fixing my antenna and just happened to notice."

"Oh!" she said. "Oh! I'll see to it right away." Sudden fear and the memory of David, swollen with anger, replaced the painted dream.

"They look pretty young. I couldn't tell for sure from this distance, but it didn't look like anyone who might be working for you."

"No," she said, her heart pumping faster, "no one's working. It's my boys, I expect. They know they're not allowed."

"Well, I wondered. I thought you ought to know. I know how boys are. Got to live dangerously, that's for sure. A lot of trouble bringing up boys in these times. Worse than it used to be, I imagine."

"Yes. Thank you for calling." She tried to cut him off.

"Well, I didn't know if you knew. I'm not sure I know just which ones are your boys. I know some who come around once in a while."

"No. I mean, I'm glad you called. Thanks for bothering."

"No bother at all."

Damn. She zipped Peter into his parka. She told herself they weren't in serious danger, not if they were careful, but David would be in a fury when he found out. He'd been so enraged the first time, and he hated to have to tell Brian anything more than once. *I don't like Rick being with Brian so much.*

With Sappho bounding and barking about their legs, she and Peter ran around the house. *Brian's all right. Good.* She craned her neck to see up. The wind was unmerciful and could make it dangerous; she amended her thoughts. She went to the back of the yard to get a better angle. The ladder was against the shed again, but there was no sign of the boys.

"Brian! Rick!" she yelled until she had no voice left. No one appeared. She gave up and went inside. They were late getting home. Where were they? She'd give them ten minutes, she decided. If they weren't home by then she'd go looking for them.

Her heart wouldn't stop racing. Anger was rising in her but she didn't know at whom. Rick? For what? For leading Brian? Where? At Brian for being late? At herself? What was she doing, sitting here waiting to accuse somebody else's child—and her own—for something she now wasn't even sure they had done? She so expected to fault them that she'd assumed the old man was right. But he'd admitted he couldn't see too well from his house to hers.

Within five minutes she heard scuffling on the back doorstep and muffled words through the door.

"Is she mad?"

"I dunno."

They must have heard her and come, she thought, as well-trained children and dogs always did when they were called. She let them get inside, smack their cold hands together, warm their pink-nosed frosty faces by the open oven. She let them worry awhile. She let her own heartbeat slow down.

She began quietly enough, telling them of the call.

"That guy!" Brian burst out. "He hates us. He's a crank. Always chases us out of his yard even when we're not doing anything. He yells at Sappho too."

"Brian! He's been our neighbor for years! What have you done that he should hate you?" She stopped. She was losing the thread. Rick stood passive as ever.

"But were you on the roof?" she persisted quietly.

Brian checked his feet, and a web on the ceiling, and Peter's block tower which was teetering. She waited. Rick waited. Finally Brian said, "Only on the shed, Mom. You used to say it was okay on the shed."

She took a breath. The shed was all right. The man might have mistaken the shed for the house roof. She wanted to believe him. "Only on the shed?" She looked from one to the other.

Four pools of translucent innocence opened wide; vigorous nodding.

"Rick? Is that the truth?" Instantly she regretted the words.

"Yes ma'am." His eyes clouded.

She was swimming upstream in a rapid river but she knew no other way. It was too hard, but if she stopped now they would be swept back to where they had started. If she stopped now they might drown. She had to work harder. She knew the hazards downstream, the fallen trees, the rocks, the falls. She must be stronger than he, stronger than she was sure she was. Part of her strength lay in finding and accepting alternatives; part of it lay in knowing when to trust and when not to; when to believe; when to compromise. To allow the shed roof had been a reasonable compromise. How many had there been in his life?

"All right," she said finally to Rick, "Mr. Kaplan agreed the shed roof was safe enough if you were careful. But I have to know when you plan to go there. You must first ask permission."

Another crisis weathered, and a new phrase was added to her mental store of disturbing phrases. *A lot of trouble bringing up boys these days.* She had not thought it would be easy.

Some of the puzzle pieces were sorting themselves out. Some still didn't fit. She tried but never did find out what had happened in his house when his parents came home. Finally when Rick tossed aside one of her questions she realized that what really happened didn't matter. Only what Rick felt to have happened was relevant. If the reunion was uneventful in his mind, that was the truth she must accept. She had her promised conversation with his mother.

Though she had to spend several hours talking herself into lifting the phone, when she finally did, it was an easy and rather boring conversation. Mrs. Lang gave her no insight into Rick's problems, had no objections to Linda's offer to help with his reading, and seemed only mildly grateful. But the call cleared her conscience.

Linda began to develop fantasies about Rick's mother. Who could have conceived this misbegotten child? A high-powered executive with brass hair and high-fashion hats one day, an alcoholic the next. She finally settled on one—a buxom, overdressed, and overmadeup imperious idiot of a woman she had met once, who had worn a rhinestone pendant on her fleshy breast and flashed her scarlet fingernails at a waiter. Having settled on that, Linda was startled to find herself in a supermarket line at nine in the morning behind a frail-boned woman in spike heels and a fine fur-collared coat; the cloud of gray-blond hair and the slender oval face were unmistakable. The voice, asking a second time for the total amount of her bill, was hardly imperious but thin and almost plaintive. Linda watched her sign the check—Mrs. Thomas Lang—and words tripped on her tongue, but the woman was gone before Linda could introduce herself.

The gun that had once seemed so important also became irrelevant. Linda decided it had either been one of Rick's fictions to woo Brian's favor, or another of his father's empty promises. When Rick spoke with any fluency it was of times past. Often when Linda tried to get him to speak of the present he became incoherent, almost mute. Eventually she understood that it didn't matter from Rick's point of view whether or not she knew anything sensible about him. What did matter was that whenever he spoke to her, she stopped what she was doing and listened.

One afternoon there were five children in the yard and she was late with dinner. Rick came to the door. She told him to play outside awhile. "I'll work with you later," she said, "if I have time." She had hardly closed the door when she heard Rick and Suzy yelling at each other. Brian, as usual, was caught in the crossfire. Before the day was over the children—with Rick in the lead, she assumed—had stoned to death half the fish in a neighbor's open pond.

The neighbor was angry. Linda called her charges home for an accounting. Brian and Suzy were uncomfortable over what had happened, but Rick was unabashed. He stood quietly while she chastised him; he looked her straight in the eye and promised never to do anything like that again. He was acting his part once more. Though she deplored what he did she couldn't help but admire his ability to stand so quietly and face her. Those words—"I'm sorry," "I promise never," "I understand," "Yes ma'am"—were his means of survival. They made reentry possible into each segment of his life: his home, his schoolroom, his friends' houses. Those words came so easily to him—words articulate Brian, she noted suddenly, could almost never bring himself to say!

When she emptied the garbage later, after the fish slaughter, she found FUCK YOU clumsily painted on her driveway. She despaired, but not totally. She remembered her old lessons: small signs were important. Overt expressions of anger, reprisals that were not actually destructive, as she'd tried to explain to David, had a certain therapeutic value. She had not been careful enough with Rick. She placated David when she told him Rick would wash it off next noon, which he did without complaint.

One afternoon when Brian was sick upstairs, she let Rick stay anyway. He swept out the cellar for her and took Sappho for a run, but wouldn't take any money. "I'd like to pay you something," she said. "You've done a big afternoon's work. I'd pay Brian for cleaning the cellar."

"It's okay," he said, and wouldn't take his hand out of his pocket.

But Brian was sullen when she came upstairs with his supper. "Where have you been all afternoon?" he asked. And when she told him he said, "It isn't fair. You shouldn't let Rick do my work. Daddy said he'd pay me to clean the cellar."

Another day when Rick was left out of a game she watched him try to break a low branch off the hemlock. Once she found three rocks from a newly planted bank removed, leaving frail roots dying in the freeze. She had to be on constant guard lest she or one of the children close him out and evoke the anger that was so close to erupting.

There were always firecrackers in his pockets. Who can get upset over a nine-year-old with a pocketful of caps and firecrackers? Except that the time and place of the explosions could alter their microcosmic world. She warned him about Peter, about glass jars, hands and faces. "Tell me when you're going to set one off," she said, "then I can get ready and won't be so frightened." He looked at her as if she were insane. She grinned. "They're fun if you know the big bang is coming."

Pieces of her own life became routine. Keeping tabs on Rick while protecting her own was as demanding and absorbing as anything she had ever done. She felt stirrings of strength and wisdom, a sense of power. She was managing after all. David was not unhappy. They got through Christmas and his mother's visit with ease and some pleasure. She had managed the shopping and preparations well. The worst of the winter weather had not been too difficult and every so often a day came promising spring.

No one had it easy, she thought as she scanned the daily papers. Students were not responding to the New Frontier or television teaching as hoped. The New Delphi fifth grade went on strike for shorter hours and refused to come in from recess. Brian's class had to stay after school one day because they misbehaved during a civil defense drill. Tempers were short. At dinner Brian wanted to know why they couldn't build a bomb shelter in their back yard. And would David take him to *Dr. No?* All the kids had seen it.

Dr. Masterson called the police one afternoon when six

high school boys sat smoking on the front steps of the school at three o'clock and refused to leave. One of Linda's high school teachers' picture appeared on the front page of the newspaper; he had been stabbed by a student.

Two languages developed—one for the playground and one for teachers and parents. Distrust was growing. Passing time was eliminated at the junior high the day after a seventh grader's leg was broken while he was on his way from math to social studies. Parents were warned not to leave their houses at night; teenage gangs crashed some parties and drank the liquor; several homes were nearly destroyed before neighbors called the police.

The New Delphi kindergarten guinea pig, named Dolly, which was tenderly taken to a different child's home each weekend so it wouldn't catch cold when the heat was turned off in the school, went to the child who lived near the Langs on Martin Avenue. While the parents were watching a football game on Saturday afternoon, the children played catch with Dolly in the rumpus room down cellar. Sunday morning the little boy's mother found the inert fur bundle in the corner of the cage. Dolly was dead, from shock or a broken back or both, the mother surmised when she pieced the story together from her sad and frightened son's account. She bought the kindergarten a new guinea pig, and saw to it that her boy neither visited out nor had visitors in for some time after. Though no one directly accused Rick Lang of killing Dolly, another house was added to the list of places he was unwelcome. An editorial in the village newspaper appeared, asking what could be expected of children for whom TV, with its nightly news of Hell Burners and Phantom Lords, acted in loco parentis. Linda, hearing one of the many versions of the story from Brian, thought of Sappho's new pups, and that Rick, like other children, needed something of his own to love and care for.

She wondered where he would spend the next weekend when he was not in her yard.

Mrs. Kaplan, there's someone on the roof.

Kennedy's ban on racial discrimination in federally insured housing, though it was not retroactive and did not cover all home-mortgage insuring agencies, did clear the way for some litigation. David and Barney proceeded with their case for Hammerman and Walker, though not as a class-action suit. David kept reminding Barney that executive power was a shield, not a sword. But, Barney countered, James Meredith was still attending classes at Ole Miss, under protection of several executive swords.

The New Delphi town board of supervisors was asked to consider a low-cost housing project for an undeveloped tract of land. The issue was opened for public debate. Linda and David went to a meeting which lasted long and became bitter. They heard one man say he didn't want any of Malcolm X's Black Muslims preaching the evil of the white man to his kids. "We didn't move to New Delphi for that," he said. A woman said that if poor black kids went to their public schools, they would resent being close to all that affluence and not having a share. "Just imagine how they'd feel, seeing cashmere sweaters lying about in the lost and found," she said. Another said it was a chance for New Delphi to help fulfill the president's dream of racial equality. Linda thought, I have only one vote, and I may not be able to fulfill the dream, but I am getting through the winter.

She finished *Summerhill*, which gave her some insights into Rick's behavior, but frightened her too, as Neill admitted that his successes came from successful families. Rick's family was a cipher. Could she make the boy enough a part of hers to succeed? She still dreamed of a summer idyll that included him.

She scanned each day for improvements, for signs, however slight, that her efforts were proving effective. She found progress. She counted fewer fights among the children who came to play. Once Rick actually joined a game of hide-and-seek without destroying it. Once he laughed out loud at something Peter did.

Sometimes she could tell, just by looking at his face when

he arrived at five after twelve, whether or not there were fresh bruises under his clothing. The belt had been used, she knew, on several occasions, including the night the calls came to his house about Dolly's demise. But sometimes the castigating voices, both present and past, had done greater damage.

A bruise is a strange kind of wound, she thought one afternoon as she fingered a blue and yellow circle on Peter's forehead. He'd hit his head against the dashboard the day before, when she stopped the car too short. Evidence of damage, but only that. There was no way of determining how deep the bleeding or, if you were not present at the time of injury, what the cause. The only sure knowledge was that the weapon had not been sharp enough to break the skin. Underneath, however, countless cells might have been damaged or destroyed. No way of knowing for sure.

Now Peter stood so still, that hardness of him, as her forefinger touched the mottled blue and yellow dome. Naked, he waited for her to dress him after his nap. He didn't blink when she touched his uncut wound. But yesterday, when she had got him home, he had cried for nearly two hours. Wet-mouthed, gasping for air between each lungburst, he had sobbed long after the hurting time. She had offered him a cookie and then turned on the television. He had screamed at the sound and hidden his soaked eyes with his fat fingers. "Look," she had tried, "look how sad you're making Sappho," holding by force the dog's head to the blurry-eyed boy.

Sappho, neither understanding nor enjoying being pulled, wiped Linda's face with her great pink tongue, yawned, and ducked away strongly enough so Linda had to let go.

"Peter, Peter, does it really hurt so much?" she had asked him, knowing that it couldn't, while a growing fear of terrible injury formed like a knot in her head.

He opened his round mouth wide, closed his eyes, and cried, throwing his whole body against her, "Nononono!" Finally she sat on the edge of her bed, setting him on her knees, her hands under his armpits, holding him hard but looking at him, talking to his open mouth until, suddenly, he licked his lips and closed his mouth. Settled. Eye to eye, buttock to knee, they sat for another hour while he emitted small sounds, unintelligibles that said everything soft and sensible to her. It was a long time that she sat with him; long, she knew, because eventually she forgot the time. It seemed that he forced her to stay until she forgot everything and everyone, until the two of them were alone in the universe. At first she tried gently to shift him off her knee, the usual parting gesture—Scoot, Peter, run and play, Peter, go find the doggy—but her slightest motion started the contractions, a shift of his eye, the opening of his mouth. She settled back again and again, until she forgot all but him and listened to the nothings that came from his throat, and answered him in quiet rational phrases. Long, she knew, because sometime during their sitting she heard the boys bang in the kitchen door, and still she didn't move. Finally, after hours, after she had given up everyone else for him and told him so, there was a little pulling in of breath, a change in the shape of the wet lips, and a puffing out of air. He smiled suddenly, and wriggled to be loose of her grip.

As she watched him strut out of her room without a backward look at his prisoner of the last hours, she said, "Oh, Peter, I'd almost forgotten who you were!"

That afternoon Brian spread three workbooks on the table. "I got marked down," he said. "They're messy."
"Show me."
"Don't blame me if I get a bad report. Miss Barker's a crank."
"I thought you liked her."
"Na-a-a, she's a crank."
"Which ones are messy? Show me."
He spread out one of his books. He had drawn eccentric circles all over the cover, camouflaging the title *Growing and Learning with Numbers*. The circles were sometimes

spectacles, sometimes eyes, sometimes arranged so as to be flowers. She turned through the book, and, seeing doodles all through, realized that Brian was restless and bored.

"I like your designs," Linda said. "Next time don't draw on the workbook, save it for art."

"I got marked down," he said frowning.

Rick came in, books in his hand. "I didn't," he said. "She never writes anything in my book."

"Let me see." Rick pushed it across the table, then wound his hair around his forefinger. His book was clear, almost devoid of filled-in blanks. Where he had done the work his writing was tiny. "Your book is very neat," Linda said.

"Barker's a pill," Brian said. "She doesn't let us sit together any more. She's a dill."

"A stupid dilly pilly."

"A boggy dog."

"Barker's a doggy."

"All right, boys," Linda said. "Get to work. What's for tomorrow?"

"Social studies." That was Rick.

"Can we take apart a battery?" That was Brian.

"I did it once. There's black stuff that got all over."

"Down cellar after homework," Linda said.

"Can we take apart a bulb?"

"No, that's dangerous."

"Why?"

"It'll explode."

"Why?"

"I don't know. Ask your father when he gets home. Brian, if you don't want to get to work, go on upstairs with Peter and let me help Rick."

"I like it here. I hate social studies."

"All right, open the book, Rick. Let's see what you have to read. Peter, please put your banana peel in the garbage."

"Nononono."

"Page seventy-four to seventy-eight. That's too much. Barker's mean to make us read so much," Brian said.

"Rick, why don't you start reading out loud?" She watched his eyes focus on the large-type paragraphs. His eyelids flicked up and down, scanning the entire page, then panicked.

"You don't have to read all the words at once," she said. "Just start at the top and take it a little at a time. When you get to a word you don't know we'll write it down and play some games with it."

"The uh—uh—"

"All right, Brian, you start the first paragraph "

"The Amazon is the longest river in South America. It runs for three thousand miles. Its source is in the Andes Mountains and it empties into the Atlantic Ocean at the equator. It runs through thick jungles. Many miles along the Amazon have never been explored. Question: What is the longest river in South America? Rick?"

"I dunno." She looked at him and realized that he was off in his own country again. Frowning, she gently put a hand on her own son's arm. "Brian, scoot upstairs awhile. Let me be alone with Rick, just for a little. Okay?"

Brian got up, looked from one to the other of them, shrugged, and took his workbook. "Okay, but I knew you wouldn't help me. You only help him."

"You don't need much help," she said.

"Yes I do. I do. I got marked down."

"I'll help you later." Cautiously pleading. "I promise."

He went up the creaking stairs with slow footsteps; from the stairwell Linda heard him say, "Come on, Peter."

Peter sat between Linda's feet, examining closely a rubber-head eraser that someone had dropped. He put his forefinger into the eraser, waggled it back and forth in front of his eyes, with his other hand removed the eraser from his finger, nibbled at it, looked at it again, and put it back on.

"Peter!"

· 197 ·

Linda touched Peter on his back. "Go on," she whispered, "go with Brian." The little boy threw the eraser across the room, and with both hands flat on the floor, pushed himself to his feet. Without turning back to look at his mother, or answering Brian's loud and impatient call, he walked to the stairs.

Linda returned her attention to Rick. "Show me the word *river* on the page. See if you can find it." He could not. She wrote it on a piece of paper in large black letters. He looked at the page again, and pointed to the word. "Now read the part Brian read."

"The Amazon is the longest river in—"

"South America," she filled in before he faltered.

"South America," he repeated.

"Go on," she said, "keep reading. It runs—"

He was silent.

Finally, "Tell me about the river again," she said.

TWELVE 〰 THE RIVER RUNS AND RUNS, AND

when you put your ear down close it sounds like a waterfall or thunder or the flushing toilet. The stick you throw in runs with the river, in and out of stones, every which way, floats with the river forever. Everything that runs away is gone forever, and I will be too. Deborah will run away from boarding school if I ever see that motorcycle out in front of my house again. Wasn't there enough trouble in California?

She cried and stamped her foot at midnight when I heard the toilet flush, and the room was black. She cried and screamed right into my dream. "You'll put me in prison. You'll lock me up." "If you were a boy I'd send you off to military school where they'd beat some sense into you."

Where was Gran?

He had reached for a doorknob that was too high so he went to get the stool to stand on and now he could reach and turn the handle that locked him in his room. He wasn't asleep. He climbed on the stool and turned the handle and went into the carpeted hall in his bare feet to the other room where the television was. He couldn't reach the knob so he went back again for the stool and then he could reach the knob. He turned it and first he heard the soft sound "baby" and he smiled and then something hit him. A scream and a blow on the side of his head. "Goddammit the baby!"

"Get out. Get out."

I'll never touch you again. I'll never let you touch him again. He'll never want to touch you again. She'll never let him touch you again. I'll never let you touch me again.

"Sh-sh-sh baby don't you cry."

Shutup! Sh-sh-ssssst. Are you awake?

Wake up! Why did you make my mother cry? My father stayed home sick in bed but my mother screamed. He walked down the stairs and out the door into warm damp air and the earth was wet between his toes, over the bridge and up the long hill. He knew where he was going then. "When I was a baby I always knew where I was going."

Where was Gran?

Two calico rooms in the back of a building with a lot of grass and an outside staircase that wrapped itself around the house. Other people lived upstairs; footsteps. Gran's door was three steps down behind a wall that was the color of lemons. When she didn't answer his banging the door with his fist until it hurt (because he couldn't reach the bell) he sat down and waited for her. He didn't remember going to sleep but when he woke up in Gran's arms they were both surprised. "What are you doing here? And with no shoes!"

"I was waiting for you."

"Poor baby." She kissed him where his head hurt so he said, "Ouch." He traveled inside high on the warm pillow of her breast, and sat on her wide lap while she washed his filthy feet with a rough warm washcloth. He stood with his face pressed against her cotton skirt while she stirred something on the stove.

"Your mother must be worried to death. I'll call her now and tell her you're safe." She looked at him while the cocoa burned his lip and said into the telephone, "You must have missed him. Oh. Yes. He's here with me."

That's where he wanted to be. But they went home in a taxi because he didn't have any shoes and when they opened the door of his house he found his mother still alive. She didn't notice the sore place on his head when she came to the door in a long green bathrobe. "Tom was sick," she said over his head. He stood between them, looking up at the two towers. "I must have fallen asleep. No, we didn't miss him until just a little while ago." The chin turned down and she said, "You were naughty to go without telling anyone, Ricky."

He heard their voices in the hall, Gran's and his mother's, while he was in the hot bathwater. Then Gran came in and stood in the steam and rubbed him dry so hard his skin hurt, but he laughed when she wrapped him in the big towel so he couldn't move, and she made him promise never to run away again.

"I didn't run away. I went to visit you. I knew where I was going." When he was a baby he always knew where he was going.

Where was Gran?

She was in the garden digging holes for him to put the bunches of jasmine in. "Pack the soil around the roots closely," she said. "Watch out. Don't step on the soft soil. Look, there's a worm for you. Careful! Don't squeeze it so hard. Look." Across the driveway Philip Cranswanger's mother was raking up weeds. His mother was inside asleep. "Don't ever go home," he said to Gran. "Give me my supper."

"I have to leave soon," she said. "But I'll stay till Vivian gets up. Poor girl, she's always so tired." When Gran was at his house Barbara didn't tease him and no one hurt him. But when she left . . .

"Play with me," Barbara said. "You have to play with me." He let her take his things, so she was nice enough. "Let's play house. You be the baby and I'll spank you for spilling the milk."

"I don't want to be the baby."

"I'm the mother and I'm so tired I could die." Sh-sh don't wake up Mother. She's been tired ever since you were born.

"I've been tired," he heard her say it so many times, "I've been tired ever since Ricky was born. I didn't expect him, you know."

"Who did you expect?" he asked once. He was standing by her side in the A&P and she was talking to a lady she'd met that he didn't know. She slapped the top of his head right there in front of the man in the store. "Don't be fresh," she said and slapped him.

Barbara went to school and he was alone. His mother went to work in an office. "What a relief to get out of the house," she said and left him at Gran's. "I'm so tired," she said when she got him every night, "I don't know how I'll ever get supper."

"Why don't you quit?" Gran asked her. "Stay home and take care of this boy of yours."

"I like you to take care of me." He wrapped his arms around Gran's legs.

His father came home while he was playing in the dirt pile where the new house was going in. He heard the deep voice a long way off, and he heard his mother crying when he came in. He hid behind the closet door in the front hall.

"He's into trouble from the time you leave in the morning. He's the one who brings in the dirt, the mud."

Barbara found him behind the door. "It's all your fault," she said. "You made her do it. Why don't you ever stay clean?"

"Why don't you try to be a mother to him?" his father roared. "Maybe he doesn't want to be alone all the time! Read to him. Clean him up. Get his hair cut. Take him to the zoo. My God, you've got all the time in the world and plenty of money, and you've got to ruin my reputation by getting a job, neglecting the house and your children."

Gran wasn't home when he got to her house, so he went to the river for a while and lay on a rock on the bank watching the water. The world was full of noise, and only the rushing water could drown the angry voices. He put his cheek on the cool rock and let his fingers trail in the water. *Where was Gran?*

There were some things Gran would tell him, and there were some things she wouldn't. "Why does my mother cry a lot?" he asked, as they climbed the last steps of the hill to the flower market. She took his hand firmly and said he'd better behave. "No more running away, getting people worried about you." She paused, caught her breath. "She's just tired," Gran said finally.

"Why does Mother cry a lot?" he asked Deborah.

"How should I know?" Deborah never cried. "It's probably your fault, just like she says. They always fight about you, Rick."

The job in the office didn't last long, and in the morning, after everyone left, his mother opened the door. "Out to play," she'd say, "and don't go wandering off. I don't want the neighborhood on a search again today. Don't get your pants muddy. Keep off the street. No fights. If anyone tries to talk to you—"

Where was Gran?

He was growing older. Gran told him, so it must be true. Be home at five. See the hands on the clock, Rick, it's three to five or five to three. "How do you know?" The clock tells you, stupid. The clock had a face that told them things it didn't tell him. Secrets. Girls looked at clocks and letters and talked secrets. The sky was so big it covered the world, covered a million secrets. Sh-sh-sh you'll wake Mother.

Don't tell her I told you but. . . . He got a book from Barbara's room and looked at the pictures. He looked at the letters, but they didn't say anything to him. "Read it to me." "You're too dumb to understand."

He was growing bigger. He knew it was true because his shoes hurt his toes, so he took his shoes off and went downstairs. "For God's sake, you can't go out barefoot; put your shoes on." They're too small. "Can't you buy the kid a new pair of shoes without my telling you?" He went out to get away from the voices.

Gran came every Sunday for lunch and brought presents and talked to Father seriously, and talked to Barbara seriously, and talked to Deborah seriously. She said, "Vivian?" and his mother walked out of the room. It was his birthday and she came in behind the giant bear, and he tried to get around the bear to hug her but she hid, laughing, until he nearly cried.

"Isn't he a little old for a stuffed bear?" Father asked.

"Oh, let him be a baby awhile." Gran shushed him. "It's over soon enough." Nobody but Gran talked to his father like that. When Deborah once said "shut up" to him he went wild, threw his paper at her, roaring so the walls trembled.

On his birthday there was a baseball mitt and a hard ball. His father took him outside. "Come, I'll teach you how to catch a ball," he said. "You stand here. Watch the ball. That's the first thing to remember." Looking across the lawn he saw his father, so tall his head seemed to touch the branches of the apple tree. When the ball came toward him he couldn't see it and it hit him on the cheek. "Get your mitt up!" the man yelled. But leather touched flesh and he cried, his arms hanging limply by his side.

"You won't even try!" his father roared across the sunny space between them. "What kind of a boy are you?"

"I'll try," he whispered. "I'll try." But tears blurred his vision and though he raised the arm with the heavy leather mitt up to his face the ball didn't go into it. Deborah, from somewhere behind him, took the mitt from his face and rescued him. He ran inside to the bathroom and by the time he came out Father had gone for a drive and Mother and Gran had finished the dishes and were standing in the hall. Gran was getting ready to go home. He stood by her side.

"Can I go with you?"

"Not today," she said.

"Your grandmother's tired," his mother said. "She's got to get some rest." That didn't sound right. It was his mother who was tired, not Gran.

He put Gran's hand to his cheek, pulled on her arm, jumped up and down. "Please, please," he said. "I'll be good. I'll be quiet."

"Stop it, Ricky." The sharp words silenced him. He heard them talk over his head, sensing fear in the air above him.

"I'll get rid of the baby, and come with you." That was his mother's voice.

"No, I'd rather go alone. I'll be all right."

"Call me."

"I promise." Gran bent down, kissed him quickly. "Happy birthday," she said once more and was gone.

In the dark he lay with his eyes open. Father hadn't come home for supper. His mother had been sad, quiet, but she hadn't been angry with him. It was his birthday, she said, so everyone should be nice. In the dark, waiting for someone to come and say goodnight, he thought about Philip Cranswanger saying, "Mothers are nice sometimes." "When?" he had asked. Now he thought, Today. Today Mother was nice. Tomorrow he would tell Philip when. Even while he was in the bathtub she had been nice. She stood in the doorway and smiled at him. "You were a good boy," she said, "all day."

"Father didn't come home to supper. He was mad at me."

His mother bit her lip, but she didn't say anything. She came in and held the towel when he got out of the tub. She ran her hands over his shoulders when she wrapped the towel around him. "You ought to be clean more often," she said, kissing his back. "You're easy to love when you're clean."

"I wish it was my birthday every day," he said.

"Go to bed," she told him.

She came into his room and he put up his arms to be kissed. For a moment she looked like Gran standing over him. "Where are you going to get rid of me tomorrow?" he asked. "Where is Gran going?"

"Nowhere," she said.

She bent to kiss him and he locked her head down to his by putting his arms around her neck. "Don't go away," he said. But already her eyes were on the door. They heard the front door open and shut.

"Tom?" she called, "Tom?"

"It's only me," Deborah answered.

"Where did Father go?" he asked, pulling the soft-haired head to his again.

"Nowhere. I don't know." He felt her soft hair on his cheek, but already she was gone from him. She strained against his arms to leave. She reached behind her and took his hands from her neck. "Hurry and sleep now," she said.

He was still awake when Barbara came upstairs and made her night noises in the room they shared. Don't blame me if the room's a mess, she said. Rick leaves his stuff all over. The sound of her getting pajamas out from under her pillow, in and out of the door, water running in the bathroom. This house is made of papier-mâché, he could hear his father say. Someday I'll have a house where you can't hear every flush of the toilet . . . someday.

Rick lay very still so Barbara would not know he was awake. "Rick?" softly. If she knew he was awake she would tell stories he hated. He had to cover his ears and shut his eyes. He must shut his eyes. The bathroom door opened; click, the light went off, and his eyes were wide open to the darkness. Suddenly a light blinded him. "So you are awake!" She was by his bed, flashlight in her hand. "Listen!"

Where was Gran?

She had not been to see them in a long time, and he had grown older without her. He went to school with Barbara in the morning now, even though he didn't want to go. There were too many people in the school who told him where to go and what to do. He was always turning in the wrong direction.

At recess the children were all together and he would stand and look for someone who might be a friend. Barbara had friends who stood in a group in their bright-colored dresses and they'd look at him and giggle. "If you get a hundred on your arithmetic," his father said at night, "I'll give you a dollar."

"If you stay out of trouble."

"If you don't get dirty."

"If you don't get into any fights."

"If you say the alphabet."

"Here's a present . . ."

"What did you write at school today?"

"What did you learn?"

"You wet your pants again!"

"The principal called. Why weren't you in school?"

"Where were you?"

"Why can't you remember?"

Where was Gran?

He did not know why he was here, smelling smells that were strange and hearing echoes of footsteps from great distances. His mother had told him, "Gran wants to see you." But this wasn't Gran's apartment. Why was he here?

A woman in white led them to a door and, stopping with her back to it, said, "Remember, she can hear what you say though it may not seem that way."

Rick reached for his mother's hand but it was not at her side. He found her skirt between his fingers, hot and prickly.

They went through a doorway and someone said, "Kiss Gran, dear."

"Your grandson is here," another voice said. There was a huge window letting in light that blinded him, but then he saw the bed with shining bars along it higher than his chest. He was told to stand on a stool and he put his hands on the cold metal bars. He looked at a thing among the white sheets, a yellowish-gray face with sharp points where bones stretched the dry skin, a few stringy strands of gray hair lying on the forehead.

"Kiss Gran, dear. Kiss Gran."

"He can't reach her."

"She can hear everything you say."

"Take the bars away." And someone took the bars from in front of him and still he couldn't find her. He stared at the thing on the bed, felt sharp bony fingers loosely grip his own hot hand; frightened, he pulled back.

"Kiss her!"

But she wasn't there! What had they done with her? It wasn't Gran, so he didn't kiss her, and he couldn't speak. He looked helplessly across the bed to his mother, biting her fingernail. She motioned to him, saying with her lips: Go on! Kiss her! Hurry! Everyone was looking at him. He wanted to hide. He wanted to climb the high hill and find the lemon-colored wall.

Where was Gran!

The wrinkled lips on the bed moved slightly; a voice that held some faint reminiscence of the gravelly sound he'd once known said, "He doesn't have to kiss me. I just wanted to say hello to him. Hello, Rick." He pulled away and ran out of the room and down the wide echoing hall past doors and tables toward the light at the end, but he couldn't find the way out. He bumped into a man in a white dress, and strong arms held him until his mother came. He felt the sting on his head, but he was trembling so, and there was a roaring in his ears that was bigger than the pain.

That night he heard her crying downstairs. Sometime

later his father held him on his lap and put his big arms around him holding him prisoner. "Gran is dead."

"No," he said. "No."

"What do you mean? I told you, Gran is dead!"

"Yessir. May I go now?"

"Go! Go on, damn you." The big hand pushed him to the floor.

He hadn't believed him then, nor had he for a long time afterward.

"But you didn't see her again?" Linda's question was a statement. "You know now that your grandmother is dead."

"Yes."

"But when she died you were too young to know what that meant."

He paused so long, and put his head down on his book, that she knew he was very tired. "I guess so," he said. He was like a swimmer who had gone a great distance under water, Linda thought, and coming to the surface, tried to see the real world again without the aqueous lens. Though he was exhausted, she pushed him one step further. "The book tells about a different river than the one you and your grandmother knew, Rick. See if you can read about it and tell me the difference."

He picked up the book slowly, blinking his waterlogged eyes, and started again. "The Amazon is the longest river in—"

"South America," she prompted softly, holding her breath.

"South America," he repeated. "It runs for three thousand miles. Its source is in the—Andes Mountains and it empties into the Atlantic Ocean at the equator. It runs through thick jungles; many miles along the Amazon have never been explored."

THIRTEEN ⚭ IT WAS IMPORTANT TO GET

Peter's bath done early. Linda was to meet David and Barney for dinner in the city. Bill Hammerman and his wife would be there, and perhaps the Walkers if they could get a sitter. Linda looked forward to the evening. It seemed forever since she had been to the city.

Peter's bath was something she mustn't try to hurry. If he took his time, quietly dribbling the water this way and that, the sitter would have no trouble getting him to sleep. Take your time, Peter, but she did not mean it. Hurry, hurry, so I can shower and dress and be ready to go at six and not in a sweat and rushing; kiss my children and walk serenely out the door like any intellectual lady of substance, poised, a promising lawyer's good wife.

Why was her heart pounding so? *He read! He read!* The special classes at school, the long hours on Nutgrove Street? Who knows why he read that afternoon? Did he feel as elated as she? Was his little heart whanging at his chest as loud and fast as hers? *I read! I read!*

Lifting Peter, a soggy lump, out of the dirty water, enveloping him in a large warm towel, she felt smiles all down her insides. Her nipples were up, her stomach sweetly tense. My stomach is smiling, she thought. Hey, Peter, your mother's belly is grinning! *He read! He read!* And when he gets on track, why I will too. I can do this well. It's what I must do. For you, Peter, my love, and for me too. Secrets she said to herself alone. I am good at this; a talent not everyone has. This will not be my last success. Others can teach the phonics, the mechanics, but I can allow a muted soul to find voice. Under the bruised skin the fruit *can* still be good!

With Peter laughing in the towel she almost missed the ringing phone. She didn't want to answer it. There had been not just the one, but several unpleasant calls. *Mrs. Kaplan, there's someone on the roof.* She caught the phone at the end of the fourth ring. Peter wriggled to get down but she held him on her hip. With relief, she heard Jean Mendelsohn settling into relaxed gossip. Could Brian go to *Peter Pan* with Suzy next week? Teachers' in-service day, so no school. Sure, why not? And Rick, Jean supposed, would be there as ever? Well, he might want to stay behind with her, Linda said. "I never know what he'll want to do."

"I suppose I can take him too," Jean said.

"You don't have to."

"Well, he's so much better than he used to be. All those fights! He just doesn't seem to fight so much any more."

"No. No, he doesn't." Did the drumbeats in her chest travel through the phone to Jean's ears?

"Did you hear the fire engines last night? They've been by almost every night this week. I thought I'd never get back to sleep— Haven't seen you in a million years. When you get time let's just goof off some morning, go to lunch or something. How about the PTA meeting tomorrow night? A professor, a reading specialist from California."

"Yes, thanks, I might go to that. Sure. Let's go together. David will be home, and I know he won't want to go out. Listen," she cut Jean off, looking at the clock, "I've got to dress. I'm trying to get out of here by six."

"Tomorrow then. I'll come by for you at eight."

She stood Peter on his fat feet in front of the long mirror and brushed his hair, black and shiny like David's, but so soft! "Stay pretty," she whispered, kissing him.

It ended a bit sweaty after all. Brian was late getting home from the playground where he'd gone after the homework was done, and Rick lingered before leaving. Peter clung to Linda's neck at the door, pulling her scarf and her hair awry; Sappho sulked when she was put down cellar with her five-week-old pups, but how much could you expect a sitter to handle? Another week or two at most and she would have homes for the five delicious wriggles of puppyhood. Rick, she knew, was still waiting to find out if his parents would let him have one. It would be good for the boy, Linda felt sure, to have something all his own to love and care for.

Then, finally, a blessed hour in total isolation in her automobile, nowhere, suspended between two lives. It began, as always, with her hands in a death grip on the wheel, her neck stiffly arched. Unsewn seams of home unraveled in her head. But gradually as the radio music filled the space and each highway bridge swept over her head, the houses marched closer and closer together until finally the vista she loved unfolded itself—a thousand gray city roofs beyond a trainyard, the lights of the Empire State in the distance sprinkling the smoking sky. The octopus began to lose its hold on her, tentacle by tentacle, allowing each freed muscle of mind and body to flex and stretch. At the end of the hour, having deposited the car against a gritty curb, she was ready for the city, for David, for men. She had even remembered to read the front page of the *Times*.

As she walked over the Roman tile floors in Nicholson's, searching for David among the maze of tables, nude statuary, torsos, fountains, and Roman heads, she almost missed them. Then she heard Barney's voice coming from a discus thrower and found them behind the tall statue. They were already drinking. Since Barney and his wife had divorced several years back, he was inevitably alone, inevitably the host. He picked this place often, liking its wine cellar and its fine filets. David stood up stiffly when he saw Linda. Had she forgotten something? Was her lipstick crooked? She searched his face for reasons. She held her lips for David's kiss, which seemed perfunctory. "Am I late?" she whispered.

He blinked, shook his head no, and finally his eyes blessed her. He held her chair.

"Bill and Janice Hammerman, my wife, Linda," he said. It was all right. She smiled and searched the faces in the half light. She nodded at Bill—she'd met him before—and put out her hand toward his wife. "I'm so glad to meet you,"

Linda said. The dark-haired woman with overdecorated eyes did not smile but acknowledged Linda's greeting with a nod and turned back to listen to Barney who was talking as usual. Barney waved his puffy hand at Linda.

"How's the country girl?" he interrupted himself. "You look prettier every time I see you." He made an effort to stand up as she settled in her chair, but the table was wedged against his enormous stomach, and all he did was shake the glasses.

"Don't get up." She grinned at him. "I'm fine. Go on with your story."

"I was telling David that what the world really needs is a return to passion. Have I told you my latest PTA story?"

"You don't have to," Linda said. "I'm quitting."

"Oh, you mustn't! How will they manage without you?"

Linda warmed to his flattery. She loved Barney's extravagant phrases, his outrageous generalizations. She always went through the same cycle with him. At first she would laugh at his jokes, keeping her distance and vowing to herself not to challenge him or become embroiled in argument. But eventually he would say something that aroused her so she wouldn't be able to stop herself. Then he would sit back, needling her now and then till she realized she had been talking too much, too loud, and David had become uncomfortable. Sometimes she would lie awake remembering with embarrassment the sound of her own voice, after all other voices had stopped, overexplaining.

Tonight she wasn't involved yet. She let herself listen and enjoy, sipping her bourbon and warming slowly to the currents around her. What had disturbed David? Where were the Walkers?

"Life is a yo-yo," Barney was saying. "So many of us do what we do, not because we have made a plan or established a set of criteria, but because someone jerked on the string and up we go again."

"Yo, yo, yo," said Janice Hammerman. "Barney's always talking babytalk. Pour me a teeny bit more of that lovely

Beaujolais, Barney dear." She leaned across the empty place at the table, putting her glass in front of Barney. He filled it. Linda looked at Bill. He sat stiffly, stared straight ahead, as if trying not to notice what was happening. His fingers rotated the glass in front of him; he was drinking clear soda, Linda surmised, vaguely remembering that he was a reclaimed alcoholic and took not even wine any more. She looked at him harder, trying to see behind the elegant mask: neat mustache and wide-set eyes under well-brushed eyebrows, enough gray at the temples to look attractive, and a high firm chest. He's older than he admits, Linda thought. I'll bet he exercises to keep that shape. Janice now rested her head on her open palm, allowing her long black hair to fall over her shoulder; she seemed to dote on Barney's words, but her eyes were unfocused.

"Women today," Barney was saying, "only respond to specific stimuli. They live such isolated lives in their suburban paradises with their children and crabgrass, and floorwaxes and viruses. Once in a while they reach for the *New York Times,* follow a front-page story halfway through the runover and say happily to the coffeepot, 'See, wasn't that fun?' and think they're intellectualizing. But mostly what they do requires neither passion nor free will."

Linda started. How did he know? How did Barney always know? Aloud she said, "Read the headline quick, Momma, before the phone starts to ring. When did you set yourself up as an expert on women, Barney?"

He grinned. "I'm an expert on nearly everything, you'll find out." David groaned, but Barney went on. "Once in a while they'll make a superhuman effort to break into the hurly-burly world—my ex-wife's best friend with an M.A. in biology got a job for a week at the telephone company, just to escape the house—but all too often they find the world a cold and frightening place. They've simply missed too many headlines."

"There'll always be another headline." Linda found herself wanting to argue with him; not all the way yet, just stirrings. She stopped and sipped her bourbon, liking the sting of it on her tongue.

"Other headlines, but that's all they have. A march of murderous headlines. Women," he warmed up, "have betrayed the suffrage their mothers fought so hard for, gone back to the kitchen, and become second-class citizens in a cultural wasteland."

"Not all of us are destined to be social movers," Linda protested. "Some mothers love taking care of their children; they don't want to desert them for great—or not so great—causes."

"But you, love, were destined; weren't you?" Barney prodded softly.

She didn't answer right away. Only one other person had confronted her that way a long time before. *You're throwing yourself away*, Robert had said. *You'll never be anything.* She had, for a time, deserted the causes of her youth, the blacks and Puerto Ricans, the poor and miserable of any color or race or country, of her city or anywhere else. Those were passionate years, when any social outrage, from a trial for rape in the South to an unjust imprisonment of an alien in the North, prompted her signature on a petition or a letter to Washington. She had aimed her education at service, not profit. Surely now she would offer more than voice and rejoin the ranks of the socially useful.

"I was," she said with her chin high and her eyes bright. "But I am not a lifelong dropout, Barney." *He read! He read!* "Besides," she said when she'd caught her breath, "what happened to all the young *men* I used to know who spent their teens shouting themselves hoarse at political rallies in Madison Square Garden?"

"Men?" Bill asked. "What men?"

"The men I went to school with." Linda found voice in recollecting those she hadn't thought of in years. "Who sang along with Leadbelly and Josh White, who marched in any picket line and acted for nothing off-Broadway. After the war most of the ones I used to know went looking for jobs with a training program, a future, and built-in benefits. They no longer wanted to save the world, but to save themselves. Whatever their cries in the battles had been, their peace cry was We Want Security.

"My friend the poet became a high-fashion leather merchant. The musician went to law school. The lawyer went into business with one of his clients. The real thinkers, those who are walking alongside James Meredith, sitting in, and changing this country, aren't my impassioned school chums, that's for sure, male or female. And if they regret their choice, it's too late now to move in a different direction. They have big families and expensive suburban houses to maintain, investments that can't be tossed aside."

As she talked she saw that smile start at the corners of Barney's mouth. She was doing it again, and when she saw David's bored expression, she stopped.

Barney shook his head. "Whew," he said. "It's been a while since we've compared notes, isn't it? You've been doing some heavy thinking." Was he making fun of her? Linda never knew. "In our town," he went on, "there was a beautiful scandal. Two of the town's most respectable wives—country club matrons and church board members—disappeared one dense, foggy night after a late meeting. They just never got home. Husbands were irate, then frantic. Children were left to boil their own breakfast eggs. Next morning the pair was found asleep in a car in the school parking lot, an empty bottle of bourbon on the floor. Truth was, they were ex-PTA presidents who found sympathy in each other. Neither had anything to look forward to after their term of office had ended."

All of them except Janice laughed. "You made that one up, Barney," Linda said.

"I? Fabricate? Nonsense! Think, lovely Linda, what *is* there for past PTA presidents?"

"Now I want to tell a story," Janice said reaching for the Beaujolais. Bill covered her glass with his hand and in a fury she knocked it out of her way.

· 215 ·

"You men talk and talk as if you know something. You do what you want to do when you want to do it. Bill, keep your hand off my glass. You may be on the wagon, but I am not. You just move lives around to suit your whimsy, without a care for who gets left."

Bill shrugged. David looked as if he would like to be somewhere else.

"I am going to tell a story of the most beautiful little girl that was ever born, a love of a girl, a doll of a girl. Her name—her name—oh, well, her name doesn't matter much. She was a sweet one, she was, and smart as she was beautiful."

Bill said, "Barney, let's order some food. That waiter hasn't been here in hours."

"Shut up, Bill, I'm talking. Her father adored her and her mother dressed her so well. And all through school her teachers admired and petted her. She won prizes. And then she went to college, the very same college her mother had gone to. And she was queen of the campus, and she took honors, and she joined her mother's sorority, and then . . ."

"And then?" Linda prompted, because suddenly Janice looked ready to burst into tears. Her voice trailed off. She seemed to be choking. Her hair is too black, Linda thought. I should have guessed it was dyed.

"I'm still hoping you'll win Walker's case," Bill said.

"So am I," David said, leaping at the chance to turn the conversation. "There's a case coming up in California that we're beginning to hear about, that seems to attack the same issue of opening private property to public use, putting the state in the awkward position of creating a 'milieu of discrimination.' It may be that this administration will be an interesting one for civil rights. The courts are beginning to hear all sorts of arguments they haven't been subjected to before."

Linda was surprised to hear David sounding so positive about the case. And pleased.

"One of the more interesting aspects of the administration," Bill said, "is that both the president and his wife are not only strong on civil rights but know that culture is our lifeblood. Without freedom, art is dead," he expounded, "and without art, freedom becomes decadent amorality. We'd be a nation of gourmands and fornicators—"

"I haven't finished my story," Janice said. "Bill, you have to let me finish my story."

"Finish then. Don't drag it out."

"Bill hates my stories, hates them and suffers through them. I tell him he ought to use them in his books. I am just full of good ideas, but because he hates me—"

"Janice!"

"Oh, all right. I'll behave. But you have to let me finish. Where was I?"

"In college," Barney said. "Your girl—I assume it's your daughter—was in college, winning honors."

"And then she graduated." Janice stopped.

Everyone was silent. She was quite drunk. Linda said politely, "How wonderful. You and Bill must be so proud."

Still silence. Even Barney was speechless.

"Yesterday," Janice said.

"Yesterday!" Linda echoed. "Then you've just come back!"

"But you see it could have been me. *I* could have graduated. *I* could have had those honors. They should have been *mine!* No one noticed me. No one cared. Bill only cares for her. She stole it from me. She stole him." Tears filled her eyes and she brushed at them.

"Have some wine, dear," Barney said, suddenly tender. "You and Bill married while you were in college, didn't you?" She nodded and bit her lip, sipping the wine gratefully. "And you never went back. Well, no matter. You are by far the most beautiful dropout I have known." His voice soothed her. David talked into the breach to save the dinner and pull attention away from the weeping woman.

"There was a good article last week on racial zoning," he said, "that may do us some real good."

"You don't have to convince me, David. I'm on your side. But it's going to be a question of whether or not those nine old men like your argument. I'm gambling they'll like it better from you than from me. They'll go for your dispassionate reasoning."

"A few minutes ago you were pushing passion," Bill said. "The more I rely on reason the less I trust it. What will win this case is timing and polemic. As you said, Barney, this is a yo-yo world. Walker wanted to join the good life even though his skin is black; he built his pyramid through careful planning. Educated himself. Now he wants his son to share the goodies. We worked it out carefully. I thought the community was ready to share—not their wealth but their good fortune. I was wrong. Those bastards have pulled every lousy trick in the book. John's life is torn; somebody else is pulling the string."

David said, "The case is clear enough, Bill. And the time is right. That's our aim, you know, to keep others from pulling the string."

"Did you know my good neighbors threw a rock through my living room window last week? The bigots have been oozing out of every drain."

Linda gasped. "Did you know, David? You didn't tell me!"

"We tried to play it down. Got the thing reglazed in a hurry and just went about our business. We don't want any publicity yet. God, will I be glad when I can find pleasure at home again."

"What we do for pleasure and principle are usually not the same." David sounded pompous.

"I'd try to juxtapose them," Linda said.

"Damn near impossible," Bill said. "The age of enlightenment is way off. Kennedy's trying to counter the evil that has been fertilized around us for a quarter of a century. But who are the victims? Well, a noble lily-white black lady by name of June Walker who's trying to raise her kid not to be a militant. Maybe even Janice is one. Maybe—"

"But what is going to happen to the children growing up in a world so sick? I feel it all around me, as if the whole nation is full of psychoses. Is that possible? For a country to be mentally ill? Everyone's afraid all the time—of Communists, the bomb, of black power, even of kids! I heard in the junior high they have to have guards in the lunchroom and study halls. If we expect kids to act like criminals we'll get what we expect. The school day is scheduled so tightly these kids have no time to think. No one trusts them or listens to them. Parents send them off to see James Bond and then are surprised when even the kindergarteners act tough."

"Trust a child!" Barney exploded in mirth. "What a romantic you are, Linda. Trust a child who's been brought up on TV and the materialistic vacuity of suburban life? Whose parents have left the training of his mind to the wasteland of our public education system and ethics to some church they've never bothered to believe in themselves? Trust a child? Preposterous! Who's training them to love?"

"Love!" David said. "You can't train someone to love, Barney. You're carrying your plea for passion too far!"

And so it went, round and round. Serious and jovial. Nerves were touched and soothed. Janice stayed quiet for a time; she was hard to ignore but it was better to pretend not to see her tears which continued to ebb and flow. Linda found she wanted to ignore Janice, wanted no part of her drama, her terrible need. Linda was having too good a time. Barney took the lead, ordering rare filets all around, and another bottle of wine. He cut into his steak, licked his lips with anticipatory relish, speared a particularly juicy piece of red meat, and held it in front of him, pausing.

"The difference between living socially and biologically," he announced, "lies in the level of frustration demanded of the psyche, rather than the stomach. We can survive a monotony of diet—so long as it is rare and tender beef—but a monotony of experience suffocates us. We continually arm ourselves for battles which we never fight. We rehearse and rehearse for plays on which the curtain never rises. Or we star in plays that have no climax and no final curtain."

"Let's hope," Bill said, his tone lightening, "that in this case life imitates art; that there is some kind of climax, and a final curtain—on this episode at least."

To Linda's relief Barney safely stowed his meat, chewed happily, and washed it down with wine.

"Art simply puts life in a box, Bill," he said. "It frames the painting, stages the drama. Have you ever thought of writing fiction which is so like life that there is no box, no stage, no frame?"

"I'd be a damn sight poorer," Bill said, "and I do like to eat well."

Linda smiled. She knew he did, and liked his yacht and his half-year house in the Bahamas. He was a lot of people, this Bill Hammerman, who'd exposed himself for a principle—or as David thought, to salve his conscience—and retreated to his various havens to write.

She was enjoying herself and these three men as if she were the only woman there. She felt she held them all; kept pace with them. She avoided looking at Janice, fearful that if she caught her eye the deluge would begin again. What had Bill said earlier about a nation of fornicators? The word stuck in her mind. Linda envisioned him and his wife naked. How they must have enjoyed each other once! Romping through their glass house in the woods, in that eden called A Woodland Place; she saw their white buttocks in her mind, remembering once she had watched a college friend gloriously chase his shrieking girl up a flight of stairs and down another.

She sneaked a peek at Janice; saw her run a pointed finger around the rim of her wine glass. What had changed them? What birth? What death? What sty? What minor misspeak? The balance of life is precarious, she thought, hearing but no longer apprehending the men's words around her. The organization of a school, the social order of a playground, the sweetness of life in her own home, the tone at a dinner table of strangers, are comparable, perhaps, to the chemistry of the human body or the balance of a water skier. All it takes is a damaged cell, a virus, an unexpected oil slick, or a Rick—she caught her thought too late—to throw the whole thing askew.

She was ready to go home. She looked at David again. She willed him to look at her but he was intent on what Bill was saying. Linda tried to catch the thread. They had moved on to some other topic.

Suddenly Janice woke up. "Talk, talk, talk. That's all that ever happens any more." She was drunker than ever. If only she had eaten. But not a bite. She twined her long bare arm around David's neck, and with her fingers turned his face to hers. "Why don't you look around you, all you serious talky men! And you too," she pointed at Linda, "so prim and proper. All the time you talk the world is full of beautiful breasts and penises, and we're missing them!" She swept her arm in a circle, taking in the stone nudes and the population of the restaurant. Bill put his hands to his head, and Barney reached for Janice's wrist. But it was David she leaned on now.

She shifted her hips neatly from her chair onto his lap and wrapped herself around him. He looked so startled Linda almost laughed.

"What's your name, darling? I've forgotten your name. Oh, yes, David. That's it. I like that name, David. If my son had lived that would have been his name." She licked her shiny red lips. "David." Barney and Bill both waved wildly for the waiter, the check.

David tried to shift her back again, but, "Oh, no, I'm not going to let you go now that I've found you. I'm not so heavy, am I, David?"

"No," David said painfully.

"What do you like to do for fun, David?" She paused and waited for him to answer. He blinked and opened his mouth but before he could speak, she said, "Fuck?"

•

Linda and David were silent for the first part of the drive. Cold now, Linda curled close to him and tucked her feet up on the seat.

"You're crowding me," he said. "I can't shift."

"Don't," she murmured. "Just stay in high." She rubbed his leg with her gloved hand.

"Um. Not here. We'll crack up."

As he turned up the ramp off the East River Drive to the Triborough Bridge she let it all out. "Oh, that poor crazy woman. That poor, poor woman. I've never known such a crazy rich poor woman before."

"Bill usually manages to go out without her. She's been in and out of institutions for a long time."

"Always an alcoholic?"

"I doubt that's the whole story. He likes to drink but never does with her. He feels he can't expect her to leave it alone if he's toping." Then, apologetically, "I couldn't cope with her, you know."

"I know." Then, "Tell me truthfully. Did you like having her on your lap? Tell me, did you?"

"I won't tell you truthfully. Either way it would come out wrong."

"You're always so reasonable."

"Without reason we'd all be lost." He touched her breast beneath her open coat.

"Not here," she mimicked. "We'll crack up."

"You should come to town more often," he said. "You were great tonight. I was watching you."

"You were?"

"You just seemed to come alive, more alive than I've seen you in months. When Peter gets to school you ought to get out and take some kind of job. You seemed so animated. Maybe you do need to be out of the house more, doing something that doesn't have anything to do with me or the children."

He read! He read! "I would like that," she said softly.

The drive through the delicious darkness lasted a lifetime.

Too long, too short, too sweet, too painful. She closed her eyes to the oncoming headlights stabbing the blackness. Wind whistled past the quarter windows. The air was too hot and too cold.

She was already in bed when he came back from taking the sitter home; covers high at her chin, she was naked and shivering between cold sheets. She watched him hang his clothes, place his shoes; heard water sounds from the bathroom. Never never did David skip any part of his ablutions, morning or evening.

"I've been warming the bed for you," she whispered when he slid under the blanket at last. "I thought you'd never get here."

His hands smoothed over her shoulders, her breasts, one and then the other, raising them, then her belly, her thighs. She arched her belly toward him, raising her arms over her head, hugging her ears to drown out sound, stretching to feel all of him, all of his strokes, as if she needed to touch him everywhere at once with every part of her. His high hard penis pressed at her legs. He felt inside her with his fingers, moved on top of her.

Oh, not yet, not yet, slowly, slowly, it's so lovely my lovely. She rocked and twisted under his warmth. For a long time they stroked and petted and stretched and rolled, extending the exquisiteness and the heat until neither could wait and when he came so far inside her, for the first time in months, she came too.

The explosions woke them out of dead sleep, so that as they both leaped to their feet they didn't know where they were or what time it was.

David was at the window as Linda raced naked down the hall to Peter's room. The baby slept soundly. Brian sat up in bed. "What is it?" he asked when he saw the light.

"I don't know," Linda answered from the hall. Then she heard David's voice out the window.

"Go home, you bastards! Go home!"

She shuddered at the tone. He came to her slowly, his bathrobe hardly around him. "Some kids with firecrackers," he said.

"That's all?" Linda asked. "It sounded so big."

"That's enough," he said in a dull voice. "That's enough."

FOURTEEN 🙂 "THE BOY TESTS HIGH," JOANNE said. "He does now and he did last fall. Corinne Alpert hasn't seen much improvement but his in-class written work is better. Right, Catherine?"

"Any fights lately?" Glenna asked.

"No," Catherine said. "Not since the first of the year. And no bad ones," she added, "since he came back from suspension."

"Mm." Glenna glanced over the record in the folder. "At the time he came back we did recommend some outside help. Either they didn't get it or neglected to inform us. If he's beginning to improve I suppose it doesn't matter." To herself, she added, Wouldn't be surprised if the shock of suspending him did the trick. Sometimes that's all it takes to straighten a child out—the shock of some real punishment. Aloud then, "Well, what do you think? Can we promote him? We've only got a couple of months to make the decision."

Catherine leaned forward in her chair with some eagerness. "He really is beginning to read. It's kind of exciting to watch now. Usually I don't get the children until they're pretty well on their way. But with Rick—well it's as if he'd been storing vocabulary in his head that he never used, kept locked up, and now something or somebody has found the key."

Glenna nodded at the special reading teacher. "Corinne, I guess your work does show even if you haven't seen the change."

Corinne Alpert, a pencil-like woman with straight black short hair and a narrow lifeless face, said, "Kids develop certain habits in my groups. Sometimes they don't bother to break out. So long as he's moving ahead, that's all I care about."

"I ran the Stanford-Binet last week," Joanne said. "His potential for fourth grade is all right, if he keeps on. He reads at 2.8 now, but usually when the block is broken the speed picks up very fast."

"How does this compare with earlier tests?"

"In October he was almost mute. I had to use the non-verbals on him to get an IQ."

"What about special schools?"

"Unnecessary. I'm sure we can handle him. Especially now that the reading block seems to be broken. That sometimes accounts for the fights too. Kids get so angry at themselves when they can't read, they'll fight with anyone."

Joanne glanced at the women in the room. She had taken the chair nearest the window so she could watch them. They were all so well meaning, these bumbling teachers. Because of her Ph.D., her scientific and medical preparation, and because they turned to her only when they were in dire need, she felt she had a certain power over them. Translating the percentile ratings into Dear Abby wisdom was a game she liked and felt expert at. Catherine, she thought, was so in love with her charges that she never wanted to let any of them go. For some, she made a great mother/teacher. Children unfolded like lilies under her warm praise. But later some might find the going tough. Missed deadlines were considered failures in higher grades, and often there were no second chances.

But that idiot Corinne, who sat in her prim jumper, mouthing the words the children in the circle were supposed to be reading out loud! She ran two groups: advanced readers and retarded readers. It was a wonder they weren't all turned off. Joanne did not know of one child whom Corinne had brought up to class level without outside tutoring. If Rick had not been sent to a tutor this would be Corinne's first success, Joanne thought.

Joanne had watched Rick carefully during the fall when there had been almost daily fights on the playground, checking for signs of paranoia or other problems outside of the school's capabilities. There were some, but not enough to make a firm diagnosis. She finally got around to running special tests on him after he pulled the knife on Glenna. That was a dilly of a day, she thought. Glenna, as usual, had made too much of it. She was fine so long as what happened fit her preconceived plans. Anything out of the ordinary threw her, and she made snap judgments that were often inappropriate and rigid. Joanne burned at Glenna's obvious delight in the fact that the boy hadn't had any fights since November. That's why she had insisted that the reading was its own therapy. At a time when the boy obviously needed extra help from all of them, Glenna had thrown him out. The father, Joanne thought, had been right for once to take the offensive against the school. Although she had placated him with the usual generalizations, she continued to believe that Glenna—and she, too, as psychologist—was vulnerable on that suspension. Glenna really was terrified of these kids, she thought, suspecting a hood behind every locker.

Joanne didn't expect children to grow up without knowing about knives and sex, about all kinds of challenges to authority. Every time she drove around the neighborhood, she saw groups of young boys smoking or just hanging around. Even the junior high children were smokers now. Kids were maturing younger. It wasn't possible to shelter them from information beyond their years. These kids didn't live in a vacuum. A boy like Rick Lang, a newcomer, could so easily fall into a rebel group. Without reading he'd probably drop out before the end of high school. But if the reading picked up early enough, and somebody remembered to keep him busy, he might get some well-oriented friends and— She suddenly remembered she had to ask Glenna about the other boy. But Rick, she thought, was on the mend. She was glad of it.

Linda came into the meeting with Jean Mendelsohn after the speaker had begun; they found chairs on the side and tried to catch the thread of thought. At first the trappings of the gym, the ropes hung high, the basketball nets, distracted her. The place was pretty well packed. Her thoughts finally tuned in. "Interesting to note that by fifth grade, two out of three children are so inhibited in their ability to express themselves on paper that the remainder of their English-language teaching through high school and beyond is an attempt to untangle their emotional knots from their writer's cramp. What are we doing in American public education today to produce a nation of literary cripples?

"Is this paralysis of the writing hand a product of work-book learning? I would say yes. The workbook—that great panacea of the teacher shortage—is creating havoc. Students are learning to fill the blanks, fix the bad sentence, put in the missing verb or adverb or adjective from the given list, even identify the parts of the sentence. But creating one simple declarative sentence out of their own thinking has become a gargantuan task. Rather than fail all of our progeny, we have raised them on the short-answer test, which they have learned to master. In most schools it is quite unnecessary to write well in order to earn an A. And A's are what kids are being taught to go after.

"I have a paper in front of me written by a second grade child. 'If I had a chance to change places with someone I would like very much to be the president because he works hard and I love to work hard. I love to make decisions of my own. I would love to sign bills all the time. I would give people permissions for doing things. I would look very tall and handsome and I would have deep blue eyes.'

"Not much question that the author had a pretty lucid

knowledge of the world, a good sense of his relationship to it, and the ability to express himself on paper. During the course of his third grade career his teacher corrected his papers in red pencil, taught him spelling, paragraphing, use of parentheses, capitalization. In his language workbook he practiced sentence structure, style, vocabulary. In an energetic approach to teaching self-criticism, his teacher required that all papers be written twice, corrected by the students themselves, and then copied.

"In the spring this same child handed in a paper which said, 'I don't know what to write.' The phrase has been uttered thousands of times by thousands of young people. And it is no wonder when all of their written work, from the simplest poem to the most critical essay, has been subjected to such scrutiny.

"How can we talk in one breath of the freedom of expression and opportunity to which this nation is historically dedicated, and imprison our children's creative processes through such a massive system of literary goose-stepping? The workbook is turning our teachers into custodians of paper, monitors, day-care center guardians, keepers of the peace and the status quo. What workbook education could prepare a child to write 'The fog comes on little cat feet' or the Gettysburg Address? In one school I know, the third grade was kept on the playground learning to march, square dance, and sing for two weeks because the workbooks hadn't arrived."

Linda's mind began to drift. He was right, of course, and it was fine that someone had the sense to bring him here. How many would hear—or understand—what he said? She glanced around the graceless room, shifted on the wooden folding chair, nodded, smiled at friends. These people made up her world. She wondered how many she would miss if she left town tomorrow. How many would miss her? The voice of the speaker droned on; then applause was around her. "If you have any questions."

A man from the audience stood to ask a question. He was over six feet tall and his barrel chest stretched the heavy brown jacket from button to button. Even though the broadness suggested strength, there were signs of softness in his jowls, and the chest was just low enough to suggest the sagging of an ex-athlete.

His voice was as big as his chest. "I've only been a resident of New Delphi for eighteen months. Before that, I was a member of the school board of another community. We dealt with problems such as these constantly, and I want to say that since we came here we have been most impressed with the worthiness of intentions, the high ideals of the citizens. I feel sure that when we settled up there on Martin Avenue we made a wise choice. This is a fine community for our children to grow up in; and we certainly have been warmly welcomed by church and school and merchants alike. I like it here. I want to admit it."

"What office is he running for?" someone behind Linda asked.

"Never saw him before."

"That's Tom Lang." Jean's whisper went through Linda like a shock. Of course!

"But we have to be careful how we label certain things. Someone here was talking about freedom. Someone else about custodial care. Now it seems to me that the first responsibility of a school *is* to keep children busy, off the streets, learning and preparing for the responsibilities that will be theirs. No custodial care? Well, why not? Do we want our children to run wild? Even our pets are shielded from the dangers of a world they're unequipped to handle. Yet in this very district, last fall a lower elementary school child was turned loose during the school day for a whole week, a whole week of school missed. That means losing state aid, mind you, for some minor infraction. I'm sure you'll take my word that the quality of the offense in no way justified the punishment. We—at least some of us—were young once." He laughed. "Well, I think we'd better talk less about freedom to learn than freedom to destroy ourselves."

The assemblage was silent.

Mrs. Kaplan, there's someone on the roof.

Linda's back was to the door and the light from the window made her blink. She knew the technique well, and tried to figure how to move her chair so she could see Mrs. Franklin's features. There wasn't space. The light glared and left the figure at the desk in silhouette.

Mrs. Franklin was not an uncomfortable woman, for a school psychologist. Though quite ugly—Brian had said she looked like a bulldog the first time he had been interviewed by her—when she smiled, Linda felt in the presence of a friend. She licked her lips between phrases, as if searching for bits of toast, and mouthed her words unmercifully. But she was a robust woman, unusual in an elementary school office because she often swore and forgot people's names.

"I'm a troubleshooter," she said to Linda. "I can watch the kindergarten kids on the playground and tell you which ones won't read next year. I couldn't care less if Johnny doesn't learn enough spelling to get him out of third grade, but if I see him throwing rocks at his teacher, I'll go to work. When did you first notice Brian stealing?"

Linda's pocketbook fell off her lap with a clatter. Clumsily she scraped her possessions off the floor and stuffed them back in. When she was in her chair again, she brushed the hair back from her forehead and said, "You have him mixed up with someone else. Brian doesn't steal."

"No?" Mrs. Franklin licked her lips and opened the folder on her desk. "Let's see." She ran her finger down the page. "Brian Kaplan, Miss Barker's third grade, 27 Nutgrove Street—last April fell in fishpond—usually quiet, well-liked by peers." Mrs. Franklin looked up. "He's got a fine record, you know. He's learned his skills, doing well in all areas. You are Mrs. Kaplan, aren't you?"

"Yes," Linda said softly.

"Now, does Brian confide in you?"

"Of course," Linda said angrily. "He's a perfectly relaxed, intelligent little boy. We get along fine. He's never stolen anything at home, at least nothing that I know of. And if he had, I wouldn't consider him a criminal anyway. You should be the first to know that it's perfectly normal for a boy to go through a stealing stage."

"Yes."

"Just what is he supposed to have stolen?"

"What do you think would be the cause of his going through—as you put it—a stealing stage right now?"

"I didn't say—"

"Is there a new baby at home?"

"No!" They were all alike, she thought, jumping to easy conclusions too quickly. "His brother is nearly two and they're quite used to each other."

"Um, well, he doesn't seem to be having difficulties with any of his subjects. Sometimes when a child is failing—"

"Brian has always liked school. Even the boring aspects."

"Look, Mrs. Kaplan, try to help. Yesterday a new silver pen belonging to Miss Alpert was found in Brian's desk. Last week he changed a five-dollar bill at the school store. His teacher was missing five dollars from her purse that day. There have been other incidents, Miss Barker tells me. All within the past few weeks."

"It can't be true," Linda murmured. True, untrue, what difference did it really make now? If they believed him a thief, that became a truth with power and effect. Avenues would be narrowed to him, some closed. Watchful, distrustful eyes would already be following him. There is nothing anyone can do, nothing believed, that does not have some effect. A wave already started. She felt beginnings of fear, as she might on a sandbar alone at dusk, the first ripple of an incoming tide, chilling her. Children do steal, she knew, even good children. But not Brian! Please, not Brian! *I don't like him being with Brian so much.*

"Mrs. Kaplan." The voice was gentle. "You're wiser than most mothers." The flattery was offensive. "You said yourself he shouldn't be treated like a criminal. If there's a problem with your relationship—"

"Oh, for heaven's sake," Linda cried, "everyone's always blaming everything on the mother. The kid's fine and when he gets an A in spelling it isn't my fault, and when he steals it isn't necessarily my fault either." She didn't like the sound of her own voice. Once, long ago, in another life, another world, another room, someone had asked her why she thought everyone was what he was because of his relationship to his mother. She had replied vehemently, "Dammit, I do, and if there's anything else that makes people what or how they are, I'd like to know it. That umbilical cord is tougher than nylon and more corrosive than salt, and people come out the way they are—right or wrong—because of the way they can or can't get along with and fight or fence with their mothers." Now, she thought, I have two of my own that I am helplessly mother to, and how can I make the end of each day come out right for them?

"Our relationship," Linda said, recovering, "is probably no better or worse than yours with your children, which I will let remain your private affair. I'll talk to my husband." She left the room.

She couldn't quite talk to David, of course. For one thing, he was on his way to Washington again, and though she had the name of his hotel, she knew he'd hate to be called. For another, wasn't this his prediction come true, though perhaps not quite as either of them had expected it? She could have told Mrs. Franklin about Rick. The teachers undoubtedly knew the boys were friends, but something had prevented her from mentioning him. She rationalized—it was against her sense of decency to blame another child. She didn't know the truth yet. She would talk to Brian. How far had he been corrupted? She didn't dare tell David. Could she just ask Brian directly? She held her chin high as she picked up Peter from the outer office and walked through the school corridor, noticing this day the faint smell of urine that pervaded the air.

Her throat was dry. Was she getting sick? Of course she could ask Brian directly. When Brian spoke, she did not doubt. She could make mistakes; she could blunder; but Brian trusted her and she trusted him. He told her everything he did and she told him exactly what she thought of what he did. Their love was complete, innocent.

Sentiment began to crowd her thoughts, and by the time she had reached the door she knew that not only would she talk quietly, calmly, with her loving, trusting son, but she would call David. After all, if you can't tell your own husband the important things . . .

In an anguish of self-deprecatory feelings, and of love for David (who would, of course, understand how upset she naturally was), she walked to the phone booth at the corner, not wanting to wait the ten minutes until she was home. She fumbled in her purse and, finding only quarters, decided to squander them. She heard the deep gong once, then twice, and dialed his office number. An operator said, "Deposit five cents please."

"But I already put in fifty!"

"How am I supposed to know that?" The voice was snippy.

"I supposed you would. I'm sorry."

"Well, I'll return your quarters. Deposit thirty-five cents."

"But I don't have change. I don't mind paying extra. Please put through the call."

"I can't return the difference, Madam."

"I know. But please!" Linda was almost crying.

The quarters reappeared; Linda redeposited them. The ringing began and eventually the girl at the switchboard answered. "I'm sorry, Mr. Kaplan is out of town. Whom shall I say called?"

"Never mind," Linda said and hung up.

Mrs. Kaplan, there's someone on the roof.

FIFTEEN ❧ THERE WERE THREE OF THEM, MARionettes without strings, she could see from the bedroom window. She opened it, letting in the crisp air and also their voices. She heard them slip from the wild west into Neverland.

"You be Wendy and I'll be Peter." That was Brian talking to Suzy.

"No, Rick should be Peter. He's the oldest."

The small girl pushed Brian aside and pulled Rick to a particular spot on the stone wall. Rick allowed himself to be moved, his arms dangling. "I'll sew a shadow on you if you don't look out."

He dodged lightly away from her, scuffled cheerfully with Brian and teetered graceful as a bird on the wall. Laughter.

How the boy had changed! Wasn't his laugh mingled with the others? The sun shone on the three, and their shadows danced on the winter grass. A glorious day, no trace of snows past, no hint of cold or damp or bitter wind still to come. The worst was over. Linda inhaled deeply the dustless air, heard Brian say, "Oh, all right. I'm not sure I'd know how to teach you to fly anyway."

"Peter was the oldest, and so am I. So I can tell you what to do," Rick announced.

"That depends," Suzy said testily, holding her braids on top of her head. "I'm the Wendy bird, remember? The mother. So you have to do what I say."

A mother already! Linda closed the window and went to check on Peter. Seeing that he was napping soundly, she retreated to the bathroom, turned the faucet, and let hot water run nearly pure. Tonight even her toenails would be clean and clipped.

Slowly she immersed herself in the old claw-footed tub, every inch of her thrilling to the sting, until high-collared by the hot water, breasts afloat, she closed her eyes, letting the back of her head submerge in the heat. David was coming home. She had missed him. She hoped Peter would sleep long enough for her to soak, manicure, wash her hair, shave her armpits.

In the quiet now that the water was turned off she remembered the laughter, Suzy's high-pitched, the boys' a few notes lower. Strange how feminine little girls were, even at seven. Suzy, without guile, had thrown her arms around Brian that morning just as if she had known what role she would play years later. "Do you like me?" she had asked. Brian, usually so full of explanations, was dumb, but he had not said no. Linda had been irritated. What right had Suzy? Then she laughed at herself. A girl-child of seven was hardly a threat.

The heat soothed. It would be all right after all. Everything. David would be home tired, happy, optimistic, tender and quizzical, arousing her. Rick was healthier every day. Even the problem of Brian's petty thievery had turned out better than she expected. He had been collecting for the social service drive and had given Miss Barker the money for safekeeping, he said. When he went to get it from her desk so he could turn it in, he had taken five of hers by mistake. He had, of course, returned it as soon as the mistake was discovered. And the pen? Linda had asked. What about the silver pen? Oh, that was a mistake too. Rick had borrowed the pen and loaned it to Brian, who had merely used it awhile and put it back.

"Do you often go into Miss Barker's desk?" she had asked.

"Oh, sure, she doesn't care. Everyone does." But everyone doesn't get accused of stealing, she thought miserably. But she believed him; he had not been at all evasive or flustered by her questions. Somewhat to her surprise, he didn't seem upset by the suspicions either. She tried not to dwell on it, and pushed other warnings away. No need, she told herself, even to bother David with the mix-up now. Stupid of her to have been so flustered during the interview. She placed the sopping hot washcloth over her eyes.

There was a sound above her head—a squirrel running across the roof. Often at night she and David heard them, worried that they might find a way into the attic. She let herself float. The sound was heavier, not like the squirrels.

Damn, the children must be on the shed roof again. And they had not asked permission! She hoped they hadn't lured Suzy up. As soon as she was dressed she'd get them down, talk to them again. She couldn't have them just popping up there at any time without her knowing. Well, at least Peter was safely asleep. She allowed herself back into the soporific complacency of the heat, her suspension, relishing stolen minutes in limbo. She belonged to no one.

She wished they hadn't gone up. Why did they like it so up there? She supposed it gave them a sense of power to be so high. They, who were always taking orders, could look down on their officers. To see without being seen. One-way glass. Both boys must be up; she could distinguish more than one set of footsteps.

Suddenly the heat was oppressive. She was perspiring. She couldn't breathe. The shed roof was below bathroom level.

Good God! She pulled herself out, soaking the towel, the floor. Hurry, hurry, hurry!

A memory pushed at her. The heat and the ringing in her ears, her wetness, overwhelmed her. What was it she feared so terribly that was not finding space or place in her brain?

A sound, a sentence, knowledge of tragedy once far removed now felt close. She struggled with her indolent, panicked mind. She would never make a lawyer, she thought, she reacted too slowly. Stupid. Stupid.

The phone rang. She would not stop to answer. She struggled with pants over her wet rump. She knew what the voice would say.

There's someone on the roof.

Icy air slapped her wet head. The breeze sliced through her wet sleeves as she ran stumbling around the house until she burst upon their rehearsal.

Another tableau: Rick, with arms spread-eagled, stood at the edge of the gutter. "Like this," he seemed to be saying. Brian, comfortably on his haunches, safely back from the roof's edge, watched him. Suzy was halfway up the ladder to the shed roof. From there it was an easy haul for the boys to pull her the rest of the way.

Fear seemed to expand like an inflating balloon in her chest. Death seemed so close it breathed on her, as close as it had been only once before in her life.

Daddy was dying in the back bedroom. There was nothing now that she could do to stop it, to help him, or Momma, or even herself. Life was seeping away, slipping, easing, sifting, drifting, out of his emaciated body. Momma hugged him, begged him, "Breathe, Ben, breathe!" She pressed her ear to his chest, listening for his heart, but she heard only her own. Momma's tears flowed for him, onto him, wetting him. Linda watched him weaken and had nothing more to offer. How many months had Momma fed him and turned him and washed him? "A pound of sweet butter," she'd say to Linda, "a dozen cracked eggs, a half-pound of pot cheese, fresh today. Stop at the Busy Bee for me, darling." But when it came time to wash him she would say, "It's enough now, darling. I'll do the rest alone. Go read."

Daddy was dying in the back bedroom after she had chosen *him* to live! How dare he die after all she had given up for him!

Daddy was dying in the back bedroom. An astringent odor emanated from the room. When his stillness could no longer be denied, even by Momma, Linda took the old woman in her arms and held her gray head against her breast. What would they do together without him to care for? What would they do without him? What would she do with death? The most dreadful moments for the living are the moments of utter helplessness.

Daddy was dead in the back bedroom. Over Momma's

gray head, still pressed against her, Linda met David's eyes. She had not seen him come in. "I came as soon as I got your message," he said. She had forgotten calling him.

But today David was not here, nor on his way. Someone would die. Lives and families would be sundered. She recollected things she had tried to ignore, signs of her impotence. The group at the railroad station the night the trains were late; David's dead voice the night of the firecrackers, and his words, "Go home, you bastards." Like dogs.

The children had not yet seen her. Their absorption was total. Outwardly calm, Linda put a firm hand on Suzy's ankle. Startled, the child turned at her touch, but did not protest when Linda ordered her off the ladder.

"Brian, Rick, come down now!" She measured the words like hundred-dollar bills. This was her home, she had control and must keep it. Brian, looking guilty, slowly let himself backwards onto the shed. Then he followed Suzy down the ladder.

Rick did not move. Did he not see? Not hear? Was he now in that other world so real to him she could not reach him? She tried to hold him with her eyes, at the same time sending the others to safety.

"Run along home, Suzy," she said without turning her head.

"It's okay, Mrs. Kaplan," Suzy chattered. "We were just pretending. See, Rick is Peter, and he is the one to teach us to fly. Like the movie. I wouldn't have jumped off, honest. I'm not that dumb."

"I know, dear, but just run on. Brian has to go in now too." Bombs seemed to be bursting in her ears.

To Brian, whose arm she gripped so tightly she thought her fingers would break, she said, "Go inside and stay there." Her voice was not gentle.

"Oh, Mom, it was only—"

"Get inside." She glanced at Brian. He was coatless. She was cold. "Where's your jacket?"

"I dunno. In the back, I guess. I got hot."

"Get it and go in." She resumed her eyehold on Rick.

"Okayee." Brian ambled toward the kitchen door.

Then, only then, when she was sure he was out of sight and sound, could she deal with the boy on the roof. Still poised, ready. For what? She didn't know. She did know. The picture would be in her mind forever, a silhouette, a night at the theater. She remembered Sartre's butcher of Auschwitz. "You do what you are and you are what you do." True, too, of a boy of nine? Already condemned? Already self-condemned?

She must talk him off the roof. He must not die today in her back yard so close to her children, inscribing their memories with horror. But tomorrow? Would he leave his blood on her doorstep tomorrow? For Peter to find? For her? Would she see him, too, in crowds?

This thing she had tried to do, worked so hard at, even placed her own family in jeopardy for, was not succeeding! What misguided self-indulgence had misled her to choose herself to be his savior? To unheed so many warnings? Now terrified, she remembered her pleas—a little time, a little love. And even up to half an hour ago she had held to her optimism. It had seemed to be working.

She loved him! Was that what had led her astray? Was that the fatal error? Does a professional succeed *because* of a lack of love, where she would be bound to fail? Distance and rationality? But, she argued, he had cried for love. No professional distance could have reached him. And if love, as she believed, was what made a person whole, why should it not have succeeded? And even now she knew her love, and she must use it, was the only way to bring him down unbroken. But she had to measure that love. It was big; it overwhelmed her. It made her weep in the night. His gray eyes followed her every moment. And yet, and yet she must withhold herself from him. As she had with Robert. How could she give all of herself to him, to Brian, to Peter, to David, and thus save them all? She couldn't; there was not enough to go around. She could not make him her own without losing those who had come first.

She pushed the thoughts around and away from her flooding brain. Now was now and now she had to talk him off the roof. Later she could think about what had brought her to this moment and left her in it alone.

"Rick, Rick." Softly, softly she spoke. Too softly; he didn't hear her, but made a quick motion with his foot that she didn't understand. Then she did, and for an incredible instant—only an instant but it seemed to last and last—she knew he could and would fly! She wanted him to; she fully expected that as she stood watching, this boy would lift off, would rise above the treetops and the roofs of her village; with his shadow trailing him would grow smaller and smaller until he appeared only a tiny pencil T-form against the March sky, flying to a distant place out of her life as swiftly as once he had dropped into it. In that instant when he kicked his shadow behind him, she believed he was no longer the boy whose memories were a tangle of pain and anger and hunger he had not nor ever would understand, victimized by a disease as insidious as a cancer with its deceptive remissions and its wrong cells crowding his psyche, denying him breath and joy; but she saw him free as Peter himself, ready to soar, to live forever in some Neverland. And in the next instant she remembered what she had forgotten, his story of Addie's daughter, if there really was such a child, who had flown from another roof and lived as still as if dead, on and on.

And so, because she had for that instant believed what he believed, she found the words she needed. "It was only a story, Rick, like one of your dreams. Tell me the dream. I want to hear it."

He looked at her and she knew he saw her. She pressed the advantage. "Come down carefully and tell me the dream about flying. I'll wait for you. Then, if you like, I'll tell you a story."

He nodded assent and, himself again, backed off the high

roof and then climbed down the ladder. She sat on the doorstep with him for nearly an hour. At first she let him talk. In his words she let herself see clearly the two people, the Rick she had tried to find, the boy he might have been, and the other one, the bitter, frustrated, already old and destitute person she had never quite touched. When he was silent, she talked of little easy things, movies, games he was beginning to like to play. Then she explained how she loved him, how she cared what happened to him. And then, finally, she explained that she could not let him play with Brian alone any more. "You may come to see me any time," she said. "You and I will always be friends. But not Brian. With you, even when you are at this house, he does things that are too dangerous, that we have forbidden, things he would not do if you were not here. I know you understand that." She felt his eyes without looking into them. "We have forbidden going on the roof." She tried to hug him, to bring him close, but he sat straight. He seemed placid enough. "You do understand about that, don't you?"

"Yes ma'am." He looked at her clear-eyed and steady. She knew she was losing him. How could she draw him close and hold him at arm's length in the same instant!

They sat in silence awhile. The sun shone no longer, but now she did not notice the cold. A blanket of gray descended, cloaking them with thickening air. Where had this suffocating fog come from? March was no season for fog.

She found her voice again. "I'll talk with your parents and we'll find someone else to help with your reading, someone more expert than I, with more time. There are wonderful people who can help children. I'll talk with your parents and make sure you get the help you need. But you must feel free to come see me and tell me how you're doing." She thought she saw him nod. She wasn't sure. "And of course," she added, "the puppy is still yours if you want him. Has your mother decided yet? He'll be ready to go home with you in a week or so."

Finally she shivered. It had to be ended somehow, and

she must do it. "Come," she said, "I'll get Peter up and drive you home."

"No!" He came to life, wary as a squirrel. He sprang away from her, disappearing into the fog so swiftly she reached out to feel the air where he had been. She would not—could not—chase him any more than she could have chased Sappho, had she ever a mind to run off.

"Wait!" she called futilely. "Wait!" Enveloped in fog, she had never felt more alone. Walking up the stairs she thought of all the times his grandmother had said to him, "I'll take you home." Would his memories now be in her mind forever?

As she picked up the phone she heard the pups squealing. Sappho must have left them again. She thought of Rick's newborn tenderness the day she had shown them to him. If he had not yet dared to ask his mother if he could have one, would he now?

When she heard Addie say, "Lang residence," she spoke past the balloon in her throat. "Addie, this is Mrs. Kaplan. Is Mrs. Lang there?"

Later that afternoon Brian found his jacket on the lawn, filthy, rubbed in fresh dog dung. She knew then that her decision had been the only one. She would press the Langs to get professional help for the boy. But she could not be his counselor or his tutor or his substitute mother any more. She soothed Brian's feelings, evaded his inquiries. But she did not know what to say to him or to herself when, as they were giving the pups a clean bed for the night, they found that one of them was missing.

David's call came at ten-thirty, long after the children were asleep. He was fogged in at Philadelphia. No getting into any New York airport tonight. "I'd take the train," he said, "but I can't get to Grand Central before the last one leaves. I'll spend the night here and go straight to the office in the morning. I don't feel like driving half the night."

"No," she said, "don't try to drive. You're tired and I'm

all right." She forced back the desire to tell him everything. "How did the hearing go?"

"Decision reserved."

"How do you feel about it?"

"Numb."

"Well." She was at a loss. Where were words to tell him that she needed him?

"Are you all right?"

"Of course."

They said goodnight, hung up. She slid between the sheets alone. Long-distance marriage. Separate lives. What held her apart from him? She opened the book by her bed. *Do you know that in my little village during a punitive operation, a German officer courteously asked an old woman to please choose which of her two sons would be shot as a hostage? Choose!* She closed *The Fall*, turned out the light. She began to tremble, then, uncontrollably, to shake. After a time she cried.

SIXTEEN &03 LATER SHE LAY QUIETLY, EX-
hausted, but there was no possibility of sleep. The heavy mist wrapped the house, coating the windows, muffling the sound of the cars that slowly passed. All right, she told herself, you love the boy and you loved Robert. There is only one thing to do. Start at the very beginning of Robert and tell it the way it was at the time.

She couldn't really do that, though she could try, because her viewpoint had changed over the years. At the time she had loved Robert so much that all she thought about was touching him. Also, she had been so young that she didn't really know him. She only knew herself.

They listened to each other, but what they heard often

· 243 ·

were reflections. He told her how wonderful she was and even though she wasn't very bright he said she would do great things. He said she had all that warmth and insight—that was a rare gift—and she believed him. When they read the same things he told her what she found between the hard covers and he made her feel she had discovered them herself. She told him he was very perceptive and very intelligent and that he was the first person who had ever made her feel smart.

She saw him first across a crowded lecture hall. She couldn't stop looking at him. She had always been partial to blond men who didn't look like her own swarthy ancestors. She saw him smile at a girl he was with and put his hand on her neck lightly, and she hated the girl and wished that someday someone would smile at her like that. No one ever had. She'd tried all the tricks and she'd practiced in front of mirrors but no one ever smiled at her with all of himself like that except her father, and she was so much taller than he that even though she loved him, when she secretly tried flirting with him to see how it would work, it didn't, because he was really quite funny-looking, short and thick-chested, and who can get romantic about a smile coming up at you from your nice round father?

Let Daddy lie peacefully now for a while, she told herself. He's not really very mixed up with Robert, except that Robert's rebellions led her away from the safe suffocation of West Seventy-seventh Street. He was all of the lives she'd read about but hadn't lived.

She saw him closer in the hamburger joint (the name was silly, like Humpty Dumpty or Piggly Wiggly) where she went to have lunch. She stared at him and he caught her staring; she looked away and wished she hadn't worn that noisy red skirt that somehow didn't seem subtle enough for a subtle-looking, sweet-faced, blond, slim, serious young man. He looked so neat. But she went back the next day, and finally he sat down across a small square table from her, and she burned her tongue on the soup.

"If you're staring at me because I'm not in uniform, you might as well know that it's not because I'm a fairy. I had an operation once and they wouldn't take me."

"I wasn't," she said.

"You were staring."

"But not about the uniform."

"Oh." His voice was suddenly soft. After a bit he said in that first accusing way, "But you're always writing things in that big black notebook of yours. You write furious-ly."

"Don't you take notes?" she asked. "How can you remember anything?"

"I only remember what I want to forget," he said. "I don't care for most of what they tell me."

"What do you care for?"

"Have you ever walked under the Brooklyn Bridge at midnight?"

"No."

"I did it once after I saw *Winterset*. Will you go with me?"

"Yes." She went home and read *Winterset*. And then they walked under the Brooklyn Bridge, and she was afraid all the time they were there but she didn't tell him.

It was like being hypnotized all the time, being with Robert. For hours they would walk the city hand in hand, sometimes down the tugboaty East River; sometimes on the Drive; sometimes through olive-oil-smelling streets below Washington Square. She felt each sidewalk belonged to them. Robert sometimes walked blocks without saying a word.

Once she asked him, "You didn't say anything for forty-five minutes. I timed you, and then you said, 'Have you ever washed your hair in beer and lain in the hay?' Were you trying to impress me? Or did it just pop into your mind like that?"

"I don't know," he said. "Once I had a girl who did that. I thought maybe you could try it. Your hair always smells of castile soap." Then he added, "I don't like to talk unless I have something to say."

"I do," she said, "I do."

He had an apartment of his own on Horatio Street, one dark eight-by-ten room with a fireplace, but the bathroom was in the hall. They studied together there, stretched out on the floor side by side. They read the same books and talked about them till three in the morning. They made love between the chapters of *Crime and Punishment,* all day or all night; they couldn't ever stop making love once they started. But when he rode uptown on the smelly subway at night to take her home and leave her at the door of her parents' apartment on West Seventy-seventh Street, he left her at the door a virgin still.

Sometimes they argued about it. "Why in God's name do you cling to that last Puritan shred? You are already a complete woman. You are. There's no difference between what we do and intercourse. What lies do you tell yourself to justify this?"

"I don't know," she said. "I just can't let you—" She couldn't say put it in though the words were in her head. "I can't. It's not even that I think it's wrong. I always said I'd sleep with a man when I fell in love, and I love you. But—I don't know. Be patient. Something frightens me."

She never knew what it was. Something in Robert always frightened her and perhaps she didn't complete that last part of the act because she knew it would bind her to him and she didn't dare let herself be bound. Robert sometimes talked to her in the dark. He wrote terrible poetry and she loved it, though his images often were frightening. He hated his mother and he hated his brother; in the dark all the fair beauty would lie unseen and he'd talk of his hatreds. "I dream of my father's coffin disappearing into the fire behind the velvet curtain and I wonder if he is really dead or if my mother just tucked him in before his time."

"But your father isn't dead," she said softly in the dark. "You told me he rules like a monarch." She never knew how to act when he spoke like this, she didn't know how to help him; but she hated his mother and she hated his brother with him and for him.

Robert's mother drove in from Long Island one day. "Brace yourself," Robert told Linda, "I haven't been home in two months so she's taking us to dinner." Mrs. Holden was like a caricature. She was big and bleached and buxom and obviously wore that terrible kind of corset that makes a woman's buttocks one and her bosom one, like a giant S. She wore a huge pink rhinestone pendant that settled into her pale flesh. Somewhere described in her puffed cheeks and chins and even visible beneath the pathetic makeup was Robert's face. Linda looked away.

Mrs. Holden took them to dinner at Longchamps and flicked red fingernails at the waiter and told Robert that his father would hold the job open until he graduated, but "he says you have to start in the summer."

"I'm not going to work for him this summer or ever," Robert said.

She flicked for the check and told him she'd give him money for a haircut if "Linda will see to it that you don't spend it on beer."

When they were alone, Linda said, "I never knew there were real people in the world like that. No wonder you left home."

"She doesn't know I've left," Robert said. "She doesn't even know I hate beer." He liked Scotch straight and wine and they both liked brandy so much that many mornings they listened to lectures with cotton mouths and taut brows.

"If you're not going to work for him what are you going to do?" she asked. Once Robert wanted to be an actor, but he decided that he hated the theater. "It's a dirty disgusting cheapening business like any other where the people who succeed are the ones with ugly souls who sell each other back and forth." Once he was going to be a writer and sent some things to some magazines. Then one day his writing teacher, who had said he was brilliant, tried to seduce him.

Linda said it didn't make his writing any less good just because the man turned out to be unscrupulous, but Robert vowed he would never write again.

Sometimes he played his clarinet with a five-piece combo and got paid for it. He was a music major that term, and Linda loved to listen to him play and go to concerts with him because he knew so much more than she did.

They spent a lot of time with some friends of his from his acting days, a marvelously uninhibited flamboyant group; only one, his friend Dominick, a dense-haired warmhearted clown, ever seemed jealous of the time Robert spent with Linda alone. All of them, Robert, Dominick, others whose faces were nameless pictures in her memory now, were very loving and very left-wing. They hated the war but fought in it; when it was over, they said, they were going to fight the rich and raise the poor. Walking across the Square one night, Robert gave his haircut money to a drunk who held out his hand. They talked over a smoky bar to a haggard woman named Tillie who said between missing teeth it was a shame only the good men got killed. Robert said she was "beautiful inside even though all her flesh was gone." Wherever they went he spoke with his charm, his soft humor and bright questions, intensely serious, to the ugliest tramp, the burliest truckdriver, the bartenders, the bums; he always smiled at them. In all the time they were at school together, Linda never saw him smile at a professor.

He got straight A's and never took notes. "How can you do so well," she asked jealously, "when you don't study half what I do?"

"I can learn anything," he said, "so long as you're with me."

She felt wonderful but she didn't believe him and wished he hadn't said it.

She tried the beer and the hay routine one summer weekend when Dominick loaned them his mother's house in the country. "I'd be there myself," he wrote from Fort Bragg, "but I can't get a pass."

They rode a bus across the factory-strewn swamps to the New Jersey farmhouse, just the two of them. Linda lied to Momma, of course, but she'd been doing that for so long about one thing and another that it didn't bother her. "Momma isn't very bright," Linda would say, "but she isn't pretentious and she doesn't ask any more questions than she wants answers to. People wander across her life and she feeds them as they go."

On Saturday night at nine a carful of friends, Dominick at the wheel, arrived. "I got a pass after all," he said. Robert and Linda looked at each other, but since they'd had their long quiet hayfield day and had followed a brook and climbed some rocks and found relics in the barn and cooked two meals together with the groceries they'd bought at the general store, they laughed and said, "Oh, all right. Get the ice."

Along toward midnight someone turned off the phonograph and said, "Let's play murder." The farmhouse rambled and became too dark with too many doors and unknown passages. Furniture loomed large and had sharp corners. Tense and miserable, Linda moved through the black spaces, bumping bodies she didn't want to touch, weeping finally because she had lost Robert in the darkness among the foreign bodies. She wanted to find him, but she was so afraid it would be his hand squeezing the back of her neck, and she didn't want him to murder her.

Someone screamed. The lights went on. Linda wiped at her eyes and found Robert on the other side of the dining room, casually leaning against the sideboard. He had not murdered her after all. They sat together on the floor during the long interrogation.

"Did you do it?" she whispered.

"Sh-sh-sh," he said. According to the rules, no one could lie except the murderer. She felt in his coat pocket to see if the short matchstick was there. He took her hand out of his pocket and tried to hold it, but she pulled away. It seemed that the game went on forever. If Robert was the murderer and had murdered someone else she would never forgive him.

Later they danced and drank some more, and someone played the old piano. She watched Robert talking to the piano player, and she wanted to cry. He saw her and said, "What's the matter? You're not drinking. You look glum."

"I wish they'd go away," she said.

"They're fun," he said. "They're having fun. What's the matter with you? You never laugh at anything any more."

"I hate them all and I wish they'd go away. I'm too old for this. I don't know. They're like silly children with their silly game. I don't want to play any more games, Robert."

He took her out of the room and into a narrow carpeted hall. He stood her against the wall and put an arm on either side of her head so she couldn't move or look away. "We never play games, you and I," he said. "At least I don't. What are you saying?"

"I don't know," she said. "I wish they'd go away."

He went into the other room and spoke to Dominick a while, and then the friends left. Dominick said he was sorry they'd butted in, that he would stay in the city. Linda said she was sorry she'd ruined their party.

The house was quiet finally, too messy and too quiet. They turned out the lights on the mess and found the big bed upstairs; they slept all the night together but when they awoke she was a virgin still.

Sunday morning they were both silent. Robert cooked the eggs seriously. Linda made coffee. "Where did you learn to cook?" Linda asked.

"I used to watch the maid. My mother hated to see me in the kitchen so I went there a lot."

They ate silently. Then they cleaned up the house. They packed all their things and still had four hours until the bus left for the city. They walked through the tall grass to the barn, climbed to the loft, and sat in the scratchy hay. Robert said her hair smelled of it.

"I know. And I washed it in beer."

"What do you want?" he asked her finally. "It's true. You never laugh any more."

She tried to remember when they had laughed together but she couldn't. "I don't know. I told you that." She wanted to do something big and she didn't know how or what it was. She couldn't make her voice right. There were ropes around her chest.

"You said they played games," he persisted. "What are you doing? Aren't you playing too? We'll play house today and tonight we'll pretend we're grown-ups but—"

"Stop," she said. "I know what you're going to say."

"But you aren't grown up. Just what is your game, Linda?"

"I want it to be real, I guess. I want all of it, every bit. I want you and your babies and I want us to be in a real house."

"With a fence and a yard and a neighbor and—oh, God, so that's it. And all your high talk of careers and futures and independence. That's all a trap to catch me and put me in the cage I just escaped?"

She lay on her back and smelled the hay and looked at the high-beamed ceiling with light cracks and birds' nests, and though the hay felt scratchy and awful she put her arm over her head and said nothing. Finally she closed her eyes. If he kissed her, she wouldn't have to think for a while.

After an eternity he spoke. "If I said I thought we should get married would you sleep with me all the way now?"

"No," she whispered, not even knowing from what depth the word came. "No, I can't. I'm afraid."

He left her at the door of the house on Seventy-seventh Street without going upstairs. When she walked in with her suitcase, all the lights were on and Momma was there in tears and Dr. Abrams was on the telephone. Daddy was in the back bedroom in a coma. He'd had a stroke an hour before and they were waiting for an ambulance.

She saw Robert once more. He made her go to dinner

with him, one night, but neither of them ate much and they became angry with each other.

"You're throwing yourself away," he told her. "You've gone uptown on me. Don't you know you'll never be anything now? I'll never be anything. They'll never let you go."

"He's so sick," she said, "and he needs me. So does Momma. I'll finish school sometime. I'll go back. I promise."

"It's your life, not theirs. To give in now is like betraying everything we've said, like betraying yourself. Everything was a lie."

"I'll be what I want to be somehow or other," she said. "You shouldn't make me have to choose. I have to do this now. Later—"

"You can't have us both," he said. "You know as well as I. Come back. I'll have a degree next year and then we'll make plans."

She knew he was right but she didn't know it either. She thought of asking him to wait for her, bringing him close to her again, but she never did. It wasn't just that he wasn't Jewish and even introducing him to her parents would have meant open rebellion. She sensed that he was emotionally fragile. She loved him, admired him; he always looked at truth squarely where she would turn her head. Though she could not have expressed it at the time, she was afraid he would, someday, become nothing, a drifter, a piece of lint between her fingers; that his passion—based so often on anger—would be dissipated on people and issues that didn't matter; that his anger would turn against himself, against her.

In all the time they had been together she had never looked at a future with Robert. She had loved only the now.

There was one more phone call. It came after her father was home from the hospital, alive and able to see, but paralyzed. The bell rang at midnight, after she'd gone to bed. She'd started *A Passage to India* which Robert had bought for her. She ran quickly so the ringing wouldn't wake Momma.

"You were waiting by the phone," he said. His voice was a feather against her cheek.

"No, I was reading in bed."

"What were you reading?" He sounded like himself again. She'd missed him.

"Forster. *A Room with a View*," she lied.

"I've not read that."

"You can borrow it when I'm done."

"No. I'm leaving tomorrow."

"What?"

"I joined the American Field Service. I'm going overseas."

"I thought the war was almost over. What could you possibly do?"

"They still need ambulance drivers."

"Oh Robert!" she wailed. "When?"

"Tomorrow morning. I have to be at Grand Central at eight." She could hear him breathing. She could hear her heartbeat. She looked down at herself, nightgown-naked.

"Where are you now?"

It was as if he had seen her. She felt his jagged laughter cutting against her eardrum. "That would be marvelous," he said. "The perfect parting sacrifice. A little late, but after all he's leaving tomorrow, so it's quite safe. No chance to get really involved."

"That's cruel," she said.

"I'm a cruel person," he answered. "Good you knew it in time. I wouldn't have wanted you to worry about me."

"Robert." This time her voice was so thin she made almost no sound. She wasn't weeping, but it was so hard to give him up when she had no one. "When you come back—"

"The word is 'if,' darling. Haven't you been to the movies?"

She put her finger quietly on the button that breaks telephone connections. How easy it was. If you didn't want to hurt any more or think any more, or feel or listen, or do or be anything but a cold numb thing in the darkness you reached out your forefinger and pressed gently on a little black button.

Eight months later she received a short note from Dominick explaining that Robert had been killed by a guerilla ambush while driving in the hill country north of Manila. After that, she used to see him in crowds.

THE LAST DAY ⚜

THE BOY BLINKED IN THE FLICKERING CHANDELIER LIGHT
and put a reluctant fork into his crumpled baked potato.
The quick saliva of nausea filled his mouth.

"Where have you been?" his mother's voice said again.
"Answer me. Where have you been?"

> *Pussycat, pussycat, where have you been?*
> *I've been to London to visit the queen.*
> *Pussycat, pussycat, what did you there?*
> *I frightened a little mouse under the chair.*

"But it wasn't frightened, Gran. I kept it in the dark of
my pocket and it only cried a little. And then I held it tight
so it wouldn't cry any more."

"What's he talking about?"

"Eat. Eat."

"I'm not hungry."

"Eat. Eat."

"Oh, leave him alone, Mother."

"What do you care if he eats?"

"Maybe he's sick. Mrs. Kaplan phoned. She was upset.
What did you do to upset her, Rick? Answer me when I ask
you . . ."

Rick stood up and walked out of the room, leaving the

voices behind him. He went up the carpeted front stairs, knowing he left a trail of mud crumbs. In the morning he would hear Addie. "As if I don't have enough to do." In the morning he could leave early, before the sound.

He reached the landing and went to his room. Something was missing. An old friend. He bit his lip. There was a strange taste in his throat he could hardly remember. He walked down the hall to Barbara's room and his old friend was there. He lifted the giant teddy bear off the satin bedspread, carried it back to his own room. He lay face up on his bed with his eyes open, the big bear beside him.

The strangeness in his throat became intense pain behind his ears, a long-forgotten sensation. How long? How forgotten?

What do you want for your birthday, dear? I want the river to be all mine. But when he opened the door she hid behind the great orange bear with glass eyes. I couldn't bring you a river, she said and laughed. Isn't he a little old for a stuffed bear? Oh, let him be a baby awhile. It's over soon enough.

The orange had turned brown, and one of the eyes was gone. Water ran from the corners of Rick's eyes. He closed them and wondered when he had last been a baby. Sometime after four. It was over soon enough. He opened his eyes to the blue ceiling, tangled his fingers in the coarse fur; the old friend that Barbara always stole, that was all he had of Gran. The bear and the memory of tears.

Sometimes the sound of her voice was in his head but it was fading, and another voice was there instead. There was something he still hadn't done, but he wasn't sure what it was. He looked at the pile of school books, the arithmetic workbook (*Do two pages tonight*), the list of spelling words he had to write sentences for inside it. Underneath was the reading-for-pleasure book from the library. Every day his special teacher said, "Now don't forget to read one half-hour for pleasure every night."

"I don't like to read for pleasure," he told Brian's mother. He remembered that she laughed, and then, even though he didn't know why, he began to laugh with her, and soon they were all laughing. She said, "I've never heard you laugh like that."

It was like flying. He looked away from the books and closed his eyes again. He tried to think of the dream about flying, because if he could do that then he could forget the sounds in the dining room, the memory of the warm fur in his pocket, cold mud on his hands.

He hid his hands in his pockets, out of sight. But he found the yellow car there, and a book of matches. He lit the matches one by one, dropping them on the great bear belly. One by one. After a while a tiny black hole appeared. Glowed and died. The matches were spent. He turned and flung his arm across the coarse fur chest and pressed his cheek against the hard-stuffed friend. A pencil line climbed, curling slightly, toward the ceiling. He fell asleep. He fell asleep before the acrid smell touched his nostrils.

Where was Gran? Would he ever find her? Did he know the way?

It was a night of sirens. They seemed to be everywhere, near and far, round and round, invading Linda's territory, surrounding her, daring her to attempt sleep against their piercing crescendoes, their whining diminuendoes.

Somewhere in Philadelphia David slept in a strange bed waiting for the fog to lift.

Somewhere in Maryland a child cried in the night and no one listened.

By morning Linda was more exhausted than when she went to bed.

By morning the room had filled with smoke. Once they opened the door and found him, the smell went through the house and clung to clothes and curtains. But beyond the smoldering bear locked in the boy's embrace, there was little visible damage. Death by smoke inhalation takes only a few minutes.

The small town went into shock. Death came too close. It could have been anyone. It could have struck any child. Why Rick Lang? Mothers and fathers re-remembered to hide the matches.

Addie watched Mr. Lang wind the clocks. He did it carefully, lovingly, the way he always had. She watched him wipe with his finger for dust on the round varnished mahogany top of the mantel clock. There was no dust there, she knew. He turned and saw her in the arched doorway, the dustrag in one hand, the Electrolux hose in the other. She saw her father in his eyes, her father's grief.

"Don't clean today, Addie," he said.

"Yes, Mr. Lang."

Neither of them moved. She wanted to hug him hard, the way she had Rick when he was bad or sad. She kept her arms tight at her sides. She tried not to cry. She couldn't stem the stream that ran from her eyes. She had watched that small box being lowered into the ground and she felt the cold soil on her own skin. She thought of Elizabeth. Did Marybelle keep her warm?

"We were going to get a doctor to help him," he said. "And we'd found a special school. It's just—well—" He moved the minute hand ahead carefully. "We were too late. That's all."

Addie nodded. "You'll stay on, Addie. I hope you won't go away. Mrs. Lang is going to need a lot of help now."

"For a while," Addie said. She fingered the bankbook in her pocket. She had nearly enough money now. Another few months and there would be enough to do what she wanted. She had all the facts, and the application nearly filled out. There was a nursing school nearby where she could live and study. Then she would bring Elizabeth up north; she would find a doctor who knew a cure.

"Stay as long as you can," he said. "We all need you."

"All right," Addie said aloud. "I'll stay as long as I can." And to herself she added, "You stay warm, Elizabeth. I'll be with you soon. I'll get help soon enough."

In the desolate days that followed Linda found herself staring out the front window again and again, watching the road where the gray-jacketed boy had so often flown by. Tears flowed. She did not know for whom she wept. For herself. For a boy she once knew. For a starving child. For all of them, all the disconnected lonely people; the dead and the lonely.

Finding her there one morning David held her close from behind. "He was already lost when he found you," he said. "You must believe that."

"I do," she said, "I do. And thank you." She rested against him a moment. Then, "You'll miss your train. You'd better go."

"No," he said, "never mind the train. I don't want to leave you." She turned and let him hold her. She felt the rough texture of his cheek against her forehead, mentally tracing the furrows with her finger.

She said, "I feel so guilty about trying to help him. I do, you know. I feel that you, everyone, was telling me all along it was wrong. As if, in a sick world, it is wrong to try to make it better, and right only to get rid of any imperfect creation. You drop a bomb. Mark the elms with an X for destruction. The boy gave Brian a bloody nose—ban him! What kind of a world is it that can't tolerate illness?"

"It wasn't wrong to help him," David said. "It was all right."

"But why did I have to choose? And in choosing, kill him?"

He was quiet for a time, until he felt her heart beat less strangely. For a moment she was his child. "You didn't kill him," he said. "I think perhaps you might have postponed his death awhile, but—"

"But?" She waited, needing him to go on, needing his arms so tightly around her.

"But," he said, and then she was his wife again, "long long ago you made the choice. You chose to share your life with me. You chose me."

EPILOGUE ⚜

IT WAS A YEAR OF REVIVALS. YO-YOS WERE BACK. PETER came into the dining room with two of them going one night, boasting that he hadn't faulted since he left work. David, seeing his grease-blackened hands, dryly reminded him that even at his advanced age of sixteen it might be good to wash. Peter said okay, and pocketed them, adding that it was a waste of time to get all clean when he was going to take apart the carburetor of his old pickup after dinner. Linda thought, A car and a yo-yo—he had always been easy to please.

The next afternoon she opened the window to the smell of new spring growth, heard a high-pitched sound that came from the yard next door, girl sounds of tease and taunt. Looking across, she saw two that must be nine or ten. Startled, she thought of Suzy, but Suzy was away—in a cabin somewhere in Colorado, Linda had heard. Like others of Brian's age, Suzy had done her time in emotional exile, survived but made choices that had not been comforting to her parents. The Mendelsohns had moved away a few years after the Langs. She didn't know where any of them had gone. She was still anchored to New Delphi, protected by her rock. As she watched her new young neighbors undulating inside their hula hoops she half expected to see Brian, with Rick right behind him, coast up on their bikes, riding the pedals with one foot as they came to a stop. The mind picture went on. Rick's hand darted out and grabbed a hoop, breaking it.

She shook her head. *The heart has its own memory.* It never took much to bring back the past. The sound of a bike whizzing past the rock; the phone interrupting a quiet stretch of work, now usually Brian calling collect from Ithaca where he was in law school; or a child with translucent eyes at the welfare center where she worked. The past was as much a part of her as the present.

She heard the kitchen door slam, looked at her watch. Peter coming home from his after-school job in the garage, needing more grease solvent than she could believe before he could appear at David's dinner table. When he went off to college in two more years, she knew she would miss the black fingerprints, while not missing them too. She still had twinges of ambivalence.

Time to put the work away. Liking the neatly typed label, she closed the folder on the report she was writing. It was always an effort to write up a case once she was done with it, like a life ending for her, when really it was a life beginning.

That had been a year! For a time she had blamed a certain madness, her shapeless confusions, on the nation's soul-sickness. It had been easy to do. That year had, it seemed, heralded such a succession of national and personal tragedies that she had been swept along, taking each one as her own loss, her own responsibility. The guilt of the lucky Jew in America; the guilt of a woman who could not control and repair every broken life she came near. What had she— or anyone—learned to do about death after all?

The painter had continued to lay broad flat brushfuls of white on the walls; the lawyer prepared his brief; the teacher corrected the spelling words. Not all children survived their parenting or their schooling or the accidental ravages of disease or social upheaval. The mother put the roast in the oven and diapered the baby.

What do you do about death? Madness was one thing,

but when you had responsibilities you fulfilled them. Rick had not made the world into which he was born, could not shape it, nor find a path through it even with her help. Since then, some others had. But it had taken her a long time to come to believe she was not solely and personally responsible for everyone, as if she could unzip the guilt and let it flow away from her.

Now, closing one more folder, writing up one more case, satisfying requirements of an organization outside her immediate family, her professional life gave her days an order and dignity they had lacked before. Now she was motivated by more than guilt, more than passion, more than love or reason or intellect. And now on a warm Saturday morning walk with David, she could miss the dead elms but happily discover hickory and oak and walnut seedlings that were finding sun-space in what was left of their woods.

The phone rang. It was Brian saying he might come home for the weekend. How nice. David would be pleased. She halloed at Peter, liking the sound of him opening the fridge. She put the folder in her desk, locking away for the night that other life. But she knew, too, that she never really put away the pieces of her life. She had not lost the people she had loved and who had died and left her. She would see them in crowds or on lonely beaches; she would hear the words they said. She knew that you lose nothing that happens to you. It is, in the end, what you are.